SARAH McCARTY

Caden's Vow

ISBN 978-1-62090-644-6

CADEN'S VOW

To the real-life inspiration for Caden:

Q, may your happily-ever-after waltz up and give you an ever-so-ladylike bite on the butt soon. It couldn't happen to a nicer man. Or a more deserving one. As I'm sure all the ladies who enjoy *Caden's Vow* will agree.

Caden's Vow

CHAPTER ONE

HELL'S EIGHT WAS doing Tia proud. Caden Miller looked around at the normally peaceful garden Tia had started and Tucker's wife, Sally Mae, now helped maintain, at all the people crammed into its well-tended confines to celebrate Tia and Ed's wedding, and couldn't help a smile. Ten years ago he wouldn't have given a snowball's chance in hell that Caine could pull off his dream. But like the others, where Caine had led, Caden had followed. And Caine's drive to succeed was evident in the sturdy outbuildings, the assortment of equally sound houses and the contentment reflected in the faces of those in attendance. The men of Hell's Eight weren't just content; they were flourishing. They were settling down, marrying, having children, sinking their roots deep into the east Texas soil. Of the original eight, only he, Ace and Luke remained footloose and fancy-free. Something that should have pleased him but instead had him feeling a pang of…envy? *Shit.* Since when did he feel envy for something he didn't even want? He wasn't a settling man. He'd always been as restless as his father before him. As all the Hell's Eight used to be.

Glancing around the garden, at the tables laden with food, at the couples standing side by side, the contented smiles where he was used to seeing hardness and purpose, Caden again felt that strange tightness in his gut. Hell's Eight was changing. The reckless rage that had driven them for so many years had smoothed into something just as durable but...calmer. Caden rolled his shoulders. He didn't like calm, but it seemed to be settling all right with Hell's Eight's most notorious members. Shadow, Tracker and Tucker, three of the most feared men in the territory, known for reckless deeds that were as dark as their looks, were hovering over their wives, every bit the doting husbands. Caine and Sam, wild men known for getting the job done no matter what, were looking as confident as rich bankers—that is, if one discounted the subtle tension in their muscles and the alertness in their gaze that spoke of men accustomed to surviving by their wits. Not to mention the guns strapped to their thighs and the knives tucked into their belts. Shit, they were all going soft, and if he stayed here, so would he.

Caden sighed and took a drink of the fancy champagne Desi had ordered all the way from Chicago for Tia and Ed's wedding. It tasted like cat piss to him, but what did he know of the finer things? He was the son of an Irish nomad, a dreamer. A man who'd sworn his pot of gold was just over the next horizon, around the next bend. Caden had a brief mental flash of his father's face. Rigid with determination as he'd told Caden to hide when the Mexican army had raged into their town. He'd been seven going on eight, anticipating the gun his father had promised him for his birthday two days hence. He hadn't wanted to hide. He'd wanted to fight, but his father hadn't given him any choice. He'd shoved him into the hidey-hole under the kitchen floor, and on a gruff "Remember who you are, son," he'd replaced the planks above him and left him in the dark. Those were the last words his father had ever spoken to him. His mother he hadn't found until…after. She'd been at the mercantile when the army came.

Caden took another swallow of the champagne, wishing it were something stronger. There were times when a man just needed something to drown out the noise of the past, but champagne wasn't whiskey, and the memories kept coming. He'd lain beneath the floorboards for what seemed hours, listening to the shouts and screams, wincing at the gunshots, straining to hear his father's voice, feeling helpless and scared until he couldn't stand it anymore.

By the time he'd climbed out of the hole, the battle was over. He'd never forget the smell that struck him as he'd stood—gunpowder, smoke and…blood—nor the carnage that spread out beyond his front door. Bodies of friends and neighbors littered the road like trash left by the wind, changing the street from familiar to macabre. He'd found his father's body lying in the doorway of the still-burning mercantile, his head caved in on the right side, blood pooled around his shoulders. His father's legs had been on fire as Caden had dragged his body into the street. The stench of burning flesh fused indelibly into his memory that day as he'd beaten out the fire consuming his father's body with his bare hands. He hadn't felt the pain, hadn't felt anything. And when he'd looked up and seen Sam, his expression had reflected the blankness that Caden felt. And then he'd learned what Sam already knew. Everything that had made up their lives was gone. The town. Their parents. Their childhood.

The only survivors of the massacre were the eight friends. By agreement, none had buried their own parents. They'd thought it would help. It hadn't. And, also by agreement, they'd vowed revenge. Extracting justice one by one as they grew up, earning the label of Hell's Eight along the way. Caden didn't know what would have become of them if Tia hadn't caught them that day, starving, stealing that pie, and taken them under her wing. They sure as shit wouldn't have become Texas Rangers. Tia was one in a million. Strength and softness mixed in one. If he ever met another woman like her, he'd marry her in a minute.

Fingers slid over his forearm. He didn't need to look down to know who it was who touched him with such compassion and gentleness. Maddie. Poor abused Maddie. Born to a whore. Raised in a whorehouse. Used by men all her life until Tracker had brought her home after one of his failed searches for Ari. Maddie was as fleeting as sunshine, here one minute, gone the next, retreating into fantasy as fast as she snapped out of it. Her fingers tightened slightly on his arm. He smiled down at her automatically. Despite the harshness of her past, there was something about Maddie that remained untouched, that drew a man to smile. That enticing illusion of innocence probably had made her a damn good whore.

Caden regretted the thought as soon as Maddie smiled back at him with complete trust, her dark green eyes picking up the deeper green of leaves of the pear tree, her wavy red hair dragging the sunlight with it as tendrils escaped her bun and blew across her cheeks. Freckles sprinkled like pale kisses across the bridge of her nose. And her smile…that sweet, gentle smile that captured the hope of the world added to his guilt. So trusting when she had no reason to trust anyone, least of all him. Fey, his da would have called Maddie. One of the special ones that bridged the space between this world and the magical one.

"Tia looks like a queen, doesn't she?" Maddie said in a soft voice that eased a man's tension. For all her differences, Caden had always found Maddie a very restful soul.

"Yeah, she does." He was happy for Tia and Ed. It'd taken Ed seven years to convince Tia he wasn't going anywhere. And Tia, well, she deserved the best of everything. Not just because she'd taken eight ragtag boys and raised them into men, but because of who she was. She stood next to her husband, petite and elegantly plump in her golden silk gown, her graying black hair pulled back into a sedate bun, her white, gold and black lace mantilla draped artfully around her face. He felt that familiar twinge of unease that came with the thought of settling.

Voices rose and fell around him, taking on an unreal quality, and the moment froze with sudden clarity. They were all settling down. Caine had his Desi. Tucker had Sally Mae. Sam with his Bella. Tracker had Ari, and

Shadow had his Fei. The wild boys of the plains were becoming the builders of the future. Hell's Eight had been Caden's focus for as long as he could remember, but looking around the ranch he'd helped build, Caden had that ever-increasing sense of "wrong." His feet itched and his nerve endings crawled impatiently beneath his skin. He'd been a part of Hell's Eight for twenty-two years, but he didn't feel as if he belonged here anymore.

"Are you worried Tia won't love you anymore now that she has Ed?" Maddie teased, her fingers sliding between his and squeezing. It was a totally inappropriate gesture. Yet it completely soothed his unease. Caden tugged at his hand. Maddie didn't let go.

Shit. The woman made it easy to take advantage of her. Her sweet nature and the fact that more often than not she was in her make-believe world where nothing bad could touch her made her an easy target. Everyone wished she was stronger, but disappearing into her own mind was Maddie's defense against what'd happened to her in her life. Caden thought they should just let her be. It was a hard world, harder if you were brought up in a whorehouse. Harder still if you had the sweet personality of a child. Too many men had taken advantage of the optimistic woman in Maddie. He didn't want to be one of them. This time he tugged his hand free. "I'm not worried, Maddie mine."

The endearment just slipped out. She blinked up at him. "If I'm yours, why do you need to lie to me?"

How was he supposed to answer that? Across the garden, he smiled at Tia and Ed before lifting his glass in a silent toast. Tia smiled back, but Caden could tell from the tension at the edge of her mouth that she knew he was leaving. He hated to ruin her day, but he was who he was. A Miller didn't let grass grow under his feet. He pursued rather than settled. He took another sip of the champagne, wishing even more that it was whiskey. "Habit, I guess."

"You don't lie to anyone else."

Everyone else could handle the truth. Maddie continued to stare up at him, her fingertips resting on his forearm, as if the pressure took his measure. The way she stared at him so steadily made him uneasy, as if she really was fey and really did see more than others.

"I'm leaving, Maddie."

She blinked slowly. He had the oddest impression she'd just gasped.

"When will you be back?"

He traced his finger over the curl spilling down her temple. It was always too easy to touch Maddie. "I don't know."

"Where will you go?"

"So many questions."

"You don't want to answer?"

Maddie could be surprisingly blunt.

With a sigh he admitted, "No."

Cocking her head to the side, her gaze never leaving his, she took another step in until the blue gingham skirts of her brand-new dress brushed his boots. She frowned as her fingers trailed down to his wrist. "You're upset."

From across the garden, he saw Tia note the familiarity with a frown of her own. Caden shrugged. They could lecture Maddie all they wanted about proper behavior, but it wouldn't make a difference. She listened, she truly did, but in the end Maddie was Maddie. Open sunshine and optimism covering a lifetime of hurt. Her conduct was as volatile as her grasp on reality. While he'd never seen Maddie actually proposition a man, she often gave the impression she was propositional. And that was a shame, because she had a heart of gold and deserved to be treasured.

Faint strains of music blended with the hum of conversation. Four of Sam's vaqueros strummed their guitars. The hum of conversation rose as everyone wandered to the grassy center where ribbons and bunches of cut flowers fluttered in the breeze, defining the dance area. Tia had declared May to be the perfect month for a wedding, and Caden had to agree. The day was beautiful, the weather perfect, and the bride and groom happy. There wasn't a fly in the ointment. As Caden watched, Ed took Tia's hand and brought it to his lips with a courtly bow Caden would have sworn the former cowhand could never have pulled off. When Tia smiled at her husband, her expression full of love, the last of Caden's uncertainty slipped away. He could leave cleanly now. Tia was happy and safe. The last of his debts were paid. The sense of excitement he'd expected failed to come.

"Don't be sad," Maddie said, her fingertips smoothing over the inside of his wrist.

"Millers don't get sad."

"I can feel—"

"I think there's some cake left, Maddie," Caine interrupted, coming up beside them, a whiskey glass in each hand and a gentle tone to his normally hard drawl. Everyone at Hell's Eight used a gentle note with Maddie. A body couldn't help it. She had that way of wild things about her that made you think one wrong move and she'd either dart to the right or leave looking for a hiding spot. Plain and simple, harsh words shattered Maddie's fragile hold on reality. "You might want to think about getting some before Tucker's sweet tooth takes hold."

Maddie let go of his arm and turned toward the cake table. Sure enough, Tucker was moving toward it.

"He's like a horde of locusts devouring all in their path," she muttered.

The comparison made Caden smile. Tucker was a deliberate man, deadly when he chose to be, but he did like his sweets.

As if hearing his thoughts, Caine offered, "He does like his cake."

So did Maddie. Brought up as she had been, she'd never had a sweet before fourteen and only that one which she'd stolen. Since she'd come to Hell's Eight, she'd been making up for lost time. Not content with just sampling what Tia baked, she was learning to create her own confections. When he'd asked her why, she'd said in a moment of total clarity that if she knew how to make what she needed, she'd never be needing again. He didn't like to think of her being without. He'd asked Tia to up the monthly order of baking supplies. No one had complained after Maddie proved she could turn anything she baked to bliss. She never ate what she baked, though. *That* he couldn't figure out. And she wouldn't say why. Which just deepened the puzzle of what made the apparently simple Maddie so complex.

Maddie glared at Caine, her eyes snapping with the knowledge that he was laughing at her. "That doesn't mean it's all his."

No, it didn't. "Tia did declare the cake fair game after the first serving."

She bit her lip, revealing white teeth and the slight gap between the top front two. She always tried to hide that gap. Personally he thought it too appealing in a far too sexual way. Maddie wavered, clearly torn between the two things she wanted. Caden took pity on her. Maddie wanted that cake, and right now he needed to give her one last thing because it might be a while before he saw her again. By the time he came back, she might be more grounded in this world. Maybe even married. He resisted the urge to stroke his fingers over the freckles sprinkling across her cheekbones.

Caden put his champagne glass on the potting table beside him. "Go get your cake, Maddie."

Still she hesitated, looking up at Caden with those leaf-green eyes, her fear in her gaze. "You won't leave before I get back?"

"No." He'd be leaving tonight, though. It was time for him to go.

"Best hurry," Caine prodded.

Maddie frowned at Caine. She looked like a kitten challenging a cougar as she ordered, "You won't tell him bad stories? He doesn't sleep well when you do, and he needs his rest."

Shit, she made him sound downright feeble. Something that wasn't lost on Caine if the smile tugging at his lips was anything to go by.

"Wouldn't dream of it."

Caden turned Maddie toward the crowd gathered at the cake table. "Go, Maddie, before there's none left."

She did, lifting her skirts and showing an indecent amount of ankle in her haste to beat Tucker to the cake. She had pretty ankles.

"I'm not even going to ask how she knows how you sleep," Caine stated with an arch of his brow.

And he wasn't going to tell. Caden folded his arms across his chest. "I haven't been messing with her."

Caine dismissed the challenge with a wave of his hand. Whiskey sloshed in the cut-crystal glass he held. Caden remembered when they used to drink it straight out of the bottle. "Hell, I know that, but that woman has a powerful affection for you."

"She's like a child."

"Maybe when she first got here. But have you noticed lately she's more here than there?"

"She's healing."

"Desi says she's forgetting."

Caden took one of the glasses from Caine. "How the hell does a woman forget being forced to serve men from childhood?"

"A woman who knows how to escape into make-believe?" Caine made a slashing motion with his free hand. "How the hell do I know?"

"Then, why are you bringing it up?"

"Because Sally Mae told Desi that I should."

Of course she had. Caden sighed and swirled the whiskey in the glass. "Life was a hell of a lot easier before we had women cluttering up the place."

Caine's whole expression softened as he looked over at his wife. Blonde and petite, her curly hair temporarily confined in a knot, Desi was the love of Caine's hard life and he was hers. If ever two people fit together like pieces of a puzzle, it was Desi and Caine.

"I happen to like the clutter," Caine drawled.

Caden bet he did, but the Miller men didn't have that kind of heart luck. They were treasure hunters, adventurers, trailblazers. Caden took a sip of whiskey. The only thing the Millers brought women was loneliness and disappointment. "I know."

"You really going to try to salvage that gold mine of Fei's?" Caine asked.

Caden swallowed the whiskey, savoring the burn. That was more like it. Enough whiskey could cauterize any wound. "Yup."

"Sam said Fei blew it to hell and gone."

Caden shrugged. There were ways around that. "Just presents more of a challenge."

"A hell of a challenge for one man."

Caden smiled and took another sip. "Since when did Hell's Eight shy away from a challenge?"

"Never." Caine swirled the whiskey in his glass. "Is

that what has your feet itching? No more challenges for you here?"

There were plenty of challenges at Hell's Eight. Just because they'd staked their claim didn't mean there wasn't someone who was going to try to take it.

His father's face flashed into his mind. Frozen in time. *Remember who you are...*

He'd done his duty by the Hell's Eight and Tia. But now it was time to do right by his family.

"More like a promise I've got to keep."

"What promise?" Caine asked.

"Nothing that involves you."

"If it involves you," Caine countered, "it involves Hell's Eight."

Caine's loyalty to those he considered family was all encompassing. Caden drained the glass and set it beside the delicate champagne flute. Such elegance where before there had been none. He turned away. "Not this time."

"The hell you say."

He met Caine's gaze squarely. "I do."

"At least let Ace or Luke go with you."

Caden could see Maddie scooping up her piece of cake. Saw her smile at Tucker shyly as he pretended to grab for it. Inside, something twisted, revealing a touch of...anger? He pushed the feeling aside.

"You can't spare the hands."

"We can spare what you need," Caine said.

Caden knew the state of the ranch as well as anyone. Knew the threats against it. They'd just expanded.

Every man was necessary. And now with the cavalry being pulled back East to deal with the discord there between North and South, they had to add the renewed threat of Indian attacks to the mix. "Too many people would draw attention."

"Two is hardly too many," Sam cut in, coming up beside them, a whiskey glass in one hand and a bottle in the other. Behind him was Ace. "Hell, it won't even get the job done. Remember, I saw the place after Fei blew it up. The woman is thorough."

Caden knew he'd eventually need help, a lot of it likely, but right now, he didn't want it. "I need to do this on my own."

"Because of that promise you made your da?" Ace asked, his dark hair flopping over his brow, giving him the look of a devil-may-care no-account. Until you looked a little lower and saw his eyes. No one that had any ability to take a man's measure could mistake the coldness and purpose that shadowed his light brown eyes. Ace could cut a man's throat with the same aplomb with which he could perform those card tricks he liked to show off. And with a smile on his face. Not that Ace enjoyed killing, but if it was necessary, he didn't have any qualms about settling a score. Caden sighed, noting Tracker and Shadow making their way over, too. This had all the makings of a well-intentioned ambush. Shit.

"Did someone send out an invite I missed?"

Sam smiled. "Nah. This is more of an impromptu party."

"What promise did you make to your da?" Caine asked, with that tenacity that marked everything he did.

"Nothing." Caden glared at Ace. Of all the Hell's Eight, he was closest to Ace, which had resulted in a drunken confession about his father many years ago that should never have been made. Ace merely shook his head.

"Don't get your tail in a twist. You're a grown man. You get to be as foolish as you want."

"The hell he does."

"Let it go, Caine," Caden ordered.

"The hell I will."

Sam leaned in and poured more whiskey into Caine's already quarter-full glass. "Drink that."

"Shit, if I drink that, I'll be drunk."

Sam shrugged and offered Ace the bottle, before saying, "At least you'll have an excuse for spouting nonsense."

"It's not nonsense. That gold mine is in the middle of Indian country, and Culbart isn't going to be any help if anything goes wrong out there."

That was true. The mine wasn't the only thing Fei had blown to hell and gone. When Fei's father had sold her cousin Lin to Culbart, Fei had taken matters into her own hands. A lot of dynamite had been blown to rescue Lin. Which meant the only white man close enough to come to Caden's aid at the mine wasn't going to be feeling that friendly toward a Hell's Eight man. Caden mentally shrugged. He'd faced tougher odds.

"Culbart's a hard-ass, but no one has ever accused

him of being stupid," Ace said. "If Hell's Eight calls for help, he'll be there. He can't afford to be that friendless with that ranch of his smack-dab in the middle of Indian country and tensions rising the way they are."

"Besides, I thought some of the problems with Culbart stemmed from the fact the man thought Lin was being kidnapped?" Caden asked.

"He's got a point, Caine," Ace offered. "Like the man or not, truth is Lin came to no harm in Culbart's care, and any man worth his salt would go after a woman stolen from his care, even if it was one of us who did the stealing."

Caine frowned and took a large swallow from his glass. His green eyes narrowed. "The man still has an ax to grind. He lost good men in that 'misunderstanding.'"

"It would have been easier if Fei had bargained a bit before up and taking off with her cousin," Sam interjected wryly. "Might have saved on the grinding."

"Culbart didn't leave her much choice," Caine drawled, taking another sip. "He'd lost good money in the deal. Holding on to Fei was his best chance of getting it back."

Ace shook his head. "Or so he thought. Fei did a good job covering her pa had gone bat-shit crazy. You can't totally blame Culbart."

Caine cocked a brow at Ace. "You sound as though you like the bastard."

Ace shrugged. "I do. He's tough as nails, but he's got a strong sense of right and wrong." He took a drink of whiskey. "Not to mention an interesting sense of humor."

"When the hell did you ever see his sense of humor?"

Caden snapped, impatience rubbing his temper raw. He wanted to go, not sit here and discuss Culbart's good qualities.

"When Caine here sent me to set Culbart straight."

"You were supposed to intimidate him," Caine countered.

"I decided to socialize first."

Caden shook his head. Leave it to Ace to turn an enemy into an ally.

"I wouldn't say he's a friend," Ace continued, "but he's not hostile."

Caden straightened. He was doing this, and to hell with Culbart and to hell with argument. If that ruffled feathers along the way, then too bad. "Well, if Culbart still has an ax to grind, let him grind it."

"Goddamn it, Caden," Caine snarled. "Why do you have to do this now when we're spread so thin?"

Because he did. Turning on his heel, Caden walked away, not answering, pushing past Shadow and Tracker, ignoring the surprised lift of Tucker's brow. As he reached the garden gate, he heard Caine say, "Would someone tell me about this promise?"

"It's personal, not important," Ace responded with a blatant lie for which Caden would owe him.

"It's important enough that the man who never breaks promises is breaking one to keep it."

Ace swore, "Shit."

Maddie. Caine was talking about Maddie. Caden had promised her he wouldn't leave the party before she got back. Caden saw her out of the corner of his eye, standing slightly apart from the others, smiling and watching the dancers, looking as pretty and as inviting as sunshine after a storm. Saw Luke head her way, and swore. She'd get over it. He shoved the gate open and kept walking. As the gate slammed closed behind him, he heard her call his name, the surprise and disappointment nipping at his feet in a tone he'd heard his mother use too many times.

Fuck.

He was his father after all.

CHAPTER TWO

HE WAS LEAVING. Maddie stood, tucked half behind a flowering pear tree, looking at the buds amid the leaves, feeling her hopes fade even as the trees blossomed. New pears that she'd come to think would signal a new beginning for her. In a few months those small, nondescript bulges would be fruit. She'd planned on picking that fruit for Caden, but he was leaving. Leaving her. Leaving Hell's Eight. Without even a goodbye. To her, at least.

Just like everybody else she'd ever cared about. The man she'd thought was her father. Her mother. Her friends. They'd all left. And she'd stayed, just as she was staying here because she always hoped things would get better. Ever since she'd made the decision to take Tracker up on his offer to come to Hell's Eight, she'd been clinging to some sort of hope. Hope that life for her could be better. That she could be loved. That she'd have a husband. A home. Children.

And yet here she was, standing among strangers, treating them like friends, mooning over a man who couldn't see her as woman or whore. Watching him say his goodbyes to others, bracing herself for his absence, for the awful not knowing if he was alive or dead for weeks on end. She shivered, the cold, sick feeling digging into her stomach. She loved Caden so. But beyond a smile whenever she came into his presence and an occasional offhand endearment that meant nothing, he didn't know she was alive. But that didn't change the fact he was her heart and he was leaving. Or that she hated it.

The protest started at the edges of her mind, subtle yet insistent, gathering strength like a storm chasing across the plains, gaining volume as it got closer. The howl dissolved to voices from her past, some kind, most of them cruel, telling her what to do, how to do it, as if her pain was nothing. As if *she* was nothing. The urge to slip away deeper into the foliage until she disappeared clawed at her nerves.

She dug her nails into her forearms, letting the pain drive back the cacophony. Caden was a strong man. He respected strong women. All the women of Hell's Eight were strong. Sally Mae with her pacifist beliefs, healing ways and defiance of convention. Desi with her fiery spirit. Ari with her gentleness that belied an inner strength that didn't ever let her quit. Bella who was just pure life. Fei with her purpose and drive. Those were the type of women that Caden admired. That was the kind of woman she needed to be.

She looked over to where Tia stood beside her Ed, the mantilla on her head fluttering in the breeze, catching the smile in her eyes. Tia, who'd lost her husband and her children, and yet had taken on eight young boys, wild boys, hate-filled boys, and turned them into men to be admired. Why hadn't God sent her a Tia?

She licked her lips and looked to where Caden had

disappeared. Maybe the good Lord hadn't sent her a Tia when she was a child sobbing into her pillow at night, but He'd given her an escape. But now He was taking that away, and she couldn't help but think that it wasn't coincidence that as her escape into fantasy stopped being effective, her love for Caden grew. She was meant to come to Hell's Eight. She truly believed that God sent her here. But she didn't believe he sent her here to be alone. He sent her here for Caden. For though he was restless and distant, part of the whole yet somehow apart from it, he was a man who needed love, who needed gentleness, and she'd waited her whole life to give her love to someone. It didn't matter if he recognized it or gave it back. She'd waited her whole life for someone to love. And now he was leaving.

She shook her head. She couldn't let it just happen. She heard a noise beside her. She looked up. Bella stood there, for once without her handsome blond, blue-eyed Sam, her belly rounded with child, her smile full of that life that gave Sam purpose. Maddie had spent a lot of time studying what attracted these men to these women and what kept them moving. And for Sam it was Bella's spirit that he cherished.

"You hide again, Maddie." It was both an accusation and a question, spoken in Bella's melodic accent that made music of her words. Even the exasperated ones.

Maddie shrugged. "I'm watching to see what needs to be done."

Bella shook her head. "There is only one thing you watch, my friend."

As always, Bella's use of the term "friend" made her jump inside. Maddie had never had a real friend. She'd been kept alive after her birth for a purpose. For a long time she'd dreamed it had been to be loved, but as the years passed, the truth had become clear, and she'd learned to stop smiling at others and to stop believing. Though the women of Hell's Eight were kind to her, she never felt comfortable with their caring. She was a whore. She might have run from her life, but all the offers of friendship in the world couldn't remove the stain. It was easy to pretend that wasn't true, protected here at Hell's Eight. Here the world couldn't touch her, but someday she'd have to leave. And when she did she wanted to be just like Bella. Confident. Sassy. Always ready with a quick response. Never hiding.

But she wasn't like Bella. Not yet. She didn't have fire. She didn't have family. She didn't have beliefs. She'd been a child lost and now she was a woman lost, but she was going to find her way. The padre said God didn't put people on this earth with no purpose, which meant she had a purpose, too. When he'd first said it, it'd been a unique idea she couldn't understand. But over time she couldn't forget it, and slowly it had grown on her and taken root. Until now, finding a purpose *was* her purpose.

"I don't know what you're talking about."

Bella smiled and glanced over to the gate Caden had just passed through. "It is easy to see where your heart lies."

Maddie licked her lip, feeling that stab of fear deep

inside. To love something was to lose it, to cause its death. Instinct had her reaching for make-believe, but she couldn't find that hazy place where real and imagination blended as easily as they used to. Ari said it was a good thing. Maddie wasn't sure.

"Hearts and flowers are so pretty at weddings." The slip into nonsense was only half-faked. It was always so much easier to act as nothing when you felt like nothing.

Bella sighed and folded her arms under her ample chest, resting them on her belly. "You will try this nonsense with others. I know you are not *loca.*"

Maddie wished she knew that. "Are you so sure?"

Bella shook her head. "There is more to you than nonsense, Maddie."

Maddie blinked. No one had ever said that to her before.

"I am sweet thighs and soft breasts and pleasure for a man." She'd heard that so much it was rote.

Bella snorted. "You're passion and temper, and when you find your feet, the only man that will find pleasure with you is the one that you choose."

"You think I'll get to choose?"

Bella, always so insightful, always so blunt, touched her hand, causing Maddie to jump again because no one ever touched her. Touching was bad, painful, death. *"Sí."*

She pulled her hand away, immediately feeling bad. She liked Bella. Bella just smiled.

"You are Hell's Eight now, Maddie. You are not nothing."

"Tracker just brought me here."

Bella smiled and looked at the big man talking to Ed. The wind caught his hair, exposing the deep scar on his cheek. "Something brought us all here."

To Maddie, Tracker was a scary man with that scar down his face and those big muscles and that dark skin, but to Ari he was her sun and moon, which just proved gentleness lived everywhere. Maddie clung to that. Caden wasn't as big as Tracker, but his hands were strong enough to bruise, break bones.

Bella grunted and put her hand to her stomach. "I swear if this child doesn't stop kicking me I'm going to let his daddy raise him."

Maddie looked at Bella. "You carry a girl."

"How do you know?" It was uniquely Bella that she didn't dismiss the thought, just asked if Maddie was sure.

It would be tactless to say she'd seen so many pregnant women over the course of her eighteen years in a whorehouse that she knew how a woman carried. So Maddie just shrugged instead and said, "Some things a woman just knows."

Bella's brows lifted, and she made an eloquent motion of her hands. "See? *Ya está.* When you don't stop to think about how you are going to be received, you say what is on your mind."

"A woman should be seen and not heard."

Bella snorted. "Idiots should be seen and not heard."

Maddie couldn't help but flinch any more than Bella could help her immediate apologetic touch on her hand. Bella was always touching. It didn't bother Maddie so much anymore.

"I am sorry, Maddie. You know I do not think you are an idiot."

So many did, though. Her glance cut to the path Caden had taken. Bella's gaze followed hers but she didn't let go of her hand this time, just gripped it tighter when Maddie tugged.

"Maddie?"

"Yes?"

"Do you believe the truth I always tell?"

Maddie nodded, used to Bella's grammar. It was actually pretty the way she spoke, clear yet a little off-kilter, like a unique music played beneath the words.

"I believe you." She tugged at her hand again. Bella gripped tighter.

"Do you believe that I would never do anything to hurt you?"

She nodded again.

"Do you believe I am not conventional?"

Maddie nodded. "I believe all that you tell me. You are a good person. You would never lie."

Bella snorted. "Good people lie all the time. So do I. I would to save someone I love, but I would not lie to someone I love for no reason."

Maddie understood that. "Yes."

Bella shook her head. "I will speak plainly now, in words I want you to hear."

Maddie grabbed a branch of the tree and braced herself. Only bad things started that way.

Bella took a step around until she faced her, her stomach touching the folds of Maddie's skirt. Maddie wanted to run and hide, but it didn't really matter what she wanted. Bella was determined to have her say, and she could see Sam searching for his wife. Soon he would be here. Maddie preferred not to deal too closely with the men of Hell's Eight. It wasn't that they were bad men; they were just men, and men made her uncomfortable.

"I'm listening."

"Forgive me my plain speaking, but you are in love with Caden."

Maddie flinched, clenching the branch in her hand, the leaves tearing and sending a slightly fruity scent into the air. "A man like that isn't for me."

Bella snorted. "He's a man like any other who needs a woman to love him."

"He has his pick of women."

"And you could have your pick of men."

Maddie shook her head. Only the naive believed that. "I am used goods, fit for the bed and nothing else. No man would want me."

Bella's nails dug into her wrist. "You will not speak such words again to me. You are my friend. You were there for that time Sam went away and my dreams were bad. You sat with me and made me tea. You run around this place like you are nothing, doing everything, supporting everyone, making sure that Sally Mae had what she needed for the wedding, organizing, finagling—"

"I am good at trading," Maddie interrupted.

"Trading, then. But everything you do supports those that you love. You are a strong force in the background making everything possible. You have changed so much here at Hell's Eight since you have come and yet you see none of this. You see yourself as nothing, as bed sport only."

Maddie looked away. Bella's finger under her chin yanked her face back.

"If you want Caden, this thinking needs to stop. You need to believe in who you are. You need to believe in the strength that kept you alive all these years. You need to believe in that part of you that makes you the one woman he smiles at whenever you are near."

Maddie hated the hope that sprang to life in her chest, hated it yet clung to it.

"You don't know—"

Bella shook her head. "No. I do not know anything for sure, but I know when you are around Caden you smile, and I know when Caden is around you he smiles. This does not determine the end, but to me it seems a good beginning."

She could see Caine and Ace arguing, she assumed about Caden. No doubt Caine didn't want him to leave. Caine thought he had a lot of power over the men, but her Caden was a stubborn man, and she understood more than Caine that Caden was also a man who needed to make his own way.

"What would you have me do? A knight doesn't look for a princess among the garbage."

"My Sam had no use for me when he first met me."

That Maddie couldn't believe. "You are Sam's princess in the tower."

"I was Sam's pain in the—" Bella smiled and tapped

her behind, leaving the word unsaid. "He thought I was too good for him, that he would only bring me trauma in my life. He denied our love, our attraction and our potential for joy."

"But you're together."

"Yes. We are. But I had to chase that man across half the state and I had to fight for him."

"You can't make someone love you. Sally Mae told me this."

"And Sally Mae is right. But you can stop someone from running away from the way they feel long enough for the truth of their feelings to catch up to them."

Who did Bella think she was, preaching such hope to the hopeless? She had no right. "Maybe I'm just too stupid to understand such a thing."

Bella let go of her hand and took a step back. "Maybe you are too stupid to be with a man like Caden, who has everything except the softness he needs. And maybe you are too stupid to know what is right and wrong and how it should be between a man and a woman. And maybe you are just too stupid for a lot of things because you foolishly believe all the wrong people told you." Bella made a slashing motion with her hand. "But I do not think so. I have seen how you have changed. How you have grown, so when I tell you this, know that I am speaking to Maddie the woman who has become part of Hell's Eight, not Maddie who sees herself of no value. It is time for you to leave here." She motioned toward the gate. "Time for you to follow your heart."

"Why?"

Bella's expression softened. "Because if you want Caden, Maddie, then you need to do whatever it takes to make him see you and what could be. Something big. And no one can do it for you."

She turned on her heel.

Maddie stood where she was anchored by her grip on the tree and the weight of the preposterous idea Bella had put forth. "Wait."

Bella shook her head and raised her hand. "No. It is time for you to make up your mind who you will be."

Maddie had the insane urge to chase after Bella, to have her tell her what to do, but what was the point? Bella was right. She had decided herself it was time she stopped being a child.

Caden was leaving as if it was nothing to anyone. The man never understood he was missed when he left. Or maybe he didn't care. Sometimes it was hard to know. Follow her heart, Bella had advised. Did she have the courage to do something that big?

Caden had told her that he wouldn't leave without seeing her. The anger that hit her was strong. The determination just as strong. She was done being left behind. Every day when she got up, life happened to her. Tomorrow, she was going to happen to her life.

MADDIE'S TREASURES WERE packed into a saddlebag along with two changes of clothes before dawn even touched the sky. Caden had left an hour earlier. She'd heard the back-porch step creak as he'd slipped out. Saw the light in the barn. It was time for her to go now, too. Sneak-

ing down the back stairs, she ducked out the same door
as Caden, but she avoided the third board on the steps.
While no one would protest Caden's departure, hers
would be sure to cause a fuss. Her redbone hound whined
and lifted his head. She smiled and made a motion of her
hand. He came over immediately. She fed him a piece of
meat left over from supper. He wolfed it down and, when
another wasn't forthcoming, drooped his head until the
loose folds all but obscured his eyes. He had the look of
his father, Boone, but was the despair of Tucker's pack.
Worthless, he'd been named, because while he could
track like his father, he wouldn't bay.

The day Tucker had cut him from the litter, she'd cried
for him. When she'd heard his name, that had been the
final straw. She'd taken the dog as hers, expecting a protest. No one had said a word. He'd become her "porch
hound," as Tucker called him. She'd tried to change the
dog's name, but he refused to respond to anything else,
which just went to prove everything had a meaning to
someone, and she had to respect his preference.

It still made her nervous having a friend, even if it
was a dog, but there was no going back. Worthless had
claimed her as much as she'd claimed him. So far they'd
been friends. Tonight, he was going to become her partner. She hoped. Tapping her hip, she beckoned Worthless to her side.

The note and IOU she'd written crinkled in her pocket.
Flower was a sweet little mare that Tucker had trained
for her. She had a gentle way about her and not a mean
bone in her body. Maddie trusted her as she trusted no

human. No matter how valuable the horse was, Maddie couldn't choose another. And not only because her riding skills weren't that good. She needed things around her right now in which she had faith. She might have decided to happen to her life, but that didn't mean she had any confidence she could pull it off.

Flower nickered as Maddie approached her stall. She opened the door, her hands shaking. She patted the mare's neck and took a breath. The only other time she'd taken her destiny into her own hands was when she'd bolted after Tracker out the door of that whorehouse. She still didn't know what had made her do it, but once done, there'd been no going back. She'd been prepared to beg the big man, but he'd turned and looked at her, appearing so dark and alien she'd almost reconsidered, then with a nod he'd held out his hand. She'd taken it full of fear, only to find beneath that harsh exterior was a good man.

He'd been looking for his Ari then, sympathy for her plight no doubt driving him to collect discarded women along the way. Tracker had brought her home to Hell's Eight the way he brought many others. Giving them a place to heal. Most had left after a month or two. Moving on. She'd stayed. She hadn't had any other place to go and she'd been afraid to start over. Or so she'd thought. Truth was, she'd just been slow to be ready.

She looked beyond the open stable door to the fading night beyond. But that was all changing. "We're going adventuring, Flower."

She snubbed the little horse to the hitching post and fetched her tack. Worthless flopped by the post. "Caden thinks he can just break a promise to me, but he can't," she told the hound. He rolled his big brown eyes at her.

Thanks to Caden's relentless instruction, she made short work of saddling and bridling the little mare. At the time she'd wanted to curse him, but now, when time was critical, she appreciated every tedious lesson. She couldn't afford to let Caden get too far ahead of her. She took the IOU out of her pocket and stuck it on a nail jutting out of the post. Stealing a horse was a hanging offense. She wanted to be sure the Hell's Eight knew she was only borrowing Flower. Over the IOU she put the note she'd written to Tia and Bella. It was short and to the point. A thank-you and a simple *I've decided to live my life.* As an afterthought she'd added, *Please, don't worry.* She hoped she'd spelled everything right.

It was a novel thought that someone would worry about her. She smiled. Taking control of her life was working. She now had friends.

Looping the leash around Worthless's neck, she tied the other end around the saddle horn. His silent tracking was going to work for her. The last thing she needed was for Caden to know she was following until they were too far out for him to send her back.

She took one last look around. Here she was safe. Beyond the door, her life waited. For a minute she hesitated. Worthless whined and stood. She nodded. "You're right. It's time to go."

She swung up into the saddle, her skirt settling around the pants Caden had purchased for her when he'd noticed how she'd been sore after that first time riding. She hadn't had pantaloons and she'd been too embarrassed to tell anybody. She'd fretted for days he'd tell and she'd be embarrassed. So much had embarrassed her back then. Gathering up the reins, she sighed. She'd felt so lacking amid the confidence of the Hell's Eight women. But that had been her own silliness, as Bella would put it.

Then, a few days after that first riding lesson, Caden had handed her a box and told her to open it in private. Her first thoughts had been shameful. Thinking he'd bought her scandalous womanly things, and it had been with great trepidation she'd placed the box on her bed. When she'd opened it, she'd cried. Stupid, silly tears. He'd bought her ugly man-pants to wear under her skirts. Made of soft wool and thick enough so her thighs wouldn't chafe. She'd lost her heart to him right then, though it took her weeks to identify what that skip of a beat had meant.

She loved those damn pants. Loved that damn man. And now she was planning on loving her damn life. So much had changed around her in the past year. So much had changed within her. She'd gone from a scared child who hid in make-believe to a woman who was learning to live. It was exciting. It was energizing. It was as scary as all get-out. Patting Flower on the shoulder and smiling at the eagerly waiting Worthless, Maddie urged the mare forward. Worthless fell in beside.

"Ready or not, here we come."

CHAPTER THREE

MADDIE'S SENSE OF adventure took a rapid downhill spiral. It wasn't as easy as she thought it would be to follow Caden's trail. Worthless would first pick up and then lose the scent. And frankly, she couldn't tell the difference. Flower didn't always want to go where Worthless went, she couldn't see what she was doing, and that damn breeze rustling the leaves kept whispering in her ears little words of warning. *Go back. Go back.* But she was tired of going back, so she plunged on, letting her mind drift so worry wouldn't eat her alive, trusting Worth to get her where she needed to go.

Flower stumbled, tossing Maddie about in the saddle. She grabbed the horn. The mare tossed her head and took two steps back. Worthless whined at the end of the leash as he was pulled off the scent. Lifting her head, she saw immediately why the horse stopped. An overgrown, impenetrable bramble thicket was just sitting there where she needed to go. Darn! She'd have to go around.

The dog whined again, straining toward the thicket as she tugged on the leash.

"We don't have a choice," she snapped at the animal. She immediately regretted the harshness. It wasn't Worth's fault that she was confused. She just hadn't expected everything to look so similar in the dark. She had no idea where she was. Flower tossed her head again. No doubt she wanted to be safely home in her stall. Maddie had a sense of day coming, but not much sun got through the thickness of the trees. Worth whined again, straining to the left. There was a slight hole in the thicket there, but it certainly wasn't big enough for the horse. Wrapping the leash around her wrist, she pulled him back. She sat deeper in the saddle and looked around. In all directions, she saw trees. If she didn't know better, she'd say the same tree just repeated itself. She didn't even know if she could find her way home from here. She had no choice but to go forward. She'd just have to take the chance that she could find the trail again. And the discouraging thought came to her that if she and her horse couldn't pass through here, neither could Caden, which only left one question: What exactly had the dog been following?

"You were supposed to follow Caden," she told Worth. He looked up at her, tongue lolling, panting slightly. No doubt he was thirsty. She was, too. The mare nickered. Poor Flower was probably thirstier than them all. Maddie reached for her canteen only to discover it gone. It'd fallen off somewhere along the way. Tears burned behind her eyelids. She took another breath, closing her eyes as the panic started deep within. She was lost with no water. Going back was no more possible than going forward. Her great adventure was a disaster. She should have just stayed at Hell's Eight.

The buzzing started at the edges of her mind. Holding

her breath, she reached for her calm place, picturing in
her mind the pond at her home outside of Carson City.
It was so easy to summon the image this time, to imagine she felt the breeze upon her face. In the summer it
was so pretty with the shade of the trees spreading out
over the water and the clover sprinkling the shore like
a smile. The breeze off the water felt so good on those
hot summer days. She squeezed her eyes tightly shut and
imagined until she could feel the sun on her face, smell
the damp earth, hear the soft rustle of the summer breeze
through the trees, feel it caress her face and shoulders.

She did love summer days. There was something so
hopeful about them that made a body feel as light as a
feather. There was nothing she loved more than sitting
by her pond, and if she were lucky, with a book to read.
She did love to read, and Mrs. Cabel, the schoolteacher,
occasionally allowed her to take a book from her library
so long as she treated it with respect. She always treated
those books with respect. They were her treat, her escape into another world.

But something was wrong. This time of day, the shade
was always on the right side of the pond, providing a
more comfortable place to sit. It'd be the perfect place
for a picnic. She guided Flower to the right. The dog
whined and went along. She crossed the rocky surface of
the stream. The horse stumbled, jostling her. She shook
her head, chuckling. She always tripped over that big
stone in the middle. It was so easy to lose track of time
here on the sunny side of the pond. In her mind's eye
she reached her spot, smoothed her skirts as she sat on

the blanket, leaned back against the tree and just let the cares of the day fade away. She loved it here by the pond.

Pain in her calf snapped her eyes open. She grabbed at her leg. Worthless was on his hind legs, clawing at her skirts. Flower tossed her head and sidestepped. Reality slapped her in the face as she looked ahead. It was not the scene at the pond but a sheer drop-off that faced her. Thirty feet down she could see a river cutting through the ravine. The mare tossed her head and took a step back. Maddie grabbed the horn.

Dear God. She'd almost driven them over the cliff. Dragging her eyes away from the drop, she looked around. She didn't recognize where she was. She didn't recognize where she was going. Didn't know how long she'd been drifting in her mind. Long enough for the sun to come up and the woods to change to clearing, but that didn't tell her much.

"Where did you bring us?" she asked Worthless. He sat down and flopped his wrinkles at her. Some help he was. She backed Flower away from the edge. "At least it's pretty."

And it was. Hell's Eight was up high on the cliffs where it was sparse and the environment was harsh, but down here things had a lusher feel. More like home. There weren't so many sharp edges to the landscape. It rolled more than cut and grass grew around rocks and summer flowers sprouted along hillsides and leaves filtered sunlight. It would be a wonderful place to stop and picnic if she weren't lost.

"What are we going to do?" she asked the hound. He

stood on his hind legs and pawed at her foot. Leather
creaked as she leaned down and petted his head. Worthless wagged his tail, his expression blissful as she
scratched behind his ear. Clearly, he shared none of her
concern. And why would he? He was used to hunting
with Hell's Eight. For sure Tracker wouldn't be lost.
Neither would Caden, Tucker or Caine. They knew this
country like the back of their hands, whereas she... She
sighed. She only knew how to create pictures in her
mind.

She made a note of another one of her needs. She
truly needed to learn how to find her way around the
wilderness. The next time she brought it up with the
men, she wouldn't be fobbed off with a ruffle of her hair
and the statement that there was no need, the way Sam
had done. Hell's Eight's protection or not, she needed
her own skills.

She didn't want to be watched out for. Protectors came
and went. She'd had a lot of protectors over the years.
Protectors had a way of losing interest, and when they
did, she was always alone again and left to her own de-
vices. At that point her choice was to rely on herself or
to find another. With no skills to sustain her, there really was no choice. But she didn't want a protector anymore. She just wanted herself. She wanted to be like the
men of Hell's Eight, like the women of Hell's Eight. She
wanted to be able to look trouble in the eye and knock
its teeth out.

She flexed her fingers, made a fist and tried to imagine what the face of trouble would look like, but it always

came at her in so many different forms it was hard to pick just one to punch. Like now, trouble tended to be a sneaky bastard. She was lost. Her current trouble was as simple and as complex as that. She tried to remember all she'd heard about Fei's mine. The stories were wild and exciting on one level, like something out of a storybook. But it hadn't been a fairy tale. Shadow had lived it with Fei. When Maddie listened to them tell the story, all she could think of was the expression of confidence in Fei's face as she talked about how she'd handled things. Maddie wanted to be that confident. She wanted people to look at her and know that she could handle things. She wanted Caden to look at her like that. She wanted to know it herself.

She remembered the talk about the climb, how hard it was to get up the side of the cliff to the mine, which meant it was high. Her options in trails that were rideable were either to go back the way she came, to travel along the right side of the mountain or to take the steep drop down.

With her heart in her throat, she turned the mare to the path along the side of the mountain. The sun was rising on her right, clearing the mountain. She didn't know if that was good or bad, wrong or right. She didn't even know if that was east or west. How could she be so ignorant about such important details? Of course, growing up in town, it was never important which way the sun came up. On Hell's Eight she'd never been left alone; always someone guarded her. Another form of protection that had not served her.

She urged Flower forward. The one thing she hated about being "here" so much was the uncertainty of the emotions that always ate at her. In her make-believe world, it was calm. It was peaceful. There were never any wild swings of emotion. No fear. No hate. No pain. No sadness. Just calm summer days by the pond or maybe an evening at a social where she'd dance with handsome gentlemen who treated her with respect and thought she was lovely. She shook her head. Sometimes she wondered if she'd known going with Tracker had meant that she would be "here" so much and what being "here" meant if she wouldn't have done it. She shook her head again as the birds sang in her ear and the horse's hooves clopped along the path. Maybe not. Her make-believe world hadn't been as satisfying even back then, and it'd been harder and harder to hold on to her peaceful feeling. Maybe losing the ability to pretend would have happened anyway and instead of being safe at Hell's Eight, she would have just been in…

She sighed as the path turned around the hill. It'd been so much easier as a child to pretend. So much easier to shirk the responsibility of living. Until the day when a customer had stabbed her friend Hilda. Maddie moaned in her mind, remembering the horror of the blood, of putting her hands over the wounds, of trying to stop the pulsing flow, her only friend's blood gushing over her hands in a steady stream. No matter which wounds she covered, no matter how quickly she covered them, she couldn't stop the blood. All she could do was sit there and listen to Hilda gasp and groan as her life was ripped from her by an act of senseless violence, while around them the brothel girls and their customers went about their business. All because Hilda hadn't undressed fast enough. Maddie bit her lip as sobs welled as fresh today as they were back then. Hilda had deserved better. It'd been so unfair. So wrong. Long after Hilda had stopped breathing, Maddie had been trying to clean up the blood, as if cleaning up the evidence would bring her back. But there'd been no bringing her back, no forgetting the words Hilda had whispered to her. *I was going to...*

It'd been a game they played. When they got enough money, they were going to buy a house. When they met a nice man, they were going to have a home and children. When they saved enough, they were going to travel the world and live high. And Hilda hadn't gotten to do anything except spread her legs for the dirty men who paid the money.

I was going to.

Maddie had closed her eyes, those words hanging in her heart. It'd been in that spilt second that Tracker had come into the saloon, and in that split second she'd found the courage to jump on his offer. And now here she was, in the middle of nowhere on an adventure chasing her life and completely lost. Somehow her escape wasn't turning out the way she wanted. But then again, it wasn't as if she'd gotten any of it right.

At first she'd thought Hell's Eight would be everything she needed—a nice house, cleaning, cooking, baking but no bedding. She really didn't like bedding and no one there expected her to. And at first living there *had* been nice, really nice, but somehow it hadn't been enough. In the past couple months, she'd been consumed with the same restlessness she so often sensed in Caden. A need for…just something. She needed more than safety. She needed her own dreams. Her own life.

Lost in her thoughts, she didn't even see the riders coming at her around the corner until she almost ran into them. Flower tossed her head, whapping Maddie on the chin. Stars shot between her eyes. Four riders pulled up in front of her, two abreast on the trail. Flower stepped back a quick two steps. Maddie would have taken six. They were a hard-looking bunch. Their clothes were dirty from the trail, whiskers sprouted on their cheeks, and they all had guns strapped to their thighs, but they weren't unfamiliar. She didn't know who they were, but they didn't look any different from any of the saddle bums who'd frequented the Red Velvet Slipper looking for companionship. The look they were casting over her didn't feel any different, either. It was the type of look men gave her when they came into the saloon parlor, hot and hungry, seeing her as a body, not a person, wanting her as a vessel, not a companion. Her stomach heaved the way it always did, and her mind rebelled the way it always did, but the pretend wouldn't come. And she was left staring at them and the reality of what was likely about to happen.

"Well, what do we have here?" the older man on the right asked, pushing his hat back and folding his hands across the saddle horn.

She fumbled for a smile and turned Flower. "I'll just move over here and let you pass."

He laughed and nudged his horse forward, cutting her off. Worthless snarled.

"Best you hush that dog up before I shoot it."

Again, Maddie wished she'd had the forethought to steal a gun she knew how to work. The two men in back pulled their guns from their holsters. The rifle in the saddle scabbard looked good, but she'd only ever fired it once. And this close it wouldn't do much good.

"Hush, Worth."

As discreetly as possible, she untied Worthless from the saddle horn.

"Are you alone out here?" the leader asked.

What to answer? Holding on to her smile, she managed to say, "I got a late start."

It sounded like a lie even to her own ears. She wasn't surprised when the men didn't lower their guns.

"You saying you're alone out here?"

"I have Flower and Worth, and I should catch up to my friend soon."

The men exchanged a look between them. Clearly, she was much better at fooling herself than others, which was a sad thing.

"Does your friend know you're coming?"

She smiled brightly at them. "I imagine he's expecting me momentarily."

"Honey, we've been riding on this path for an hour and a half and haven't seen a soul."

"You wouldn't if he didn't want you to." That was the

truth. Caden was like a wolf in the night, slipping in and out of the shadows, being seen only when he wanted to be seen but always dangerous except when he was with her. She reached up and tucked her hair behind her ear, holding on to the strength of the memory of the brush of his fingers.

"And who is this friend you're trying to catch up with?"

She licked her lips. Flower, sensing her tension, shifted her feet. Seconds seemed like hours as Maddie debated her options.

"Don't lie, girl. Just tell the truth."

Habit made her answer to the snap in that voice. "Caden Miller."

Another look exchanged between the men. "Caden Miller of Hell's Eight?"

She nodded.

"You think Caden Miller of Hell's Eight is here?"

She nodded again. At least they knew Caden's name. There might be some protection in that.

"Shit. Come here, girl. Let me have a look at you."

There wasn't any choice but to go forward. She kneed Flower in a gentle urge. The little horse walked sedately forward, showing none of the trepidation that she had. Why didn't anyone but her see the danger here?

As if on cue, Worthless growled, low and deep in a way that said he meant business. The leader pointed his gun. She had to do something. It was easy and natural to slip back into the role of coquette. Shameful, even, the ease with which she did it. Dropping her shoulders, tilting her head to the side, leaning just that little bit forward, Maddie angled the horse between the dog and the man.

"Here, now. He doesn't mean any harm."

"He's not going to do any, either."

"But you might."

He cocked an eyebrow at her. "How's that?"

"Flower here isn't used to guns." She flipped her braid back over her shoulder and trailed her fingers across the top of her chest. "If you just go firing shots randomly, I might end up thrown, maybe even—" she ran a hand down her thigh "—breaking a leg."

The transition from weary to interest was subtle, but she could see it in the set of the men's shoulders, the tip of their chins, the relaxing of their hands on the reins.

The man in the back with the faded brown hat spat and said, "Would be a shame to break such pretty legs, boss."

As she suspected, the older man was the leader. His clothes were of better quality, and his face sported less stubble, as if he took more frequent care of his appearance. With a press of her knee, she shifted Flower's direction, putting herself closer to him. This was the man she had to influence.

His eyes traveled from the top of her head down to her waist and then back up, stopping at her breasts. Men always liked her breasts. She hated them. Fingers clawing, pinching; mouths slobbering. But there were advantages to having big breasts.

"You're lying, girl."

Yes, she was, but not in the way he thought. He brought his horse forward. The gelding towered over her little mare. He towered over her. He rode all around, checking her gear from front to back.

"That horse doesn't bear the Hell's Eight brand."

No, she didn't. Because Maddie wouldn't let her be hurt that way. Caine had fussed. Tucker had pointed out the reasons. Even Shadow had tried to tell her that it was okay, that it was necessary. Only Caden had understood. Flower was hers. She wasn't bringing her pain.

She smiled wider, showing her dimples. Men loved her dimples. Sure enough, the man's eyes dropped to her mouth.

"I rode up for the wedding celebration."

"Rode up, hmm? Hell's Eight's a day and a half away from any town."

She shrugged. "I didn't ride up alone."

"But you're riding out alone."

She shrugged. "It wasn't what I expected."

"I hear they aren't too particular about the company they keep."

She was used to men hating others because of the color of their skin. It was always a cause for a fight in a whorehouse. The proprietors learned quickly to separate out the Indians, otherwise they'd be replacing the furniture every day. Maddie wasn't sure the violence really had anything to do with the color of the skin. Men just seemed to like to fight. Any excuse would do. Skin color was just the easiest one.

She nodded. "A girl's got to have her standards."

One of the other men snorted. He was wearing the same dirty, dusty brown shirt and pants as the others. The only thing that distinguished him was his blond hair. "No way in hell the men of Hell's Eight let a pretty little thing like this slip out."

"I heard all of them were married up anyway."

"Not all of them and they've been hiring help." She shuddered delicately, feeding their assumptions. "Not a lot of single women up there."

"You think the married ones would let a whore in their midst, boss?"

She raised her brows at the man. "Are you calling me a liar, sir?"

She didn't know what she'd do if he said yes. She wasn't used to confronting people head-on. She thought of Bella and her fire and added for good measure, "Because if you are..."

"If I am, what?"

So much for Bella's inner fire. She couldn't copy that.

"Then I would have to tell you, you're wrong." She put her hand to her chest, drawing the man's gaze back to her best assets. The feel of her cotton dress was a shock when she'd been expecting skin. It was hard to flaunt your attributes when you were covered to the chin, but Tia had insisted nice girls didn't wear low-cut dresses. It had been useless trying to explain to Tia that she wasn't a nice girl, and while rape was something to be avoided, it wasn't anything she couldn't handle. But Tia was Tia and she always got her way.

After Maddie'd gotten used to thinking of herself as

unavailable, she'd loved her dresses. The material was
cool and comfortable, and while men smiled at her, none
had touched her. None had tried to corner her when their
wives weren't looking. No one treated her with anything
but respect. And even better, women didn't pull away
when she came close. She'd started to form friendships.
As a result, she'd begun to think of her coming to Hell's
Eight as a new beginning, a wiping clean of her past.
She'd kept herself pure. Felt good about it, even. Having a choice made her feel so…strong, in a unique way
she'd never had.

But it had been just another illusion like so many others. As, predicably, the men leered at her, Caden's face
flashed in her mind. She saw his frown as she smiled
back, and her heart sank. He wouldn't want her if these
men touched her. The knowledge was a stab through her
heart. Around the edges of her consciousness, the opportunity to escape presented itself. Worth whined. She
shook her head. She couldn't give in. Worth was Hell's
Eight. He would die for her. She was Hell's Eight. She
couldn't abandon him. She checked to make sure Flower
was still between the man and her dog. She was. "May
I ask your name, sir?"

"Who I am's not important. Who are you?"

She tossed her head again, wishing her hair was free
so it could flow about her shoulders. Men loved her hair
almost as much as they loved her breasts. "They call me
Ginger," she said, giving them her saloon name.

His eyes went to her hair. "Your spirit as fiery as
your hair?"

She smiled the smile she knew he expected from her, the one she'd been taught to give, the one that came too easily for the proper woman she'd been training to be.

"So I've been told."

"Hell's Eight owes us, boss. We lost our last woman because of them."

Last woman? That sounded ominous.

"True enough." The boss stared at her a moment. "She's got more meat on her bones than the last one."

"I gotta say I like the idea of a sporting woman better than I do a virgin."

The boss snapped, "The woman never said she was a virgin. Would never have brought her home had she mentioned that."

What kind of men were these?

"I say we keep her," the man in the back said.

She kept her eyes on the leader. The others could say all they wanted, but until this man spoke, nothing was going to be in stone. She knew it. So did they, which was why they were angling so hard.

The leader looked at her.

"You really a working girl? Because I don't want no misunderstandings this time round."

The answer lodged in her throat as the reality of where she was sank in around her. *Once a whore, always a whore.* She'd heard that so many times. She'd stopped believing it when Tracker had taken her away and the acceptance of Hell's Eight had settled around her. But just ten hours away from Hell's Eight, she was back to where she'd started.

"Yes." It was hard to get the word out.

"The men's humor would sure improve with a woman around the place."

The guy in the faded brown hat offered, "Morale has been down. Comanche's got everyone working double time."

"How much do you charge?" the boss asked.

"For what?" she stalled.

"I've got a camp of ten men who need satisfying."

"Around the clock?"

"You get Sundays off and from sundown to sunup. Other than that, the men come in, and you'd be available."

"And who would I be working for?"

"Frank Culbart of the Fallen C here." He made a token touch of his finger to his hat. She didn't get the impression that he was being disrespectful but that he was just rather gruff.

Culbart? Dear God. These were the men who'd purchased Fei's cousin and held her captive! "I don't cook and clean," she said.

"Girl, you'll pretty much do what I want."

She raised her chin, thinking of Tia. "I'm a working woman, sir, not a slave. I'll expect a decent wage."

"I yank you off that horse you're whatever the hell I say you are, so you best take what you get before you find yourself in a position you don't want to be in."

She didn't want to be here at all. She wanted to be with Caden.

One of the men rode forward and grabbed Flower's

reins, slipping them over the horse's head, and pulled
Flower forward.

"We'll leave the dog here."

"He won't stay."

He pulled his gun out. "Then I'll shoot him."

"No! "

"Don't you be telling me what I will or will not do."

She yanked at the reins, panic gathering in her stomach. Worth snarled and charged the man holding Flower's
reins.

With a calm that she couldn't fathom, Culbart pulled
the trigger. Worth howled and fell, whimpering before
lying still.

"No!"

Culbart took aim again. Kicking Flower forward,
Maddie grabbed for that gun before he could fire again.
Culbart swore.

"Goddamn it! Hold her, Dickens."

She screamed when somebody's arm went around her
waist and yanked her off her mare, hating the laughter
that flowed around her, mean, vicious chuckles that declared their superiority. She clawed at her captor's hands,
but her nails raked harmlessly over his gloves. Before
she could get her bearings, she was thrown around. She
automatically splayed her hands, but she didn't hit the
ground; instead, her stomach hit the saddle, and the slap
on her ass was hard enough to arch her back.

"Calm down. The dog's already dead," Dickens ordered.

She didn't want to calm down. *Caden!* The scream

came from her heart. The ground spun as the man wheeled his horse.

"We keeping her, boss?" someone asked.

"We'll see how she works out."

"And if she doesn't?"

"Nobody'll miss a whore."

The truth of that sat like ice on her soul.

CHAPTER FOUR

UNDER THE BEST of circumstances, mining was back-breaking work. Under these circumstances—one man trying to discreetly salvage a mine that had been blown to smithereens—it was brutal. Caden sighed and tied the rope to another boulder, hooked the harness around his shoulders and dragged the stone away from the hole, muscles straining with the exertion. The job would have been easier with help, or with equipment, and he knew he was going to have to break down, eventually, and get both. But right now he needed to establish his hunch as true. He had a pretty accurate description of the layout of the tunnels from Fei, but the reality was the explosion had collapsed everything. Even part of the mountain had caved in. When Fei decided to blow something up, she did a thorough job.

It was hopeless to think he could restore the natural caverns that had formed the basis for the original mine, but Caden was banking on the explosion having freed up a lot of that gold embedded in the rock walls. His plan was to dig and sift until he had what he needed to set up a full operation. Fei had given the mine a lyrical name in her native Chinese. When asked, she explained it meant "fresh start." He grunted as the boulder caught and jerked him back. Fei had found a new start for her life here with Shadow. Now it was going to give him one, but instead of love, he'd take cash. Cash was power. Cash was the future.

He hauled the rock to a preexisting pile. Fei had kept the mine secret. He wanted to maintain that secrecy, at least until he had something to claim. Too much disturbance of the surrounding area would draw curious eyes, so he was working slowly and steadily and just dreaming of a less laborious process. When he got the rock to the edge of the pile, he dropped the rope from his shoulders, flexing them against the stiffness and pain. It would have been easier if the secondary mine exit had survived. But it hadn't. Nothing had. Except Fei's hopes and dreams and her belief that spirits of good fortune rested here. Being half-Chinese, Fei had a lot of strange beliefs, but when you boiled it down, they weren't any more fanciful than his da's belief in the wee folk.

He glanced around the barren rock-strewn area. The impression was the opposite of hope. "If you could see your way to sharing, I'd be mighty grateful."

He didn't know who he was talking to, Fei's spirits or his da's wee folk. In the end it didn't matter as long as someone listened. As he stood there, the midmorning sun beat down on him like a fist. The hot, humid air pressed in on him, a bead of sweat rolled down his spine. Damn, it was hot for June. Felt more like August. Taking off his hat and wiping his forearm across his brow, Caden looked to the southwest where storm clouds gathered low on the horizon. It was late in the year for tornadoes, but that didn't mean one wouldn't come calling. Shit.

The breeze kicked up and blew dust across the site. Another chill went down his spine, and the knowledge that something was wrong settled in his bones. Walking over to the side of the clearing, he picked up his rifle, checked to make sure it was loaded and the barrel clean before he cocked it and looked around. Nothing moved except the leaves on the trees and the birds in the sky. Everything appeared normal. It was only the hairs on the back of his neck that said differently.

He climbed to the top of the rise, his tired leg muscles protesting the effort. Standing on an outcrop of rock, he covered his eyes with his hand and looked around, slowly and methodically scanning for any signs of movement. Any sudden flight of birds. Anything to explain the lifting of hairs on his nape. He saw nothing, which didn't mean he was in the clear. He sighed and rested his rifle in the crook of his arm and checked again. It wasn't the first time he'd felt a threat before he saw it. As far as the eye could see, there were only trees, sun and the sparkle of light off the river below. Whatever it was, it wasn't close.

He half slid, half walked back down the hill, jumping off the small ledge near the bottom before setting his rifle back against the stone ledge. He'd already taken precautions, booby-trapping the trails coming in. Whatever trouble was coming, it wasn't going to interfere with today's work. More's the pity.

Putting his hands on his hips, Caden stretched his

back, groaning as the muscles unknotted. He looked at the opening again. Two days' work and he'd managed to go in about two feet. Not exactly an impressive pace. As a matter of fact, it'd be discouraging but for the incentive. He reached in his pocket and pulled out the piece of inconspicuous rock he'd found yesterday. It looked like any other rock until he turned it over and saw the veins of gold running through it. Disturbing the mountain might have changed where the gold was, but the gold was still there and—Caden closed his fist around the rock—it was going to be his.

He looked heavenward. "Soon enough, Da, the Millers are going to be worth something."

It wouldn't make up for much, but at least one Miller was going to fulfill his vow. A swirl of wind blew dust and leaves up around his feet. The hairs on the back of his neck prickled again. The hilt of his knife settled into his palm with familiar comfort. Either his da approved of his plan or trouble was walking in tandem with that breeze. Since he wasn't a man given to fancy, he was banking on the latter. Whether that trouble meant claim jumpers or Indians, he didn't particularly care. Whatever it was, it was welcome to come try to take this mine. While Millers might have trouble finding their pot of gold, they didn't give it up once it was theirs.

Grabbing his canteen, he took a drink of the tepid water, his pleasure in the day's work fading under the new tension. He put the cork back in the canteen and hung it up on the shady side of the outcrop of rock. He paused as he hung it, seeing the cuts and bruises crisscrossing the back of his hand. It'd been a long time since he'd worked like this. Not since the early days of Hell's Eight when they were building rather than sustaining. It felt good to work again, to do something with his hands, to do something for himself. Hell's Eight had been Caine's baby. This was his, and he had the deed to prove it locked up in the vault at Hell's Eight. The work might be backbreaking, but whatever the results, they were his. And he needed to get back to it. If trouble was coming, it would get here in its own time. He pulled his hat down over his eyes against the bright sun. In the meantime, he had a load of rock to move, a ton of dirt to sift through and a future to build.

TROUBLE DIDN'T COME the way he thought it would or from the source he expected. It came in the form of Ace riding up the path a week later on his big black stallion, his shirt torn, his jaw set, wearing a sense of urgency that only those who knew him well could detect. Caden knew Ace very well. Caden set down his sifting pan and took off his gloves.

"Afternoon, Ace."

Ace pulled up his horse. "Did you have to booby-trap every damn bend in the trail?"

"Seemed appropriate at the time," Caden drawled.

Ace plucked at his torn sleeve. "That second branch you had following the first on that switchback is a nice innovation."

"Thank you." Caden pushed his hat back. "What brings you here, Ace?"

"Maddie."

Caden sighed. "I know she's got a soft spot for me, but I'm not coming back just to keep her peaceful if she's gone loco again."

In her first few months at Hell's Eight, Maddie had often slipped away, either going into a blind stupor or raging fit. Turned out he'd been the only one who could settle her down. All it had taken was a hug. He didn't know why no one understood that. Maddie just needed to feel safe so all her sweetness could flourish. Her face flashed in his mind. Big green eyes, freckles, upturned nose and a mouth that would turn a saint sinner when she smiled and showed those dimples. Damn, he missed her smile. The way she'd touch his arm when she thought he was upset. The calm she brought him. His cock stirred. The passion she incited. That passion was the reason he'd been staying away from Hell's Eight more and more of late. Maddie had had enough men lusting after her in her life. She didn't need someone like him joining the queue.

"I wish it were that simple," Ace said on a sigh.

That sense of something being wrong started howling. Caden froze. "What about Maddie?"

Ace didn't immediately answer. Never a good sign. He swung down off his horse.

"Let me get my cup. We'll talk about it over coffee."

Fuck. Caden nodded and walked over to the fire on which the coffeepot swung suspended. Caden knew Ace well enough to know there was trouble. He had a habit of putting his hand on his gun when he was agitated, and right now that hand was firmly planted.

"What about Maddie?" he asked, using his gloves to shield his hand from the heat as he lifted the pot.

Ace held out his cup. "I was hoping to find her here."

Caden paused midpour. "Why the hell would you expect to find her here?"

The camp was little more than a fire, a tent and a lot of dirt. It was no place for a woman.

Ace sighed and motioned for Caden to finish pouring. "Coffee."

As soon as the cup was full, Ace brought it to his mouth. Caden had to wait for him to take two sips before he continued.

"She left the night you did, and knowing how she feels about you, we kind of thought she followed you."

"Why would she follow me?" Caden's mind had been racing with all the possibilities of what could have happened, where she could have gone.

"She and Bella had a talk, apparently."

Caden wanted to close his eyes and groan. He set the pot back on the hook over the fire. Bella was a whole different woman than Maddie. All fire and bold spirit captured in a lushly curved body. Maddie admired her tremendously, had taken to emulating her. And Bella would have followed Sam. Shit. *Had* followed Sam. The ins and outs of that courtship were legend on Hell's Eight, and not a week went by that some part of it wasn't rehashed. Caden had a feeling he didn't want to hear the rest.

"So Bella and Maddie talked, and from that you think

she lit out after me in the middle of the night?" It was only half a question.

Ace nodded. "Her horse, Flower, is also missing."

There was more. Caden could tell from the tone of Ace's voice that there was more.

"And?"

Ace motioned with his cup. "You might want to sit down for this."

The hell he did. Caden spread his feet apart and braced his shoulders. "I'm good. So the night I left, Maddie left, too, taking the horse with her."

"And one of the tracking hounds."

A hound? "Which one?"

"Worthless."

"Hell, that one doesn't even bay." But Maddie had a fondness for him. She had a fondness for anything left out or underappreciated.

"Yeah, we thought that was pretty telling, too."

"How so?"

"He'd be my choice if I wanted to follow someone but not be detected."

Caden's, too. "Tell me she took a gun." The thought of Maddie being out there alone undefended was intolerable.

"I wish I could for sure, but unless you gave her one that nobody else knows about, she didn't pack one."

Caden shook his head. It wasn't that he hadn't tried. "That woman's fear of guns is unreasonable, especially if she's going to take off on her own. Did you check to see if she went into town?"

"First thing, but no one's seen her. And there's more."

Of course there was.

Ace took another sip of his coffee. "This part's not so good."

"What's not so good?"

Ace cocked a brow at him. "Sure you don't want to sit down?"

"Just fucking tell me and quit stalling."

Ace sighed and turned the cup in his hand before saying quietly, "The dog came back shot, Caden."

"Fuck." A cold knot formed in the pit of his stomach as Maddie's name whipped through his mind. *Maddie!*

"Pretty much." Ace set his cup on the ground.

"Who'd you put on her trail?" He didn't doubt someone had gone after her. Maddie was Hell's Eight. Had been since the moment she'd burst out of that hellhole of a whorehouse and asked Tracker for help.

"Tucker took a hound and backtracked along the trail."

"Where was she heading?"

"Damned if Tucker could figure that out." Ace took a coin out of his pocket and began to walk it over the backs of his fingers. "But if she was following you, that woman has no sense of direction."

She didn't. It'd taken her a week to learn her way back from the creek. "What did Tucker discover?"

"Not much. The trail was old and the ground not the best."

"Which dog?"

"Boone, who else?"

Boone was the best. "Good."

"Boone's good, but there's only so much he can do after rain and weather have their say. We did figure out that at some point midway between here and there it looks like she met up with someone. From there Tucker couldn't follow the trail more than a mile east. Hell, he's not even sure by that point whether it was her Boone was following."

Someone. A nice way of saying Maddie met up with trouble. The knot in Caden's stomach froze over. A woman alone out here was fair game for every piece of scum that decided he wanted her. "Where was it?"

Sam pointed north. "That row of hills between here and there. It looks like she went right instead of left."

"Did anybody check the houses along that way?"

"Shit, Caden. You know there isn't anything along that way. The Indians drove them all out."

Caden nodded. That was true. As more troops were pulled East in preparation for the conflict there, the Indians were getting bolder. He knew exactly the spot that Ace was talking about. There were three ways to go off that peak. To the left toward San Antonio, down into the wilderness, and to the right toward the Culbart ranch and here. It was a good day's ride from both.

"Has anybody gone to San Antonio looking for her?"

"Sam."

"And?" As unreasonable as it was, Caden couldn't kill the hope Sam had found something.

"He's not back yet."

"It's possible she went to San Antonio. She wasn't happy with me leaving."

Ace looked at him as if he'd lost his mind. "Maybe."

"There's more."

"Of course there is." Caden sighed. "What?"

"It's more the nature of what Bella talked to her about what goes on between you that has Tucker convinced she followed you."

"What did Bella tell her?" With Bella there was no telling.

"Bella told her to follow her heart, and we're all pretty sure she's infatuated with you."

She was, and it was a measure of what a selfish bastard he was that he'd never discouraged that infatuation. Being loved by Maddie was…incredibly sweet. Hot and tender at the same time, and when she looked at him as if he was wrapped in icing… Fuck! He wasn't a total bastard. He'd never encouraged her but…his cock throbbed. He'd thought about it once or twice.

Shit. Caden walked over to the grassy patch where Jester was tethered. "You say she left the night I did?"

Ace stood. "Yeah."

He grabbed his gear. "And you think she got lost and ran into trouble."

"Pretty much."

Which made it his fault. He tossed the saddle and blanket onto Jester's back, giving it a tug back to settle it. He'd promised to say goodbye and he hadn't. Maddie was fragile. He should have had more care. Something like that would have thrown her. "How long has the dog been back?"

"About a week and a half."

Which meant she'd run into trouble immediately.

Ace took Caden's saddlebag and started stuffing essentials into the pockets. "You going after her?"

Caden looked up. "Hell, yeah."

Ace nodded and kicked dirt over the fire to put it out.

"What are you doing?" Caden asked.

"Keeping you company." He slung the saddlebags over his shoulder. His hand dropped to the butt of his revolver. "I've got a bad feeling about this, Caden. I have since the minute we discovered she was gone."

"What kind of bad feeling?"

Caden didn't want to hear Ace thought she was dead.

"I don't know." He handed Caden the saddlebags and bedroll. "But it's not good."

"Well, it's not going to be more than we can handle." Caden tied the bedroll and bags to the saddle, grabbed his rifle and slid it into the scabbard tied to the left side. "Maddie's been hurt enough."

"Agreed."

Caden swung up onto Jester. "So let's go get her back."

He refused to believe she was dead.

"And if we find she's been hurt?" Ace asked.

"We bring her home." Caden smiled as rage poured through his gut in an icy torrent at the thought of anyone touching his Maddie. Thunder rumbled in the distance. "And then we bury the bastards who hurt her."

Ace tipped his hat and backed his horse around in a tight circle. "I'm good with that."

Because they left late in the morning, it took them a day and a half to get to the spot where Maddie had met up with *someone*. There were still remnants of hoofprints on the hard-packed earth thanks to the ground being soft when the confrontation had occurred. It had dried up since then, leaving plenty of signs there'd been others, but no path that led anywhere because of the rocky nature of the surrounding area.

"Nothing." Caden squatted beside the footprints, tracing them with his finger, looking for any identifying mark, anything that would give him a clue.

"That's what Tucker said," Ace drawled from farther out, where he circled looking for signs.

There was no better tracker than Tucker. No better scent hound than Boone. Caden knew Tucker had searched the area thoroughly, and if Tucker couldn't track from here then Caden couldn't, either. But he had to look. He had to try. Maddie was gone. He couldn't grasp the thought. Couldn't stand the possibility that it was real.

"Fucking hell." Nothing. Grabbing a handful of dirt, he threw it and stood. Why hadn't Maddie stayed where she was safe? "Which way did Tucker say they went?"

Ace pointed down.

"Into the wilderness?" That didn't make sense. There was nothing that way except emptiness and hostiles.

Ace shrugged. "He said Boone lost the trail about a mile down that way."

It didn't make sense, unless they were just pulling off to rape her. The icy knot in Caden's stomach swelled, choking off his voice as he imagined Maddie being held down and abused. Maddie, who was kindness and hope. Who'd already endured so much. He swung back up on his horse. Ace followed, the way he always did, a silent, deadly companion. It was hard to get to know Ace. He kept so much of himself inside, but if there was a battle, he was there, and if there was trouble—like now—he was ready.

The path was rough. Rough enough even Rage, Ace's horse, protested. Negotiating the terrain would have been hard for Maddie's little horse, Flower, who had never traveled along anything more difficult than a meadow.

As if reading his mind, Ace asked, "Would that mare of hers be able to make this?"

"She might not have had a choice."

"True enough."

FEAR TANGLED WITH RAGE as Caden broke through a copse of trees and emerged in a clearing. The clearing was a small oasis in the middle of the darker woods. Cool and inviting and, most important, hidden. It would be simple to rape a woman here in peace. Gritting his teeth against the images in his head, Caden swung down.

Hold on, Maddie.

It was easier to see the disturbance in the soil here caused by many hooves. Harder to sort them out as one smeared into another.

"Is this where Tucker lost them?"

Ace looked around. "Looks like what he described."

Caden crisscrossed the clearing, step by step. Tucker had already decoded what was in the dirt, but what he needed was a clue, something to give him an idea of who had Maddie.

He was on his third pass over the small clearing when Ace called his name.

"Caden?"

"What?"

"If there was anything to find, we'd have found it by now."

Caden shook his head. "Keep looking."

"For what?"

"Anything." There had to be something here, something to show where Maddie was, but if there wasn't, he'd simply search house by house, town by town, until he found her or someone who knew where she was. And then there'd be hell to pay.

He pictured her face with her big eyes, rosebud mouth and that smattering of freckles across her cheeks. Kisses of the fairy folk, he'd say. He looked around the little glen, the sunlight filtering through the leaves in small rays, giving it almost a magical feel, and whispered, "If she is one of you, give me a goddamn sign as to who has her."

He waited in vain for a clap of thunder, a whisper in his mind, a touch on his shoulder. His da always said the wee folk were particular, but then, as he turned, out of the corner of his eye he saw a gleam of metal. It took him four steps to get there. Four steps in which he thought he must be losing his mind, but when he got to that spot, the shine didn't go away. It grew stronger until he was standing on top of it, and then he couldn't see it anymore, covered as it was by a low-growing fern. He squatted.

"What is it?"

"I don't know yet." He moved the fern aside, and there, camouflaged against the rock, was a button. He picked it up. He felt more than heard Ace arrive at his side. The man was as light as a cat on its feet. He held the button up.

"Hard to see as it was against the rock."

Ace nodded.

The button had a unique design. Almost a cross but not quite.

"A button," Ace said, his disappointment as strong as Caden's should have been.

"Yeah." Caden whispered a thank-you to the fate, God or whomever had brought him to that button.

Caden stood. Ace cocked his head and observed his face.

"Except you recognize it, don't you?"

"It's got a distinct pattern."

He closed his fingers around it, his mind consumed with all the reasons a man's button would pop off his shirt. None of them were good.

He ran his thumb over the raised design. "It's the Culbart brand, a lopsided cross."

"Culbart has her?"

"So it would seem." Culbart was a bear of a man. Rough around the edges. Not known for his soft ways with anything, let alone women. His crew was rougher still. And he had Maddie.

"That button could have fallen off for a wide variety of reasons," Ace pointed out with an utter lack of conviction.

That was true, but in his gut Caden knew what that button meant.

He dropped the button in his pocket and swung up into the saddle. He spun Jester in a circle and kneed him back up the trail.

"But there's only one that matters to me."

CHAPTER FIVE

LYING LOW ON a hill above the Culbart spread, Caden surveyed the goings-on below. He'd liked to have seen chaos, but for the day and a half he'd been observing, Caden hadn't seen anything that he wouldn't have seen at Hell's Eight. Animals were tended on schedule, guards were rotated through shifts and buildings were maintained. What he hadn't seen were any signs of Maddie, but Caden knew Culbart had her. Had had her for two weeks doing Lord knew what to her.

Caden tried to remember what Fei had said her cousin Lin had endured when her father had sold her to Culbart to pay a debt. He couldn't remember much. Fei had been sketchy on those details. Not surprisingly. There were things a good woman didn't want revealed. Besides, whatever had happened to Fei's cousin wasn't particularly relevant because a man approached a woman of good family differently than he did a known whore. Whether the woman had been sold or not, virginity had value. Hell, women had value in general, but if Culbart and his crew saw Maddie as a whore…

Caden closed his fist around the spyglass and ground his teeth. If they treated her like that, he'd gut them and skin them and leave them out as buzzard bait. Maddie

might not have had a good beginning, but she was better than anyone down deep where it mattered, and he'd
made her a promise when she came to Hell's Eight. He
promised her she'd never have to serve a man again unless she lay down by her choice. He remembered the
disturbance of footprints in the dirt, the isolation of her
location. The popped button. The blood in the dirt from
the dog. Fuck. Nothing about her being with Culbart
was her choice.

Putting the spyglass back to his eye, Caden surveyed
the Fallen C. He had to give Culbart credit. He might be
a son of a bitch with some questionable morals when it
came to women, but he ran his ranch with an iron hand.
The evidence was in the well-kept buildings, the tidy
outhouses, the numerous corrals and the condition of
his animals. Probably the only thing that kept him from
giving Hell's Eight a run for its money when it came to
stocking the cavalry was the fact that the Fallen C was
smack-dab in the middle of Indian country. The man
didn't just have to battle wolves and drought. A tribe
could decide anytime that he was trespassing on their
land, and with the unrest in the East over separation,
fewer and fewer cavalry were being sent to protect the
West. In the coming years, Culbart would be lucky if he
got out of this with his scalp intact. Of course, that was
always supposing Caden left anything for the Indians to
scalp. Caden popped his elbows on the ground and continued his surveillance. He needed to know the routine
to get Maddie out of there.

It was early morning and the men of the Fallen C were

going about their usual business. Men were going in and out of the bunkhouse, heading up to the cookhouse for breakfast. For the day and a half that Caden had been surveying the place, he hadn't seen any sign of Maddie, but her little horse, Flower, was in the corral and not looking too happy with that stallion next door. Caden sighed again. Obviously from the stallion's behavior, the mare was coming into heat, which complicated things because another promise Caden had made Maddie was that Flower would also not have to lay down with any man unless she wanted to, and from the looks of things, that stallion was about to take that corral fence down.

"That's a mighty big sigh," Ace said.

"Looks like we're going to have a romance to break up, too."

"You see Maddie with one of the cowmen?"

"Nah. I haven't seen her yet, though I imagine they'd be keeping her under lock and key."

"Maybe. So what romance are we breaking up?"

"That stallion and Flower."

To his credit, Ace didn't bat an eyelash. One of the things that Caden enjoyed about Ace was that the man was unflappable.

He took the spyglass from Caden and trained it on the corrals.

"Nice-looking stud. Might be worth letting it happen."

"I promised Maddie her mare would be safe."

Ace lowered the glass and raised a brow at him. "You promised a woman her horse wouldn't be...deflowered?"

Caden grabbed the glass. "Maddie's sensitive on the subject."

"Uh-huh."

It was a ludicrous request and he'd been stupid to make the promise. Knowing it didn't mean Caden wanted it shoved in his face. "Shut up, Ace."

"Didn't say a word."

"Good."

"If you're planning on ending a romance, though," Ace drawled, "then you'd better get over there soon."

"Yeah. That'd occurred to me."

"Got a plan?"

"Besides ride in and take her?"

"How about something better than suicide?"

"Not yet." The ranch was well guarded with men who wore their guns in a way that said they knew how to use them. Short of walking up and knocking on the door, he couldn't think of anything.

"We've been here two days," Ace pointed out. "We haven't seen a sign of her."

"I know."

"You think she's still here?"

"I do."

"Based on what?"

Caden put the spyglass in his pocket. "Based on my gut and the fact that Culbart hasn't come out of that house for more than two minutes in two days."

"I had that thought myself."

Caden nodded and crawled back off the edge. "The

only thing keeping me from charging in is the fact that Culbart doesn't have the look of a satisfied man."

Ace smiled. "You think he's finding Maddie's flights of fancy a bit draining?"

Caden stood, brushing off his pants. "For his sake, I sure as hell hope so."

"How are you intending on getting her out of there? Storming the place isn't exactly our best bet."

"Yeah, I've come to that conclusion."

Of course, Ace had to pin him down that first day to keep him from charging in, but now that he was a little calmer, he could see the foolishness of that plan.

"So what are you going to do?"

"First, we're going to break up that romance."

"Steal the horse?"

"Uh-uh. It's not stealing if it's ours to begin with."

"Gonna be tough to prove to a judge if Culbart put his brand on Flower."

"Let him be so stupid as to take me to court."

"That man has a fierce temper and strong will. Rumors are, nobody crosses him and gets away with it. Reminds me a lot of Caine."

"Caine doesn't hold women prisoner."

"We don't know that Culbart is, either," Ace pointed out with that reasonable side that grated on Caden's nerves.

"Maddie's the second woman he's taken against her will." He shifted his hat on his head.

"To be fair, Lin's uncle sold her."

"Doesn't mean she didn't say no."

"True enough, but I got the impression she wasn't raped."

"Only because Fei slipped Culbart saltpeter." Every man who heard that story cringed on the telling.

Ace chuckled. "She's a resourceful bit of a thing."

She was, but Maddie didn't have Fei looking out for her. She just had him. "She is that."

"Not to keep grating on your sense of vengeance without reason," Ace drawled, walking that coin over his knuckles the way he did when he was thinking, "but Maddie's been here two weeks, and Culbart's not looking like the cat that ate the canary. Are you really so sure that he's forcing her?"

Caden spun around and swung, his fist connecting with Ace's jaw. The man stumbled back four steps before he landed on his ass. Instead of coming up swinging the way Caden wanted, he sat there and rubbed his face.

"You imply she's a whore again and you won't get up for a week," Caden snarled.

Ace wiped the blood from his hand on his pants. "The only one who jumped to that conclusion is you. I meant she might be a welcome guest. Women are scarce out here, and Maddie is pretty enough for Culbart to overlook her past."

"Maddie's beautiful."

Ace cocked a brow at him. "All the more reason for Culbart to be thinking marriage. A man building a spread like this will want someone to pass it on to."

"Over my dead body."

"Culbart'll probably arrange that for her."

"Like hell."

Caden held out his hand to Ace. The other man didn't take it.

"Feel better now?" Ace asked.

No, he didn't feel better.

"You get up and take a swing back, and I'll let you know."

"I'm not fighting you, Caden. We both know I'd win anyway."

"Like hell."

"You've had too much coffee, too little sleep and too little food."

"Whereas you've slept."

Ace shrugged and took his hand, getting to his feet. "I always sleep. Best way to be ready for a fight. But yes, I've got my head straight on my shoulders and we're about even matched in the best of conditions. You," he said pointedly, "are not at your best."

"Anybody ever tell you you're damn irritating?"

Ace smiled, revealing even white teeth and a charm the ladies appreciated. "Nobody whose opinion mattered."

"What do you think we're going to do?"

"Culbart isn't an idiot."

"No, he's not."

"You're going to have to do something."

"I could just walk up to the front door. Say hello."

"There's a slight chance he'll shoot you down before you get halfway across the yard."

"Why? He won't like the set of my hat?"

"He won't like the fact that you're Hell's Eight. Don't forget what Fei did to his men."

"There's always a chance he doesn't know that Fei married up with Shadow."

"A very faint chance."

Yeah. News did travel fast. "Well, one way or the other, I've got to get into that house."

"I could go."

"Why you?"

"I'm more even-tempered."

"Somehow I don't see Culbart appreciating your even temper."

"You think he's going to appreciate you swinging?"

"I think I'm going to want you with that rifle up here on the hill covering my ass in case I have to break out of there fast."

"So you're using the excuse that I'm a better distance shot."

"You're always bragging on the skill. About time you proved it."

"This isn't much of a plan, you know."

Caden nodded. "We have to know if she's there."

"True enough."

Ace reached into his saddlebag and pulled out a derringer. Caden looked at him.

"You been chewing on locoweed?"

Ace handed the weapon to him. Caden took it reluctantly. A derringer was a woman's gun or, worse, a cardsharp's.

"They're gonna search you for weapons, but they

aren't going to expect you to be hiding something this small."

"And where would you have me put it?"

Ace looked up. "Under your hat. I don't know, down your pants. Stick it wherever the hell you want. Just stick it somewhere you can reach it quickly in case things go bad. You're not going to do Maddie any good if you're dead."

That was true enough. Caden took the gun. He debated putting it under his hat, but really, that wasn't a secure option. Instead, he slid it up his sleeve and tied the wristband tighter.

"What time you plan on going over?"

"No time like the present."

It was early in the day. Everybody was there. There'd be less suspicion.

"If we waited until later, the hands would be out."

"If we waited until later, they'd be more gun happy. I want them to feel safe. For now."

"I don't like this plan."

"I don't like it, either, but you got another option?"

"I still think I should go in."

"And I still say no."

Maddie was his responsibility. And she'd waited long enough for him.

CADEN HADN'T EXPECTED to be able to just walk right up to the door, so he wasn't surprised when within a quarter mile of the ranch he was met by two men on horseback, guns drawn. Culbart wasn't a fool and these were dangerous times.

"Stranger," the older man with the graying beard greeted him.

Caden nodded back. "Mornin'."

"What brings you around these parts?"

Caden took the measure of the men, their hard eyes, their dirty appearance and the way their fingers rested on the triggers of their well-tended guns. Culbart didn't hire fools.

"Business."

"What kind of business could you have way out here?"

Caden smiled. "Nothing I care to talk about with you."

The other man with him, not a youngster but clearly younger, maybe even family because he had the same muddy-colored eyes and the same set to his narrow mouth, spat.

"Well, if you want to get any farther than six feet under right now, I suggest you be telling us the nature of your business."

"I came to talk to Culbart about a filly." He figured it was a safe gambit. Everyone knew Culbart aimed to beat out Hell's Eight as a breeder of horses.

The younger man rode around until he could see the brand on Jester's side.

"Since when do Hell's Eight go searching for fillies?"

"Since we're always on the lookout for new breeding stock. Can't improve the herd without it."

It was the truth. The older man grunted. "What's your name, stranger?"

"Caden Miller."

Only by a blink of an eye and a tightening of his hand on the trigger did either man give any indication his name meant anything. Caden made note of the response. Only hired guns had that instinctive shoot-first-and-ask-questions-later attitude.

With a motion of the gun barrel, the older man indicated to go forward.

"I can find my own way. No need to give up your post."

"You let us worry about the guard here. You just worry about keeping your hands clear of those guns."

From that Caden deduced, they were done with their shift, and their replacements were in position. Another thing to note. Culbart's men weren't slipshod when it came to switching the guard. That was going to complicate things.

Nobody attempted to make conversation on the ride up to the ranch. Caden didn't, either. Silence worked for him. It gave him time to study the lay of the land, looking for potential dangers, spots to hide and whatever he might need to utilize on the escape. There was no telling what condition Maddie would be in. He had to prepare for any eventuality. His index finger pulled on an imaginary trigger. If she was hurt at all, they were all going to die. Maddie was Hell's Eight. More than that, she was his friend.

Caden was the center of attention when they rode into the ranch. He wasn't surprised. He doubted the Fallen C got many visitors. The remoteness of the location, plus the hostiles around, pretty much guaranteed that. Under the watchful eyes of his guards, he swung down from Jester. Cutting a glance at his guards, he mentioned too casually, "I expect to be leaving with all that I came with."

The younger man spat to the side. "I'd worry more about leaving with your life."

He looped Jester's reins around the hitching rail in front of the wide porch. "I make a habit of taking it with me."

The man said something under his breath. Caden ignored it.

No boards gave under Caden's feet as he climbed the three steps to the porch itself. It was built solid, the planks evenly spaced. More evidence of Culbart's attention to detail. The door opened before he could knock. Culbart himself filled the entry. He was a big bear of a man, with a bushy beard, bushy mustache and piercing gray eyes under shaggy brown hair. He looked more mountain man than prosperous rancher, but one thing a body learned fast out here was that a man couldn't be judged by his appearance.

"Who the hell are you?" Culbart demanded.

The man not only looked like a bear, he had the growly voice of one.

Caden touched his finger to his hat. "Caden Miller."

Culbart's eyes narrowed. "From Hell's Eight?"

"Yes."

"What the hell you doing out here?"

"Says he's got business about a filly."

Culbart said to the older man, "I imagine the man can speak for himself, Dickens."

Dickens snapped his mouth shut and his shoulders tensed. No love lost there, Caden deduced. He made a note of it.

"Did you bring money?" Culbart asked.

"I brought the word of Hell's Eight. That not good enough for you?"

Culbart hesitated and snorted then stepped back. "Leave your guns on the porch and come on in and we'll discuss it."

Caden unbuckled his gun belt. "Not very hospitable, are you?"

"I'm offering you a drink rather than a meal of lead. Count yourself lucky."

As Caden put his guns on the chair by the door, he took in the rancher's size and muscle and aggressive posture. A prudent man probably would count himself lucky. There weren't many men who could take him in a fight, but Culbart just might be one of them. Too bad he wasn't prudent.

He stepped through the door. The inside of the house was just as utilitarian and rough as its owner. The space was large but efficiently laid out. The kitchen opened to the living room with its large fireplace. To the left he could see a short hallway with doors off it. From the number of chimneys on the outside of the house, he had to assume those were the bedrooms and that each had its own fireplace. Culbart was a man who liked his creature comforts.

"Nice place," Caden observed.

Culbart grunted and waved him into one of the big horsehair chairs. He might like his creature comforts, but the man's social graces were lacking. Caden recalled Ace's speculation about Culbart's need for a wife. A woman to soften his edges would be an asset for sure.

Culbart walked over to the chest against the wall and pulled out a whiskey bottle and two shot glasses. Without any fanfare, he poured two glasses and brought them over. Caden took his glass. With another wave of his hand, Culbart motioned him into his seat and then took his own.

"So Hell's Eight is looking to improve its breeding stock, huh?"

"In a manner of speaking, yes."

"What sort of filly are you looking for?"

Caden took a sip of the whiskey. Despite the simple glass and the rough presentation, it was quality. Another indication Culbart intended to go somewhere. A man who wanted to go somewhere wasn't a man who wanted it known he was holding a woman hostage unless he had a sense of self-importance as big as all outdoors. Culbart struck Caden as a confident man but not a vain one.

"The Fallen C has some of the best stock around," Culbart said before taking a sip of his own whiskey, pausing just long enough to imply otherwise before adding, "Next to Hell's Eight, of course."

Caden smiled the same fake smile that Culbart gave him. "Of course."

"So what kind of horse are you looking for? What stock?"

Caden dropped the pretense. "A pretty little redhead."

Culbart's eyes narrowed. "What makes you think I have such a thing?"

Caden's smile slipped just as fast as Culbart's did. Leaning forward, he placed the button on the arm of Culbart's chair.

Culbart eyed the button speculatively before picking it up and putting it in his pocket. "Thank you for returning that. They're custom-made and expensive."

Caden was done with games. "You've got something that belongs to Hell's Eight. We want it back."

Culbart didn't pretend to misunderstand. "Last I heard, Hell's Eight didn't believe in slavery."

"We don't. But we keep what's ours."

"The little filly in question didn't say a thing about being yours."

Caden would have a talk with Maddie about that just as soon as he saw her. The first words out of her mouth ever should have been a claim to Hell's Eight.

"It doesn't change the fact that she is."

"Matter of fact," Culbart continued, "she seemed quite pleased to be with us. Set to homemaking right off. Started baking bread and even demanded the ingredients so she could fix us a cake."

Baking had become Maddie's refuge. Caden didn't find the news comforting.

"She's a right fine baker."

"That she is. Hard thing to come by out here."

"She can't cook worth a damn, though."

That was an idiosyncrasy that drove Tia crazy. She couldn't figure out how anyone who could bake a cake to light as a feather couldn't complete a meal without smoking up the house. It was a mystery to Caden, too.

"I've already got a cook."

And through that statement, Culbart let it be known he wasn't going to give Maddie up easily. It galled the shit out of Caden to even make the suggestion, but his first duty was to Maddie, and if an exchange of cash would do the job, then he'd do it.

"Hell's Eight, of course, would be happy to compensate you for your loss of a baker."

Culbart leaned back in his chair and steepled his fingers before him, tapping them together. He gave even more of an impression of a bear, and not a friendly one.

"Well, if it was just her baking skills that would be missed, that might be adequate. But we've grown right fond of Miss Maddie."

"We?"

"Myself and the boys. She's a woman of many skills. We wouldn't want her going off just anywhere and maybe being unhappy because promises that were made to her weren't kept."

The only promise Caden had made Maddie and hadn't kept was the one where he said he wouldn't leave before she could say goodbye. That wasn't one he'd be breaking again.

"Then it appears to me we have a problem. You have something that Hell's Eight values highly."

Culbart stopped tapping his fingers together. "It's not Hell's Eight I see sitting here."

"It doesn't matter what you see, Culbart, it matters what is. Maddie is Hell's Eight and we want her back."

"You're not going to get anywhere with me with that tactic."

The derringer weighed heavily in his shirtsleeve. It would be so easy to put a bullet between the other man's eyes. "What tactic would you like?"

"Well, boy, it appears to me that I have something you want, and unless you come up with something I want, one of us is going to end this meeting unhappy."

Fuck. Nowhere in all the information he'd collected about Culbart had anyone said the man wheeled and dealed, but looking into his eyes, it was easy to see this was a skilled negotiator.

"What do you want, Culbart?"

"That's not a very friendly attitude."

Caden stood. "I'm not feeling friendly."

Culbart remained sitting. "The Indians ran off with my prime stud the other day."

"And? You want me to get it back?"

"If I thought there was a chance in hell of that, I'd do it myself, but I heard tell that stallion of yours threw a new foal that looks to be just as promising as his dad."

Dammit to hell and back. "That horse is worth more than this whole ranch put together."

Culbart shrugged, a shrewd look coming into his eyes while the rest of his expression remained unchanged.

"You told me to name my price and I did. A stud for

a filly. Seems a fair trade to me." Setting his glass on the table, he stood. "You can get back to me in a couple days on it."

That horse'd already been promised to someone else. "We'll settle this now."

"Dickens," Culbart hollered.

Dickens came through the door, a rifle cradled in his arms. "Escort our guest off my property," Culbart ordered.

What the hell? "I want to see Maddie."

Culbart motioned Dickens forward. "You're in no position to be making demands."

"If you've hurt her—"

"If I hurt her then all the threats in the world won't undo it."

The son of a bitch. The only thing that kept Caden from tearing into Culbart was Dickens's rifle in his chest.

"Don't do it, son."

"I'm not your son."

"No, you're not, but I'd still advise against it."

Caden snarled under his breath. Fuck it. Knocking the barrel aside, he drove his fist into Dickens's mouth. The man dropped to the ground, the rifle clanking on the floor beside him. Caden turned, ignoring Dickens's curses.

"You're going to regret this, Culbart."

"Maybe." Culbart stood and came over, stepping past Dickens's prone body, meeting the anger in Caden's eyes without a flicker of fear. "But Hell's Eight aren't the only ones who watch out for what's theirs. Best you remember that, lad, before you come back in two days."

"What the hell does that mean?"

He placed his hand on the door. "It means when you come back, you'd best bring your manners."

"Fuck you."

"Better ones than that."

The door shut behind him with a decisive thud.

CHAPTER SIX

ACE WAS WAITING for him at the campsite. In his hand he held four rabbit carcasses. Since Culbart knew they were there, there was no need to hide their presence any longer.

"Is she there?" Ace asked

Caden nodded and dismounted. "As far as I can tell." He pointed to the carcasses. "Supper?"

"Beats jerky."

It sure did.

"What does 'as far as I can tell' mean?" Ace asked.

Caden shook his head and dropped Jester's reins to the ground in a grassy spot, letting the horse graze. "The hell if I know."

"Is she there or not?" Frustration bit through Ace's tone. Caden knew exactly how he felt.

"Oh, she's there."

"Is she all right?"

"I assume so."

Ace's eyes narrowed. "What the hell happened?"

Caden hunkered down on the opposite side of the fire. "We've got an invite to come back in two days."

"Why two days?"

"I don't know."

Ace sat back. "I knew I should have gone in."

"You any good at avoiding a bullet from one inch away?" Caden asked, cocking a brow at Ace.

"No. Then I wouldn't go hoping to do any better."

Caden shook his head again. "No, I didn't get that impression."

Ace looked up. "Well, what exactly do you know?"

"That Culbart isn't what we were led to believe."

"He isn't a conscienceless opportunist?" There was a touch of mockery in Ace's tone.

"I've got a pretty good idea he's an opportunist, but it's the conscienceless part I'm not sure about."

"That will complicate things."

Caden grabbed some wood and threw it on the fire before grabbing one of the rabbits off the rock. "Tell me about it." It was always cleaner to deal with scum. Caden took his knife from his sheath. The blade glinted in the sun.

"There isn't much to tell. I went in, pretended I was looking to buy a filly and as soon as I said a redheaded one, Culbart knew what I was talking about."

"Then he has her."

Caden nodded, remembering that glint in Culbart's eye. He slid the knife under the skin of the first rabbit. "Or knows where she is."

"You didn't demand to see her?" Ace took out his own knife.

"No, at that point we were in—" he gutted the rabbit in one smooth motion "—negotiations."

"Shit."

Ace ripped his knife up the dead rabbit's stomach with controlled force. "Since when does Hell's Eight bargain for what's theirs?"

"Since we're outnumbered twenty to one and Culbart has what we want."

"What's he want for her?"

"Baron's foal."

Ace froze. "That horse is worth a king's ransom. Every rancher in five states and two territories is drooling over that foal."

"I know."

"Caine is counting on the money he makes from that sale to cover next year's expenses. Getting Shadow out of that mess drained the ranch's coffers."

He knew that, too. "Then, I'll have to make it up to him."

Just one more reason the mine had to pay off.

"You didn't tell him you'd trade, did you?"

No, but he would have. "He didn't let me."

Ace picked up one of the sharpened sticks propped against the log they'd dragged over for a seat and passed it to Caden.

"Let me get this straight. The man has Maddie, but he won't show her to you, he makes an outrageous demand for her, but when you get set to agree or disagree, he doesn't let you answer?"

Caden took the stick and considered the point. It'd feel damn good right then to shove it up Culbart's ass. "Pretty much."

"What the hell is his game?"

"I don't know, but I'm guessing I'm going to find out in two days."

"Why the hell wait two days? Let's just go in tonight and get her."

"While I was socializing, I had a chance to check out the guards."

"And?"

He slid the pointed stick into the carcass. "Culbart hires men that would do Hell's Eight proud."

"Shit." Ace grabbed a stick and skewered a carcass with it before stabbing it into the ground in front of the fire. "So what are we going to do?"

"I'm going back, and if he plays more games—" Caden looked up "—I'm going to put an end to him."

Ace relaxed. "That's going to take planning."

Caden smiled and placed the rabbit over the fire. "The man gave us two days."

TWO DAYS LATER Caden was back at the Fallen C. His reception wasn't any more welcoming than the first time around, but then again, he hadn't expected it to be. He nodded to Dickens as he stepped up onto the porch. The man glared at him over his swollen mouth. He'd made an enemy there. Caden didn't care. He was wound up tighter than a clock. He wanted in and out, with Maddie safe in his arms and this whole mess behind him. Culbart's expression wasn't any more cheerful when he opened the door. When Caden reached the top of the steps, the man cleared his throat. "Wipe your boots."

"Excuse me?"

"I said wipe your damn boots. Maddie doesn't like it when you track dirt through."

Maddie didn't like it? "She's here?"

"Of course." Culbart stepped back and motioned him in.

There was no "of course" about it. Caden stepped through the door. The house smelled of beeswax and lemon and—he took a sniff—chocolate cake. Culbart closed the door. Caden couldn't help but notice the man was...groomed. Gone was the mountain man of two days ago. In his place was a close approximation of a successful businessman. His clothes were neat and pressed, his beard and mustache were trimmed and his hair was cut. It still had a wild look about it due to its natural wave, but it was noticeable that it had been trimmed and combed. He wasn't an ugly man.

Caden didn't go another step. "What the hell is going on?"

Culbart ran his hand down his chest and then over his hair. From the kitchen came an Irish ditty sung in a voice Caden would recognize anywhere.

"Maddie!"

Culbart glared at him. "Don't you be upsetting her. She's been preparing for two days for your visit."

That preparation was evident in the well-scrubbed floors, the dusted furniture set out in a new arrangement. That only left one question: "Why?"

Culbart stubbed his toe on a newly placed hassock, glaring at Caden again as if it was his fault.

"Damned if I know, but she wanted everything just perfect."

Maddie, Caden decided, must have drifted into one of her flights of fancy. "She does like order and a clean house."

Culbart nodded. "Soothes her nerves."

Stranger and stranger the picture got. A kidnapper worried about his captive's nerves?

"You got any more of that whiskey?" Caden asked.

"I do, but you won't be seeing it."

"Why is that?"

The question as rude as Culbart's response.

"Because Maddie is preparing tea."

"Tea?"

Culbart grimaced. "Swears it's the thing all proper households serve to guests."

Caden hated tea. "So Tia says."

"That's a good woman, Tia."

Why were they talking about Tia? "You know Tia?"

"I know what everyone knows, that she took you boys in, made something of you."

They liked to think they'd made something of themselves, too.

"Not many women would do that," Culbart said gruffly, going to sit before he realized his chair had been moved. He swore under his breath.

"No, it takes a real big heart for that."

"Yes, it does." Culbart found his chair. "Good to hear she's married up with Ed. A woman like that needs a good man."

There seemed a deeper significance to the words. "You thinking of marrying?"

Culbart looked to the kitchen where Caden could make out flashes of yellow as Maddie worked. "It crossed my mind."

He'd better not be thinking with Maddie.

With a motion of his hand, the rancher indicated Caden should sit. Caden did, waffling between rage and confusion, feeling a bit as if he'd stepped into one of those fairylands in his da's stories where everything should be recognizable but wasn't.

Culbart's brows lowered over his eyes. "Maddie's a good woman with a big heart."

That sounded like a warning.

"We're fond of her."

"Everyone? Not just you in particular?"

He wasn't discussing his relationship with Maddie with anyone, least of all her kidnapper. "What's between Maddie and me is our business."

The rancher's face turned red. "I'm making it my business."

Caden smiled. "Tough."

Culbart came to his feet. "You ungrateful pup. I ought to take you out back and beat some decency into you."

Pup? Culbart was probably only five years older than him. "You're welcome to try."

"Try my ass. Any man that'd take advantage of a sweet woman like Maddie needs his ass kicked from here to Sunday."

Sweet woman? "Who the hell said I took advantage of her?"

"Just because you're Hell's Eight doesn't mean you can't be held accountable."

Caden had heard a lot of things about Culbart, but not that he was insane.

"Maddie!" Caden hollered. "Get out here!"

A fist connected with his jaw, knocking him ass over teakettle. Culbart stood over him, fists clenched. "You will not be hollering at a lady in my house."

Son of a bitch, the bastard had made him see stars. Caden shook his head to clear it and glared at Culbart. "Lady?"

Caden heard a scream and saw a flutter of yellow. Fuck. Maddie.

"Step away from him, Maddie," Culbart ordered, grabbing her arm.

"Yes, Maddie. Step away." Caden did not like the familiarity of Culbart's hand on her arm.

Maddie yanked at her arm. "Uncle Frank, what are you doing?"

What the hell? Maddie had convinced herself Culbart was her uncle?

"This man of yours. He needs some learning."

Caden was still reeling from the "Uncle Frank" when he got hit with "this man of yours."

"What the hell are you talking about?" he asked, shaking his head to clear his vision as he grabbed his hat and struggled to his feet. Culbart packed a punch.

"Caden!" Maddie bent down to help. Culbart grabbed her arm again and pulled her back.

"There'll be time enough for tender touches when I'm done with him."

Maddie stamped her foot. "You can't hurt him. He'll be all bruised for the wedding."

Wedding? Caden sat back down. "Who's getting married?"

The door burst opened, Ace came in, guns drawn. "Nobody move."

"Ace!" Maddie said, a big smile on her face. "I'm so happy you could make it!" She ran forward as if he weren't pointing two six-shooters into the room, catching his right hand in hers. Caden's heart cramped. Ace's guns had hair triggers.

"Goddamn it, Maddie," he yelled. "Get back."

"Son of a bitch!" Ace jerked up the gun and pushed Maddie away. As if she hadn't just risked her life, she went flying back toward Ace, her face glowing with happiness.

Ace swore and turned.

"You knock her one inch off balance, boy, and your head will be rolling next," Culbart growled.

"For the love of Pete, Maddie! Get off!"

A shadow came up behind Ace. Before Caden could call a warning, Dickens brought the butt of his gun down on the back of Ace's head. He went down hard. Maddie grabbed Ace's shoulders as he went down, landing in a heap on the floor beneath him. Maddie glared at Caden as if it were all his fault as she struggled free, and accused, "Shame on you, Caden, riding so hard that Ace is completely tuckered out!"

Caden blinked and looked at Ace's crumpled body. Maddie clearly was on one of her mental journeys.

"Don't you worry about it, Maddie," Culbart soothed. "I'm sure your fiancé isn't any too tired to get hitched."

"I'm not her fiancé."

Maddie looked at him, her gaze so soft it could melt stone. A tear hovered in her eye.

"I'm sorry, Caden, I know you didn't want us telling anybody just yet, but when Uncle Frank found me, he wanted to know why I was out alone. I had no choice but to reveal our elopement."

Caden swore and got to his feet. She had it wrapped up as pretty as a picture. "You know damn well I'd never leave any fiancée of mine to travel alone," he growled at Culbart.

"I don't know shit, son, except that pretty lady over there thinks you made her promises and she's expecting me to make sure you keep them."

"Maddie?" She didn't answer. Caden ran his hand through his hair. "She's not right in the head."

"She seemed clear enough to me," Culbart countered. "Especially when she described your sleeping habits."

"She sneaks into my room in the middle of the night!"

Ace groaned and rolled over. Maddie gasped. Culbart jerked his chin up. "That's enough for me. Dickens," he barked. "Let the preacher in."

Caden rubbed his jaw, wincing at the immediate ache. *Fuck!*

Dickens stepped aside, making room for another of Culbart's men. Both he and Dickens kept their guns trained on him while a third, wearing a preacher's collar, brought up the rear.

Caden shook his head, capturing Maddie's gaze with his.

"I'm not marrying you, Maddie."

She stared at him for the longest second, her expression as soft as dandelion fluff, before smiling with all the sweetness he remembered, and said with perfect clarity, "You don't have a choice."

A FUCKING SHOTGUN WEDDING.

Caden jerked at his bound hands as he stood in front of the preacher. Maddie stood beside him, soft and sweet in her yellow dress, smiling up to him as if there weren't men pointing guns at him from all directions and Culbart wasn't standing over there looking like a cat that just ate the cream. They'd dragged Ace out to clean him up when Maggie declared blood bad luck at the wedding.

He tugged at his bonds again. Culbart's smile widened. Maddie's finger brushed over his.

"I told you, you shouldn't have picked those flowers for me," she said. "There's poison ivy there."

He hadn't picked any flowers, he hadn't done shit, but Maddie was off in her dreamworld, and nothing he said seemed to make any impression. He tried again. "I'm not itching. I'm struggling."

"It will be over soon."

That sounded suspiciously sane. He looked down at her, but all he could see was the top of her head. Dammit! "Maddie, you don't want to do this."

She looked up then. Her expression was the perfect mix of hurt innocence. Right down to the hint of moisture in her eyes. Maybe too perfect. Even when Maddie was at her most distant, there was always that hint of confusion as if she wasn't quite sure where she was supposed to be. A confusion that was completely missing now. And had been since he'd arrived.

"You've changed your mind?" she asked.

"I never made it up in the first place."

Her fingers wrapped in the sleeve of his shirt but didn't slide down to his wrist. Maddie always slid her fingers down to his wrist.

"You can't change your mind." She looked over at Culbart.

"He's not going anywhere, honey."

As if on cue, three sets of guns tightened their aim.

That woman has a powerful affection for you. Caine's words came back to haunt him. Was it possible Maddie had set him up? He looked down at her. There was no guile in her face, but a lot of women could make pretend seem real, and Maddie was real good at pretend.

A knock came at the door. Dickens yanked it open. Ace stumbled into the room, his hands bound behind him, his hair dripping. Blood still stained his shirt, but his neck and chest were clean.

"Here's the best man," Dickens said, shoving him

into the room. Ace tossed his head, flipping his hair out of his eyes. He didn't look any happier than Caden felt.

Shit. Ace pulled up short, taking in the preacher, the arrangement of the furniture, Maddie standing by Caden.

"Shoot, boys, if you'd have told me it was a wedding, I'd have dressed better."

"If we'd have told you it was a wedding, you'd have hightailed it."

Ace flashed that smile of his. "I like weddings as long as they aren't mine."

"Your friend doesn't feel the same."

"Caden's always been ornery."

"Shut up, Ace," Caden snapped.

"Well, he can be ornery and hitched," Culbart interrupted.

Caden yanked at his bonds. "And you can be dead."

"Marriage is good for a man."

"Then you marry her."

"Caden!" Maddie gasped.

She could gasp all she wanted. It didn't change the facts. He was being forced into a marriage with a woman he didn't want.

"I asked, but she's got her heart set on you."

Fucking hell. "Then she's going to be disappointed."

Culbart smiled. "No, she's not."

"You have to marry me," Maddie said, her fingers gripping his sleeve. He waited. They still didn't drift down to his wrist.

Certainty lodged like lead in his stomach. Maddie was faking pretend. "Why?"

"Because."

He laughed. "Because? Is that what you told Culbart?"

She nodded.

"Hell," Ace said. "Even if advances were made, it's not like she was a vestal virgin."

For the first time ever, Caden didn't come to Maddie's defense.

Dickens elbowed Ace in the stomach. "Watch how you talk to the lady."

"The lady forcing my best friend to marry on a lie?"

"If it's a lie, how does she know so much about him?"

Ace's brows went up. "I wasn't aware that she did."

"She does."

"And if it's a lie," Dickens continued, "why was she out traveling on her own, following him?"

"Because she's crazy?" Ace countered.

Maddie gasped. No matter what stunt she was pulling, it still bothered Caden to see that hurt in her eyes. And that pissed him off.

"When this wedding's over, Culbart, what then?" he asked.

"You're going to write me an IOU for a horse, and we're going to have the party Maddie arranged."

"We're having a party?"

Maddie nodded up at him, her eyes shining. "With chocolate cake. Just like Tia had."

Just like Tia had. That wedding had been the fantasy of Maddie's life. She'd thrown herself into Tia's plans, sharing the excitement as if it was her own, which might explain why he was now standing beside her facing a preacher with the world believing they were promised. That's how make-believe went with Maddie. A little bit of reality turned into a whole lot of pretend. *If* she was pretending

Caden looked over at Culbart. "You're letting us go?"

"Any reason I shouldn't?"

He exchanged a look with Ace. Ace shrugged, clearly having no better idea than Caden as to what was going on, but the goal was to get Maddie out of here, and if a fake marriage succeeded in achieving an actual escape, then who was he to argue? For sure no one would hear of this, and even if they did, it would be a simple matter to bribe the preacher to make the papers disappear, assuming there even were papers.

Setting his jaw, he bit back his pride. It'd been a long time since anyone had been able to force him to do anything. "If this wedding's going to happen, then someone get talking. Daylight's burning."

And so was his temper, because as the reverend started the ceremony, as Maddie repeated the vows in her sweet, low voice, happiness written all over her face, he couldn't shake the certainty that he'd been set up. It wouldn't be the first time and it likely wouldn't be the last. But to think that he'd fallen into a trap of Maddie's making, betrayed by one of Hell's Eight, soured his stomach. From the expression on Ace's face, it wasn't sitting too well with him, either, and as much as he wanted answers, now wasn't the time to search for them.

The ceremony was short, to the point. No rings were exchanged, which didn't stop Maddie from holding out her hand and expecting one. The expression on her face was crestfallen when he didn't produce one, but then just as quickly, she tucked her fingers up into her palm and smiled at the preacher.

"He's saving up to get me a special one. I'll be the envy of all the women."

She was going to be something. She'd be lucky if he didn't put her over his knee.

"I bet he will, pretty thing," Culbart said, "but if he doesn't, you come give your uncle Frank a visit."

The threat was thinly veiled.

"Do you really want to be on the wrong side of Hell's Eight, Culbart?"

Culbart gave Maddie a hug, tilted his head to the side. "Seems to me I just forged an alliance with Hell's Eight."

"One that lasts only as long as this wedding."

"Never known a Hell's Eight man to break a promise, and you just promised to love and cherish this lady forever until death do you part."

Son of a bitch. So he had.

"A promise made under duress."

"A promise is a promise," Culbart cut in.

Caden had to agree. He really had promised to love and cherish and protect Maddie forever.

"Dickens, put down that shotgun," Culbart said. "No need for it anymore, and fetch the whiskey. Bob, go fetch your fiddle. I fancy a dance with the bride."

Maddie giggled and blushed. "I'm sure my husband will want the first dance."

Caden flexed his shoulders as Dickens cut his bonds. "Dance with whomever you want."

Maddie's smile faltered but then steadied. "He's such a considerate man."

Culbart's frown didn't match the lightness of his tone. "A regular prince."

"Yes. My prince."

The men pushed the chairs back and Culbart put his arm out. Maddie cast him one uncertain look before taking it, her smile more forced than before. The strains of the fiddle picked up speed. Culbart twirled her forward. He danced the way one would expect for such a big man, more enthusiasm than grace, but after a couple spins, Maddie didn't seem to mind. She tipped her head back and laughed. Her hair came out of its elaborate bun and flowed over Culbart's arm. The sight was just one more aggravation in a day of them. The man was entirely too familiar with his wife. When Culbart and she stopped dancing, the next Fallen C hand was in line. This one was more graceful. He'd obviously danced a lot. Maddie's tongue peeked between her lips as she concentrated on following his intricate steps, but follow them she did, her laughter rising above the music, landing on his pride, galling him.

When the next man would have stepped up, Caden had had enough. Shotgun marriage or not, Maddie was his wife, not some floozy for all to handle. He strode across the room, tapping the man on the shoulder.

"My turn."

Maddie stood there, looking impossibly sweet, fragile, treacherous. For a moment he thought he saw fear in her eyes, but then her smile was back, soft and gentle, the way she only smiled for him. She held up her arms. He put one hand around her waist and grabbed her hand with the other. She blinked when she didn't get the kiss she expected, but as he led her into a slow waltz, she fell in step with him. Now that he had her in his arms, Caden wasn't sure what he wanted to do with her.

She sighed. "Our first dance as husband and wife."

"Likely our last, too."

She blinked, but that smile didn't shake.

"You think the fiddler is getting tired?"

She was deliberately misunderstanding him.

"I think I'm tired." Tired of this charade. Tired of believing she could betray him. Tired of accepting it was more than likely she had. Maddie hungered for respectability, and today she'd found a way to get it.

Shit. He'd been a fool. They'd all been fools. But there was no undoing this, no getting out of it right now.

He danced Maddie over to one of the hands and passed her off. He'd had enough of this crap.

"Giving away the bride so soon?" Dickens sneered.

Caden dropped her hand and turned away. "Yes."

Maddie gasped, and a reflective growl rose in one of the men. Caden flexed his shoulders and smiled. He could use a good fight. Before Caden could take anyone up on the challenge, Ace threw his arm around his shoulder and shoved a whiskey into his hand.

"What the fuck are you doing, Caden? Trying to get

us all killed?" he muttered, shoving him toward the door and out.

"She played me for a fool, all of us for fools."

Ace shrugged. "Maybe. Or maybe this is all some scheme thought up by Culbart."

"She didn't need to go along with it."

"Hell, Caden, it's Maddie. Half the time she doesn't know if she's here or there. You can't be blaming her for this."

Caden remembered the moment of satisfaction on her face at the end of the ceremony. "Yeah, I can."

"Well, whatever's going on, we can't do anything about it now, so let's just get the celebrating done, get Maddie loaded up and get the hell back to Hell's Eight."

"I'm not taking her back to Hell's Eight."

"Why not?"

"One, because I can't afford to lose the mine to claim jumpers, and two, she wanted to be my wife, then she can be my fucking wife and deal with all that means."

"And what the hell is that?" Ace asked.

Caden shoved his hat back down on his head, glaring into the house through the window at Maddie, who was dancing with yet another cowboy, her smile not as light as before, her step not as merry.

"I have a feeling we're both about to find out."

CHAPTER SEVEN

CULBART INSISTED ON providing them with an escort. Maddie was grateful. Caden was not. Every clop of their horses' hooves just scraped along his anger, until an hour from the mine, Caden reached the end of his patience. Culbart might have forced a wife on him, but he wasn't going to force the revelation of the mine. Caden pulled Jester up so short, Maddie's little mare ran into its ass. Habit had him looking over his shoulder to make sure she was okay. She wasn't the best rider, and if he gave a thought to how she'd left in the middle of the night from Hell's Eight, he'd probably have a fit of apoplexy.

"What's the problem?" Dickens asked from farther back.

Leather creaked as Caden turned in the saddle. "This is as far as you go."

Dickens's horse gave a toss of its head the way an animal did when the grip on the reins got too tight, too fast.

"Boss said we were to see you home."

"Consider us home."

"It wouldn't be right to send them back without supper," Maddie whispered.

Ace just shook his head. Caden didn't answer. The silence grew heavy with Culbart's men determined to fulfill their role, Maddie fretting about a nonexistent meal and Caden's sense of betrayal growing. If any other woman had pulled that stunt, he would have been pissed but understood. But Maddie? He shook his head. That was betrayal of Hell's Eight. Of their friendship. Of him. It was Ace who finally broke the silence.

"Maddie, honey, your uncle Frank needs his men home tomorrow. I saw Indian sign back there."

She frowned. "Indians wouldn't bother Uncle Frank. He gives them cattle."

No amount of cattle was going to settle the unrest swelling in this land, and from the looks Dickens gave his companion, Michael, that Indian sign had him worried, too.

"Maddie," Caden said, drawing her attention.

"Yes?" Her voice was soft and clear, as if a world of tension wasn't lodged between them.

"Culbart's men are leaving. Now. This is as far as they go."

"But—"

Dickens cut in, way too agreeably for a man carrying the grudge Dickens was. "Ma'am, truth be told, we are needed back at the Fallen C."

She sighed and turned her little mare around in the tight confines of the trail; he could only assume she was smiling at them as she said ever so properly in manners that Tia would admire, "Thank you very kindly for your time."

Dickens cut Caden a smile as he took her hand and brought it to his lips. Caden bared his teeth in response.

"It was truly our pleasure, ma'am."

With a tip of their hats, Dickens and Michael left. There was a brief moment of jostling when Dickens's horse had to get past Ace's on the narrow trail—Caden had a feeling it was intentional—but finally the men left and it was just the three of them. Maddie didn't turn even after they'd vanished from sight.

"Maddie."

No response beyond the slight stiffening of her shoulders. The sun glinted off the red of her hair, giving the impression of fire. Caden sighed. It was too bad Maddie's inner fire was extinguished before it even got to flicker

"You're going to have to turn that horse around and face me sometime, Maddie."

With a slow breath that expanded her ribs beneath the yellow wool of her dress, she did, and when she faced him, her expression was blank, totally and completely blank. No mischief. No dread. No nothing. Unlike her moments of pretense, that expression bothered him. He didn't know what to do with it. Son of a bitch.

"What's wrong?" Ace asked.

Caden shook his head and sighed. "Maddie needs a moment."

Ace looked down the trail. "We don't have one."

"Then we'll make one."

"I don't trust that Dickens as far as I can throw him."

Neither did he, but they didn't have a choice. Turning Jester, Caden rode up beside Maddie. The trail was so narrow their knees touched. The sensation that snaked through him was pleasure, pure and simple. It pissed him off. He slid his fingers under Maddie's chin and turned her face to his. Her gaze looked right through him. Stroking his thumb over her lips, he shook his head.

"Why, Maddie?"

She didn't answer, just kept staring. He had the oddest sensation she was bracing herself. Way down deep where no one could see. The guilt was no more welcome than the pleasure. Grabbing the reins from her hands, he looped them over his saddle horn before switching his grip to her waist and dragging her off the mare and across his lap.

"I wasn't kidding about that Indian sign," Ace stated quietly.

"I know." Ace was the type that took precautions in the middle of his recklessness. With a sigh, Caden settled Maddie in. She fit against him perfectly; the side of her breast pressed into his chest, her hips rested on his thighs. Soft. Everything about her was soft. Grabbing Flower's reins and wrapping his arm around Maddie's waist, Caden directed Jester with a press of his knee. The big horse responded as he always did. Immediately and without hesitation. He was loyal to a fault. Unlike Maddie. Fuck, that was hard to swallow.

"She all right?" Ace asked once they were moving.

He glanced over his shoulder again, but there was nothing to see except the set of Ace's shoulders, the top of his hat pulled down low over his brow and the firm set of his mouth.

"She's fine."

Ace grunted. Caden could tell Ace wasn't pleased

with him. He didn't really give a shit. Ace could afford to
be chivalrous. Ace wasn't saddled with a wife he hadn't
expected or wanted, one who wasn't even in her right
mind. And while Caden hadn't spent much time spec-
ulating what kind of life he might have, the few times
he'd gone down that road, the woman he'd pictured had
at least been sane.

A scent that reminded him of wildflowers drifted
up from Maddie's hair. It was as natural as breathing to
press a kiss to the top of her head. So natural he wasn't
even aware he'd done it until her fingers found his wrist
and she was looking up at him with hope in her eyes.

"I'm sorry, Caden."

He pulled his hand free. The hope drained from her
face, leaving it once again starkly blank. They rode on
for several minutes like that, neither speaking, her body
tense against his. His tense under hers. Anger where
there had once been trust.

He nudged Jester into a trot, forcing Maddie back
against him. Her elbow dug into his stomach, her head
collided with his bruised chin. For a second, he saw stars.

She stiffened more, which just caused her to bounce
more.

"Relax before you get us both killed."

She did immediately, on a harsh gasp that sounded
distinctly like a sob.

Gritting his teeth, Caden urged Jester into a canter,
letting the sound of the horses' hooves drown out the
sound of her crying. It didn't drown out his anger. He'd
trusted her, and she'd turned on him quick as a rattle-

snake. Goddamn her. She was lucky he didn't wring her neck. Her tears soaked through his shirt, cutting into his conscience. Before he knew it, he was stroking her shoulder, soothing her. The woman who'd betrayed him. Caden stilled his hand.

Fuck.

BY THE TIME THEY GOT BACK to the campsite, Maddie was quiet and Caden was seething. Ace pulled his horse up beside them, dismounted and smiled at Maddie.

"Good to have you back, Sprout."

As far as Caden could tell, Maddie didn't respond. Ace looked between him and her and shook his head. "Go easy on her."

Caden unwrapped Flower's reins from the saddle. "I wasn't even planning on talking to her."

Ace snorted. "You're so ready to talk you're about to explode."

"She's my wife and none of your concern."

He gave the reins a little tug so Flower recognized who held her. Maybe that was what Maddie needed. A leash so she wouldn't forget to whom she belonged.

Caden pulled his hat down over his brow and held his hand out for Ace's horse's reins. "I'll water the horses."

"I'll scout around and make sure everything's the way we left it."

Caden nodded. Ace hesitated, glancing between Maddie and him. Shaking his head, he pushed his hat back.

"Hell, Caden, just remember half the time she doesn't know what she's doing."

Not this time. "This is none of your business, Ace."

"Maddie's Hell's Eight. That makes her my business."

The anger knotted in Caden's gut as truth he'd been chewing on for miles settled. "She betrayed Hell's Eight. That changes everything."

MADDIE'S QUIET LASTED until they reached the pond. Then as if he'd flipped a lever, she slid off the horse and grabbed the reins down by the bit. Holding Jester for him, he realized. As if that was necessary. Hell, maybe she wasn't in her right mind. She looked around.

"We're home?"

He should be used to her mental comings and goings but he wasn't.

"If you're willing to call a tent in the middle of a pile of rocks home, yes."

She blinked at his tone. "You must be hungry."

What he was was pissed. "What in the hell makes you think that?"

"You're hard to live with when you're hungry."

"Noticed that, did you?" He swung down off Jester. "I'm even harder to live with when I'm played for a fool."

He grabbed the gelding's reins out of her hands, keeping ahold of the other horses', as well. The last thing he wanted right now was her help.

"I don't understand."

The hell she didn't. "Go back to the camp, Maddie."

"I can help you with the horse."

"Right now the only thing that will help is you disappearing."

She stopped walking beside him. "A wife's place is with her husband."

The cliché snapped the last of his control. "And a whore's place is on her back. What's your point?"

Caden regretted the words as soon as they left his mouth. Maddie gasped and stepped back, her pale skin bleaching a ghastly white. Guilt lashed at him. He'd never thrown her past in her face before. He ran his fingers through his hair. The woman flat-out drove him crazy. "I'm sorry, Maddie. You didn't deserve that."

She deserved a hell of a lot, but not that.

She didn't respond, just kept looking at him as if her world was crumbling. Inside, the wild anger twisted in a lash of guilt. Needing release. Before he could say anything more, Caden turned and walked away, leaving Maddie there, forcing himself not to look back. He heard the slide of soft rock under her feet as she started back up the hill, heard the ping of stones as they tumbled down behind her. Heard her sob.

Fuck. Why the hell did he care?

Letting the reins slip through his fingers, Caden stood while the horses drank their fill, his thoughts so dark he couldn't feel the sun. One by one he relived the events of the afternoon, but no matter how he shook it out, there was no way in hell Maddie hadn't played along with Culbart when it came to the marriage, maybe even put the idea in his head. Hell, she had to have put the idea in his head. Why else would Culbart consider marrying him to her? There was more for him to gain by marrying her himself in the form of an alliance with Hell's Eight.

No, any push toward marrying had come from Maddie herself. Damn her.

Who the hell was Maddie? The sweet, abused woman who'd come to Hell's Eight for shelter or the gold digger who'd conned her way into a marriage with a man she expected was going to be wealthy.

Caden took the nugget out of his pocket, rolled it over his fingers, looking for that faint trace of gold within the hidden depths. He thought Maddie had depth, but maybe he was just fooling himself the way men wanted to fool themselves when it came to women. He closed his fingers around the nugget and squeezed. He shoved the nugget back into his pocket. Or more than likely Maddie was both sweet and conniving, and who could blame her? Brought up as she was, the one thing in this world she'd want more than anything was security, and nothing brought security like a husband. A wealthy one just that much more.

Caden looked up the hill toward the campsite.

Well, Maddie had the husband she wanted now, just maybe not the one she was expecting.

CADEN LINGERED WITH the horses longer than he needed to, letting the peace of the day work on his anger. He hadn't gotten too far with that when he sensed another presence. There was only one person who snapped his senses to attention without sending off warning tingles. Flower lifted her head and whickered, looking over her shoulder. He turned, knowing who he would find.

Maddie stood awkwardly, farther away than he was used to. "I don't have any flint to start a fire."

"I've got sulfurs."

She rubbed her hands on her skirt. There was a dirt smudge on her sleeve and some small leaf particles clung to her bodice. Obviously, she'd collected wood.

"I couldn't find any supplies to eat."

"I have some hidden."

She nodded. "I thought so."

There was no vapidness about her expression, so she was here with him now.

"Why'd you do it, Maddie?"

She didn't pretend to misunderstand. "Culbart said I had to."

"He threatened you?" He'd kill the son of a bitch.

She shook her head. "No. He didn't have to." Her smile brightened, and that fast she was back in pretend. "Now I really am your Maddie."

"Maddie mine." He sighed. He still hadn't figured out how that endearment had slipped into his speech, and now she'd turned it into a reality.

"Maddie, this marriage is not going to last."

Her smile broadened. "Only until death do us part."

"Maddie, look at me."

She did, all smiles. He felt like the biggest heel as he laid out the truth along with sulfurs. As she took the small tin, he reiterated, "Maddie. This marriage isn't going to stand."

"Of course it is, silly," she stated calmly, walking past him with the confidence that had been lacking before to grab Flower's reins. "Till death do us part. That's what the preacher said, and you can't go against God."

Flower followed her easily up the path; the bond between the two was strong. Behind him Jester snorted. He hadn't gotten any further making friends with the little mare than Caden had gotten with Maddie.

"I know just how you feel," Caden muttered.

Caden followed Maddie back to the campsite. Sure enough, she had sticks stacked in front of the fire pit. Signs of Maddie were all over the campsite. Everything was arranged, neatly aligned, nothing out of place. Maddie had a penchant about neatness. He liked that in her. Maybe because of the chaos of what her life was, maybe because of the chaos his life was—whatever. That quality in her resonated with him.

To the right, two bedrolls were set side by side. Like a red flag to a bull.

"Oh, hell, no."

The only hope he had of getting out of this marriage was to not consummate it.

As fast as he was, Maddie still beat him to the bedroll, plunking herself down over both of them, spreading her hands over what her hips didn't cover, and her hips covered a lot. The woman had a nice ass.

"Stop it," she told him.

"We're not sleeping together, Maddie."

She set her chin. "This is our honeymoon."

"This is a farce."

That chin quivered then snapped up.

"You're not going to ruin this for me."

"Ruin what?"

"My wedding night."

"Dammit, Maddie, we're not having a wedding night. We got married because it was the only way to rescue you."

"You could have come in guns blazing."

"And gotten myself killed, yes, but that wouldn't have been much of a rescue."

"You didn't fight the wedding."

"I had a goddamn gun in my back."

"Gentlemen don't use bad words around ladies. Tia said so."

She glared at him as if that was the end of it. The automatic retort that she wasn't a lady stuck on his tongue. He unclenched his hands and squatted in front of Maddie, touching his finger to the curl by her cheek. Her lids flickered over her eyes and her lips trembled. Some of his anger melted.

"You here, Maddie mine?"

She nodded a nod that could have meant anything. He asked the question he'd wanted to ask first off.

"Did they hurt you, honey?"

She pulled away, cutting him a glare out of the corner of her eye as she smoothed a wrinkle from one of the bedrolls.

"Women like me can't be hurt."

Dammit to hell and back. Caden kept his drawl soft. "Anyone can be hurt."

Especially someone as gentle as Maddie. She had no defenses, no ability to stand up for herself. She was as easy to squash as a bug, and he'd taken a swing at her. Maybe he ought to go back and let Culbart kick his ass.

"Nothing happened."

He remembered the clearing, the story told in the disturbance in the ground, the button... Did he really need to make her relive that? He settled for "Let me ask you this, then."

Another glance out of the corner of her eye, sunlight splashed across her freckles, making him realize how pale she was. For all her bravado, she was tired, she was scared and she was trapped, had been for most of her life.

"Did you ever tell Culbart you didn't want to marry me?"

She shook her head.

It was the answer he expected. Caden pushed the loose curls away from her face so he could see her expression, but seeing only her profile. She looked so young with her head tipped like that, exposing the roundness of her cheek and the delicacy of her neck. "Why not?"

Maddie smoothed a nonexistent wrinkle, not looking at him, not pulling away, but so tense. "It would have been a lie."

And Hell's Eight didn't lie. He shook his head. "What am I going to do with you, Maddie?"

MADDIE DIDN'T KNOW what he was going to do, but she knew what she wanted him to do. She wanted to tell him to hold her, to keep her, to cherish her, to look at her the way Ed looked at Tia, but the words stuck like mud on her tongue. She was a whore. Men didn't cherish whores. They used them. They abused them, they discarded them, but they didn't cherish them. Especially ones that forced them into marriage.

Oh, dear heavens, what had she done? It'd seemed the right thing at the time. She remembered thinking Caden was so alone. That he needed someone and no one would work harder than she to make him happy. She remembered talking about it, hearing Culbart agreeing. She shook her head. She didn't remember more. Didn't need to. Oh, Lord, what had she done while she'd been "hiding"?

Her breath rattled in her lungs then lodged in her throat. The little girl's voice in her head screamed *run*. The woman she'd just started to become acquainted with said *stay*. Of the two, the child's voice was louder. The gray of the bedroll filled her vision. So ugly when she wanted pretty. She started to picture her pond in her mind, letting the gray wool blend into the reflection of a storm cloud chasing over the water, the harshness of Caden's breath becoming the rustle of the wind through the leaves...

"Don't you fucking dare."

The image wavered. The child cried louder. Out of the corner of her eye, Maddie looked at his fingers. Scars cut across the back of his knuckles. Old scars blending with new, the new abrasions from where he'd fought Culbart's men. He'd come for her. She followed a scrape down the back of his hand to his wrists where muscle and tendon were clearly defined. Her husband. The one to whom she owed loyalty. The one who owed her. The one she'd betrayed. The woman in her reached out. Grabbed his hand. Clung. His start shot up her arm. His curse blistered her ears. The child quieted. Maddie took another breath as the image of the pond faded and once again she was staring at the gray bedroll. And her nails biting into Caden's skin. She still didn't know what to say. The only words that came out were, "I'm sorry."

His finger slipped under her chin, forcing her to look up at him. She hated when he did that. It made it so hard to pretend. "What the hell is going on in that head of yours?"

A question that didn't expect an answer. The kind of question a man posed to an animal or an imbecile. She wished she dared push his hand away. Instead, she concentrated on relaxing her grip on his hand. It took a lot of concentration to accomplish the simple task. How did others do this so easily? Argue. Fight… Confront.

She had a choice. Retreat or go forward. There was nothing for her in going back. She forced a smile. It shook on her lips. "I was thinking it was a pretty night for a honeymoon."

"We're not married."

They had to be. She couldn't face a future without him in it. This was her life. She might have made a mess of it, but it could be salvaged. "We stood before the reverend and promised our lives to each other."

It hurt way down deep that Caden didn't see that moment with even a speck of the beauty she did, but when she recalled the day, she'd just fill happiness in. Coloring bad memories with something pretty was all right,

Tia had said, as long as she didn't forget what had really happened. And the reality was they were really married. "That makes us married."

"That can be undone."

Could it? "Hell's Eight never breaks a promise."

Caden grabbed up one of the bedrolls, yanking it out from under her hip, and stood. "There's always a first time for everything."

If Caden hadn't stomped off while saying that, Maddie might have been worried. The man only ran when he had mixed feelings. It was a small thing to hold on to, but it was something. Feigning a confidence she didn't feel, she called after him, "But you won't."

He made a sound that could have been a curse and then, "That promise was made under false pretenses."

It took her a moment to figure out what that meant. She stood and brushed off her skirts. "You knew what you were doing."

Caden always knew what he was doing. She liked that about him. The indecision that seemed to surround her like a cloud never touched him. He saw things with a black-and-white clarity that was brutally honest. And he saw her as a betrayer. She sighed. Inside, the child whined an explanation. She hushed it. Making the decision to claim her life meant she claimed responsibility for what she did in it.

"I've changed my mind," he snapped before turning and heading back toward her. A broad-shouldered man with a purpose. Her heart leaped in her throat. His shadow crept over her as he got close. Her heart expanded, cutting off her air.

Digging her nails into her palms, she held her ground. "You can't if I don't let you."

It felt good to draw so powerful a man up short. The thrill almost made up for the terror that took over when he pulled his hat down low with a deliberate tug and asked in a soft, dangerous drawl, "You're threatening me?"

Her courage spilled like so much water off a cliff. Biting her lip, she stood completely still as he tipped her face up with a finger under her chin. Men always did that, thinking if she was looking at them she couldn't make them go away. But she was better than they thought. Stronger.

"Yes."

"You think you can back that threat?"

Be strong in a way that serves you.

Bella had given her advice, and remembering it now gave Maddie courage. She'd followed Caden to claim the future she wanted. Hiding from it now wouldn't accomplish her goal. Besides. She was Hell's Eight. Hell's Eight never backed down.

"Yes, I can." *I hope.*

His gaze narrowed. "How?"

She had no idea, but she lifted her chin farther, forcing herself to meet his gaze. His eyes were so bright with sun striking off them. This close she could see the gray was flecked with blue, and not just one shade but variations. No wonder the women sighed when he came about. His eyes were fascinating. The kind a woman could stare into forever, lured by the illusion that she could see his soul if she just looked long enough.

The thought was as seductive as the way his shirt fit across muscular shoulders. Caden was a handsome man, as rugged as the hills, as harshly beautiful as the plains. The stark cut of his cheekbones under his eyes just added to his appeal. Beautifully handsome, she corrected as she dropped her gaze to his mouth. In repose his lips were firm and well shaped, not girlie but not too thin in that way that made a woman think of a mean spirit. They were, she decided, just right. A firm stroke of his thumb across her chin and his sigh brought her back to the moment.

"If you're going to piss me off, the least you can do is stay for the fight."

She blinked. She had drifted off but not in ways he thought. It was a small personal victory. She added it to her mental hoard. "I'm sorry."

His head titled to the side. A sunbeam cut a path beneath the brim of his hat. If she'd thought his eyes were stunning before, they were mesmerizing now. "No, you're not."

She actually wasn't, and what a pleasant surprise that was. It seemed she'd been apologizing her whole life, starting with the fact that she'd been born. "I don't like to fight."

His thumb crept up until the tip just grazed the underside of her lower lip. The strangest of tingles spread out from that spot. Her breath caught in her throat. His eyes narrowed, and suddenly there was a different kind of tension between them. "Then, why are you picking one?"

This she could answer. "Because you're breaking your promise to me."

"I never break a promise."

"You promised you wouldn't leave before I got back."

"Shit." His thumb stopped moving, but the tingles continued. "So you tricked me into marriage to get revenge for a broken promise?"

She stepped back, breaking the contact. For a second she thought he was going to follow, but then his hand dropped to his side. "No, I didn't, but I can't let you break another promise to me."

"How do you intend to stop me?"

"I don't know." She thought of Bella and how she faced down Sam when he was being unreasonable. She couldn't put her hand on her hip with the same flair as Bella, but she could imitate her bravado. "Yet."

That "yet" snapped his chin up. "I don't like you like this."

She didn't imagine he did, but *she* did. "Well, get used to it." She snatched up her bedroll and dragged it over to where his was, laying it out beside his again. "I'm not a child."

His gaze dropped to her breasts. She was used to men looking at her breasts. It didn't mean she had to like it. She put her hand to her bodice. "I meant inside."

The expression on his face could only be described as surprised. She was not an ugly woman, and he needn't act as if looking at her breasts was the most shocking of things.

"What the hell are you doing?"

She had no idea. She couldn't seem to settle between wanting and running. "I think I'm getting stronger."

"You always were strong." He made that claim with a nonchalance that stunned her. With a motion of his hand, he indicated the bedrolls tossed on the ground. "Do you think sleeping with me is going to make you more a woman in my eyes?"

"Men don't remember women they fornicate with."

"Honey, there isn't a man that would lie down with you and forget."

He was completely wrong. So many had. "Then, the night should go well."

"It's not even dark yet."

He was making excuses. "You don't think I'm pretty enough."

"You're beautiful."

Her heart did a little flutter. She sat on the bedroll with a plop. "Good."

He reached down and pulled her to her feet. "But Ace might have his own opinion."

Oh, good gravy. She'd forgotten about Ace.

"Unless you were intending on giving him a show?" Caden asked with a mocking tilt of his head.

The question hit her like a blow. He could be so cruel. She could feel the pull of her pond, the tranquil and cool water, smell the sweet breeze of the wildflowers around. It would be so easy to slip out from under the humiliation of the moment into that soft dream. She wouldn't have to even close her eyes. Just let her mind flow… And so unfair.

"Maddie?" Someone shook her.

She blinked, reality coming back into focus. "Caden?"

"Who else?"

She shook her head to clear it. She'd slipped away. For how long? She licked her lips. "No one."

His grip eased on her shoulders. She looked at his hands and then his face. "You were shaking me?"

She had such a hard time putting together the spaces in the time between her fancy and what was real.

"Yeah." He let go of her arms slowly as if he was afraid she was going to bolt. Or fall.

She licked her lips again, and his gaze dropped to her mouth. For no reason, she remembered that tingle.

"You really do slip away, don't you?"

What did he want her to say? More important, why did he want her to say it? "Sometimes."

"Wonderful. Something to look forward to over the next forty years. I'm going to get the supplies." He turned and stalked away.

Instead of following, she stood there and smiled.

Caden was thinking of a future.

CHAPTER EIGHT

FIVE HOURS LATER Caden was still at an impasse with Maddie. Dark had fallen, supper was cooked, edible because Caden had done the honors, and Maddie was singing softly, an Irish song that put a lilt in her voice that was only faintly there when she sang. Caden sat in front of the fire and gave it a poke with a stick. The night was warm, they didn't really need it, but keeping it going was giving him something to do other than take potshots at Maddie. She drew him, angered him and just generally threw his orderly world into chaos, so why couldn't he just walk away? Why the hell did he feel as if he owed her an apology?

Ace entered the camp, his boots making soft scuffing sounds on the rock. He took one look at Caden and said, "At least the horses are settled."

"Shut up, Ace."

Ace waved to Maddie. "Evening, Sprout."

Maddie waved back. "I set aside supper for you."

"Thanks."

Ace grabbed one of the freshly washed bowls off the rock by the fire and asked, "Who cooked?"

"Maddie made the biscuits."

Ace immediately piled three on his plate. He hesitated over the stew.

Caden sighed. "It's safe. I made the stew."

Ace loaded up his bowl. "It's a damn shame that woman can't cook." Dipping a biscuit in the stew, he moaned, "But she sure can bake."

"She can do a lot of things."

Ace raised a brow at him. "Maybe even make you happy."

"I wouldn't bet on it."

Ace took a bite of stew. "You're in a foul mood."

"It's my wedding night."

"Yeah."

"I've got a right to be testy."

"Not what most bridegrooms say."

"Most bridegrooms aren't forced to marry at the end of a shotgun."

"Yeah, but you got to marry up with Maddie."

"What the hell does that mean?"

Ace dipped his biscuit in the juicy gravy and took another bite, chewing slowly, making Caden wait until he swallowed before answering.

"It's a pretty good deal. She can bake." He held up a biscuit, which Caden knew from the one he'd had were better than Tia's cooked in an oven, and Maddie had done it over an open fire.

"She's pretty. She's sweet."

"She betrayed me."

"What makes you think she had a choice?"

"I asked her."

"Hmm." Ace dipped the biscuit in the gravy again. "I see."

"What do you see?"

He shook his head. "It's not my place."

"Since when has that ever stopped you?"

Ace looked at Maddie and looked at him, as if measuring the possibilities.

"I'm thinking you're being a fool, Caden."

"I didn't notice you standing up to marry her."

"She didn't want me."

"No, she wanted me, and she arranged it so she got me."

"Can you blame her? With the life she's had?"

No. On one level he really couldn't. On another, he did. Completely.

"She doesn't want a divorce. Said you can't break your word to God."

"He's not someone I'd be breaking my word to."

"It was a promise I shouldn't have made in the first place."

"Convenient way of thinking."

"Whose side are you on?"

"Between you, Maddie and God? I'm siding with God."

"Since when did you find religion?"

"About the time you started thinking promises convenient."

Fuck. There was nothing he could say to that.

"She is a pretty little thing."

Caden followed Ace's gaze. Maddie was sitting cross-legged, her braid drawn over her shoulder, threading her fingers through the strands, a hairbrush sitting in her lap. If this really were his wedding night, he'd stroll over there and take over the job. Cuddling that soft ass in his lap while he ran his fingers through those silky strands before picking up the brush and running it from crown to end, letting it glide over her nipple again and again until it was as hard as he was.

"Turn around," he ordered.

Ace smiled. "Feeling possessive?"

"She doesn't need men gawking at her."

"Really? Because it seems to me that's one woman built for love."

Caden couldn't argue that. Thick, wavy red hair, sweet face, full breasts and hips that flowed to that narrow waist, and just that certain something about her that made a man think of hot sex. Maddie was definitely a woman made for love, but there was always a catch.

"She's had enough of men."

Ace finished off the last of his stew in three bites. "Did you ask her about that?"

"It's not something anyone needs to ask. She's been raped her whole life."

"A husband might be different. A husband can't rape his wife."

Caden wasn't so sure about that. It was so easy to imagine making love to Maddie, touching her with the tenderness he wanted to, slowly unbuttoning her bodice, kissing his way from her mouth down to her breasts, taking those full globes in his hands and plumping those nipples to his lips, rolling his tongue across the tips until they were hard and demanding and then biting them just a little, just enough to make her gasp, before unbuttoning that dress the rest of the way. Sliding it off her shoulders. Pushing all her clothes away until she was naked on the bedroll in front of him, legs spread, lips parted. Anticipating. His cock throbbed and he damn near groaned out loud.

And then he imagined how she'd really look if he did that to her. The fear and loathing that would be on her face followed by that blank stare a whore got when they were doing their job. He never wanted to see any of that on Maddie's face. "She's not going to have to worry about that from me."

"So you plan on just giving up on making love?"

"Hell, no."

"You're a married man, Caden. Stepping outside your marriage, that's breaking a vow."

Caden poked the fire with a stick. "Did you sit over here to needle me or help me?"

Ace ladled more stew into his bowl. "I haven't decided yet."

Maddie finished that side of her hair and, with a graceful move, pulled it all over to the other shoulder and started brushing the other side. Looking closely, Caden could make out the shape of her breast beneath her dress. If he focused on the curves, he could figure out exactly where her nipple was beneath the material. Two inches left of the decorative button that draped the bodice. His fingers tingled. He rubbed them down his thigh.

"Fuck."

Ace shrugged. "She's your wife, Caden. For better or worse, and from the way I'm looking at it, you could do a hell of a lot worse."

"You shouldn't be looking at anything."

"And you should be looking at everything. What's your point?"

Caden shook his head and changed the subject. "Find anything out there?"

"As far as I could determine, nobody followed us. I went back to the trail and set a false trail. You should be good for a while up here."

Caden nodded. "Yeah, up until somebody remembers at some point that Fei had a mine up here."

Ace nodded. "Yeah. Someone's bound to put that together with your presence."

"Any signs of Indians?"

Ace nodded. "Plenty."

"Wonderful."

"Can't be blaming them. The army's been pushing them hard for years, trying to clear the land for settlers. Now, with that fracas in the East rising up, they're getting some room to make a statement of their own. It might not be safe to have Maddie out here."

Hell, it wasn't safe to have Maddie out here even if the Indians weren't pitching a fit.

"Well, there's not much we can do about it now. I've got to get this mine started and get it certified as Hell's Eight's. To do that I need money."

"Don't you mean get it certified as yours?"

No, he didn't. Caden cocked a brow at Ace. "So you do have something else on your mind besides my marriage."

Ace hesitated, cursed and set his bowl down. Picking up the spoon, he started weaving the spoon through his fingers. "Why did you leave Hell's Eight?"

"It was time."

"For what?"

"To build something of my own."

"So it didn't have anything to do with that promise you made your dad?"

"Maybe."

"You don't have to repeat your father's mistakes, Caden."

"Who said he made mistakes?"

"I do and so would you if you didn't feel so damn guilty about the way he died."

"I should have helped him."

"You were eight."

"I could shoot a gun."

"So could I, but my parents didn't want me in the battle. They wanted me to live. Just likes yours did you."

"And I am."

"Like they did without settling anywhere, chasing rainbows instead of building a home."

"I'm a Miller."

"No." Ace tossed the spoon in the bowl. "There are people that spend their whole lives looking for a home without finding it, Caden." Ace looked over at Maddie and stood. "You've found yours. Don't throw it away."

"The marriage wasn't my choice."

"That doesn't make it any less real."

That was true. "This is none of your business, Ace," he repeated.

"Maybe not, but in my opinion, you're still married to one of the sweetest women I've ever met." With a jerk of his chin, Ace indicated Caden's bedroll. "So when you go over there tonight, don't bring your anger with you."

Caden stood. "Are you threatening me?"

Ace didn't flinch. "Do I need to?"

Caden dragged his hand down his face. It was a measure of how far he'd wandered from himself that he couldn't snap out an answer.

THE TEN YARDS to the bedroll did nothing to provide an answer. His anger still seethed. The tenderness still struggled. The urge to lash out still raged. Caden expected Maddie to scramble away in fear as he got closer. Instead, she smiled and patted the blanket beside her. She was dressed in her thin camisole. The woman definitely took chances.

"You want to talk."

The hell he did. He wanted to shout. He wanted to holler. He wanted to pound something. But talk? No.

"Not really. Scoot over." She scooted but not over, just back.

"You want to sleep?"

Her unconstrained breasts shimmied with the move. He couldn't take his eyes off the sight. "Not really."

She looked up at him. He didn't hide anything in his

expression. Her fingers stilled on the ruffle of her pantaloons. He expected her to disappear into that place she went. If she had any sense at all, she would. He was on edge. Wild. Instead, she said in a voice so rational it was almost cold, "You want to start our honeymoon."

"I admit the desire is there."

She started to unbutton her camisole with a calm he'd have believed if it weren't for the pulse pounding in her throat and the barely perceptible shake in her fingers.

"But I've decided against it."

Her head snapped up. Those pretty green eyes widened.

"Why?"

He hadn't expected the question from her. Hell, he never knew what to expect from her. He took off his hat, tossed it to the upper right corner of the bedroll and ran his fingers through his hair. He finally just gave her the unvarnished truth.

"Because I don't know what the hell to do with you."

"You don't know…?" She looked at him, mouth open.

"Aw, hell. I mean I'd know what to do if I wanted to do something with you, but short of that I don't know what to do with you."

"I'm your wife. You promised to love, honor and cherish me."

"You betrayed Hell's Eight."

"You think I betrayed *you*."

And just like that, Maddie cut to the heart of the problem the way she always did.

"You did."

"I guess so."

"You could at least feel guilty."

She licked her lips, her hands tightened into fists, and those respirations were doing double time. "It's hard to talk like this. It takes all my concentration to not… drift away."

"And?"

"I need to tell you something."

"What?"

"I can't feel and do…*it*."

That was a very soft, quiet admission. *Jesus.*

Caden put his arm around Maddie's shoulders and pulled her to him. She didn't exactly help, so instead of sliding gently into his embrace, she tumbled, her head hitting his stomach, her elbow driving into his groin. Pain slammed through him. He grunted, held his breath, lifted her up and then placed her beside him.

She pushed her hair out of her face. "I'm sorry."

"Give me a minute," he said, his voice tight even to his own ears.

"What's wrong?"

He cut her a glance. Her camisole was half off her breast, exposing all but a hint of her nipple. His fingers itched to trail over that softness, to tease and tempt, to tug that thin fabric down until she was fully exposed. Vulnerable. Eager. His senses came alert. His balls spasmed in protest. Her eyes dropped to his groin. She rubbed her elbow as she put two and two together.

"Oh."

"Yeah, oh." A lock of hair was hanging in her eyes. He

resisted the urge to push it aside for all of two seconds. The problem with Maddie was she was just too darn touchable. Tucking the hair behind her ear, he asked, "Making sure you don't receive any unwanted advances tonight?"

Another lick of those tempting lips. He wanted to lean in and capture that moisture on his lips. To feel her hot breath brush over his skin with the same intimacy of the humid night.

"What makes you think they'd be unwanted?"

He glanced up, catching...something in her eyes. Desire? Fear? Resignation? "Probably the fact that I'm not seeing the kind of softness a man sees from a woman that desires him."

She raised her eyebrows. "That's probably because I'm not seeing a lot of softness from you. The kind a man shows when he desires a woman."

That shot hit home. He didn't have much to say to that, and she didn't have much follow-up, which just left them sitting there on their respective bedrolls, side by side, on their honeymoon with nowhere to go. As the minutes passed, so did Caden's anger. Her touch on his arm, the slide of her fingers down the inside of his wrist, her fingers meshing with his before giving a gentle squeeze polished off the last of it. He squeezed back. They did all right when they weren't talking.

"Maddie—"

"Don't."

"Don't what?"

"Don't start talking. Don't start hating me." She made a cutting motion with her hand. "Just don't."

"I don't understand why you did what you did."

She shrugged. "If it helps, neither do I."

He sighed and put his arm around her shoulder. She jumped as he pulled her to his side, sitting as stiff as a spinster. As if she didn't know what to do, what to make of it. Of him. And probably she didn't.

"Haven't you ever cuddled with a man before, Maddie?"

Her hair rustled against the cotton of his shirt as she shook her head.

Shit. "Never?"

"I never had a beau."

A beau. A quaint term for what for most was part of growing up. He thought of the firsts that came with a beau—first grown-up dress, first courtship. First kiss. First love. First broken heart.

Truth was, he didn't have much contact with above-stairs girls, but enough of them married and left the business that they had to fit romance in there somewhere. "No one ever came calling? Wanted to take you out?"

She shook her head again. He couldn't imagine it. Prostitute or not, some man must have wanted Maddie.

"No one?"

She sat as stiff as a board under his arm. As if each word were glass dragging across her tongue, she whispered, "Men don't cuddle whores."

She'd come to a lot of conclusions about what men did and didn't do over her eighteen years. There was a time when he'd told himself she was too young for him. Now he wasn't so sure. That much bad living left a woman with scars too deep for a younger man to handle.

"Maybe that's true, but I didn't ask about whores. I asked about you."

She shrugged and looked down. "It's one and the same."

He tipped her chin up. She still managed to avoid his gaze. He didn't let that deter him. "No, it's not."

She grabbed his wrist, holding on tightly. "Don't."

"Don't what?"

She shook her head. In her eyes he could see the glint of tears. "Please don't make fun of me this way. I know you're mad, but please, don't pretend you see me as I'm not."

See her as she wasn't? She was begging him not to humiliate her. Son of a bitch. How had he let things get this bad?

"I'm not trying to upset you, Maddie."

"I know. You're just working it out in your mind."

"Working what out?"

She clasped her hands in her lap. "The fact that you don't have to worry with me. It's all right."

"What's all right?"

She shrugged. "Whatever you want to do."

She thought he was working around to giving in to his baser instincts. He tried to imagine that. What it was like to sit with a stranger and watch him decide you didn't deserve respect. That you were there for his use, however he saw fit. To do with as he saw fit.

"Maddie—"

She cut him off. "All men do it. Even the decent ones."

He guessed it could be difficult for a man looking at Maddie's sweetness to be all right with releasing the animal in him. But he bet they all managed.

"They're the worst." She shrugged. "It just takes them a little longer."

"For what?"

She looked away. He could actually see her withdrawal.

"To do whatever it is they want to do. Sexually."

He'd called her a whore to her face, then argued with her when she said she wasn't worth anything because he'd expected her to see herself as something. Yet her whole life she'd sat waiting to be shown the opposite. *Fuck.*

From the time she was eight, she'd been learning that lesson. With every customer the madam had sent up, she'd been taught she was worthless. He tried to imagine her at eight. How sweet and innocent she'd have looked. How innocent she'd have been. It was all too easy to imagine that. What was hard was imagining any man looking at her at that tender age and seeing a woman.

"But they always gave in, didn't they?"

She nodded. He caught her chin on his finger and focused her eyes back to his. It wasn't as easy as usual. She was ashamed. "You give me their names and I'll handle it."

"There's nothing to handle. They paid their money."

And bought her soul.

"Give me their names, Maddie."

Her whisper was barely audible. "I don't remember them all."

"Then give me the ones you do."

They'd have to have been real memorable for her to hold their names close.

"Jasper Mason."

One name, just one, but said with such hatred he didn't ask if he was a happy memory. "What does Jasper Mason look like?"

She glanced up, her eyes big with doubt, as if she'd long since accepted no one would ever fight for her. "You'd kill him for me?"

He didn't hesitate. "Yes."

"You don't know what he did."

"I know."

Her hand slid across her lap, fingertips skimming material and skin, touching his fingers, sliding up over his hand, encircled his wrist before settling against the inside, connecting them in a tenuous grip. "He's evil."

"Describe him to me."

"Tall, a little shorter than you. Long blond hair, light blues eyes and a bushy mustache." She shuddered as if assaulted by a bad taste. "He always carries a quirt. His horses are always marked up." Again she looked away. "He liked me."

"Did he use that quirt on you, Maddie?"

She didn't answer. He didn't need her to. A man who marked his horses wouldn't hesitate to mark a woman. He cradled her cheek in his hand, pulling her against his chest. Holding her close, thinking of all those years she'd needed him and he hadn't been there. Thinking of her at Culbart's, needing him again.

"You don't want me now."

There was only one way to respond to that small-voiced statement.

"I always want you. Why do you think I stayed away from Hell's Eight so much?"

She didn't look up. "Because you're restless."

He snorted. "Wanting you made me restless."

She shook her head. "It's not the same."

He kissed the top of her head and debated how much to confess. He finally settled on everything. "I have the same baser instincts as every other man, Maddie, but I want you to understand something."

"What?"

He tipped her chin up, not saying a word until her gaze met his. "When I look at you, I don't see a whore."

She blinked. "But you do see a traitor."

Hell, did he? "I don't know what the hell I see you as, Maddie, but it's not a whore and it's not a traitor, and that pisses me off."

"Why?"

Such a simple question to raise such turmoil in him. "Because I used to know exactly who you were, and I was comfortable with that." The insight came out of nowhere, but as soon as he said it, Caden realized that it was the truth. He wasn't mad at Maddie for being caught up in circumstances that she couldn't control. He wasn't mad at her for her past. He was mad at her because she wasn't who he'd decided she should be, and he didn't know what to do with her.

"I'm still your wife."

"Yeah, you are."

"You can change that, though, right?"

"I expect so."

Silence for a bit and then, "So you don't have to be mad at me for that."

"No. I don't have to be mad at you for that." He could barely see her in the dark, and he had a feeling now was a really good time to be able to see Maddie's eyes.

"What are you thinking?"

"I'm thinking I don't want you mad at me."

"Why did you follow me, Maddie?"

"Because I don't belong to Hell's Eight, either."

That was news.

"But you were safe there."

She nodded. "Yes. And Tia and Desi and Ari and Bella and everybody have been very kind to me, made me very strong, taught me what I need to know."

She played with the ruffle on her pantaloons.

"But?" He let his finger drop from her chin to her shoulder, his palm naturally cupping the curve.

"Now I know who I want to be. I know how I want to be. I just don't know where I want to be it." It should have been said with tension.

"You sound excited."

"You sound surprised."

"I am."

She scooted off his lap to kneel before him. It was

an unconsciously seductive pose his cock fully appreciated. "Caden, my whole life I've been locked in a room,
locked in a name." She shook her head. "I'm not locked
in anymore. Tia says I can be whatever I want. Bella
says I can do whatever I want, but I don't even know
what there is *to* want."

"You don't have to risk your life in Indian country to
find out what you want, Maddie mine."

"I know now. I just didn't think any of this would
happen. I was just going to follow you, catch up." She
shrugged. "Have an adventure."

"If I'd known you were back there, you would have
been safe."

She shook her head again. "Culbart's men just came
out of nowhere. One minute I was alone on the trail and
the next they were all around me."

He caught her chin on his finger again, drew her face
back to his, shifted more so that the faint light from the
fire rippled across her features.

"Did they hurt you, Maddie?"

She shook her head. "No."

A man could take that no at face value unless he knew
a woman's past.

"Did they touch you?"

"Not really."

"There's a whole lot of room for wrong in that 'not
really.'"

"They dragged me around a bit by the arm, put me
on a horse behind somebody else and rode back to the
ranch."

"And what happened when you got there?"

She looked at him and her eyes went blank. "Culbart threw a welcome-home party. It was very sweet of him. I haven't seen Uncle Frank in ages."

Fuck. He was going to kill Culbart. A party? What kind of party?

"That's nice, Maddie."

"It was."

He could believe she was totally lost in her pretending unless he looked down at her hands. Her short nails were digging into her skin. Whatever was going on in her mind wasn't as pleasant as a welcome-home party thrown by a loving uncle.

"Maddie."

"Yes?"

"Come here, honey."

He opened his arms and in a heartbeat she went, her hands slipping around his neck, her chin going instinctively to his shoulder as if it belonged there. Hell. She fit his arms as if she belonged there. He held her close, feeling the tension inside her draw tighter.

"I'm glad you liked your party."

That tension started to dissipate. Maybe there were times it wasn't so bad to go along with her delusions. He rested his cheek on her hair. She felt so small in his arms, so soft. A woman who'd gotten shit her whole life but deserved love. He waited a good ten minutes before she relaxed. That was because, he realized belatedly, that was how long it'd taken to feel safe. Shit.

"I'm ready," she whispered against his throat.

It was his turn to blink. "For what?"

Her fingers went to work on the buttons of his shirt. "For our wedding night."

He was dog tired, and from those circles under her eyes, so was she, but she was ready to do her duty, let him give in to his base nature, let him do whatever he wanted. He remembered the way she said that. The disgust for those men, the loathing for herself.

He stilled her hands.

"Well, I'm ready for something else."

Ace was right. Maddie was sweet and she'd never had a choice. But she was his wife. A man owed his wife a hell of a lot more than a choice. He owed her passion. Security. Tenderness. Respect. Love.

"Would you be terribly hurt, Maddie mine, if instead of—" He waved his hand. What word did a man use that wasn't crude?

"Fucking?" she asked.

He winced. "I'm sorry I used that word with you."

"It's all right."

No, it wasn't. "Ah, Maddie, come here."

He pulled her close and then leaned sideways, taking them down, her on top. As she lay there stiff as a board, he grabbed the blanket and pulled it over them. The night air was fast cooling. With pressure on the back of her head he tucked her face into his neck. She didn't resist. Not then and not as he dragged her thigh over his and her arm across his chest and settled his head on the back of a rolled-up blanket he was using as a pillow.

"What are you doing?"

"Going to sleep."

"You don't want to—"

"Give in to my baser instincts? No. But let me know when you want to make love."

She didn't have a thing to say to that then or an hour later, but when her breathing evened out and her body relaxed as she finally drifted off, he didn't care. A woman only slept in the arms of a man she trusted. Caden brushed his lips over the top of her head, tangling his fingers in her hair, holding on, matching his breaths to hers, smiling as he fell asleep.

CHAPTER NINE

THEY WEREN'T ALONE.

Caden came awake instantly, his senses straining to catch any clue as to what had awakened him. Beside him, Maddie dozed. Across the fire he could see Ace, from all appearances still asleep. From the angle of the moon, they were three hours from dawn. Sliding his free hand under the blanket, Caden pulled his revolver clear. There was a blankness of sound to the north end of the campsite. Even the crickets were quiet. Whatever the threat was, it was located there.

"Ace," he whispered under his breath. If Ace weren't awake, he wouldn't have heard the call.

The response was immediate and just as soft. "I'm on it."

Years of working together hunting bounties had made Ace and Caden a team. Caden heard him slide out of the bedroll. A shadow amid shadows. Caden eased Maddie's arm from across his chest and slipped out from under his own blankets. When her eyes opened, he covered her mouth with his hand. She jumped and instinctively struggled. He shook his head. When she was fully awake, he placed a finger over her lips, and bringing his mouth to her ear, he breathed, "Don't move until I tell you to."

She nodded, eyes big.

Caden eased back, careful not to snap any sticks or otherwise give away his location. He knew Ace was doing the same. It could just be a bear. The intruders could be Indians or claim jumpers. There was only one way to find out. He knew Ace was working his way around the right flank of whatever was out there. Caden's job was to cover the center, draw them in. Only this time Maddie was in the center. Confident no one lurked by the fallen log, Caden crept back to Maddie. She'd pulled on her dress. They'd talk about that later. After giving her another sign to keep quiet, he motioned her behind him. Shielding her with his body, he backed them into the shadows. With a touch to her shoulders, he indicated she should lie down beside the log. It was the best cover he could find.

Clearly terrified, she propped herself up on her elbows and mouthed, *What is it?*

He kissed her quickly just because. "Push up tight to that and wait for me. And this time *don't move.*"

She scooched down. He could barely make out the glint of her eyes in the dark. Satisfied, he nodded. The log wasn't perfect, but it would be some protection if bullets started flying.

The crickets stopped chirping over to the left. Ace had gone right.

With one last graze of his knuckles down Maddie's cheek, Caden faded back into the night. He was willing to bet his last dollar that an attack like this was perpetrated by white men. He smelled them before he saw them, the acrid scent of stale sweat and whiskey broadcasting the accuracy of his guess. He slipped his knife from its sheath and set it between his teeth before grabbing the young sapling in front of him and pulling it back. The man walked like a bull in a china shop, twigs crackling under his feet, scuffing his boot along the ground. Not a professional killer, then. More likely a claim jumper.

Shit.

He was hoping to have more time. The man was just a darker shadow among the shadows. Caden let the sapling go. It made a rustling sound before it slapped the man in the face. With a shout he stumbled back, arms flailing. Caden jumped him before he could recover.

Someone yelled from across the campfire, "Did you get 'em, Burt?"

Caden drew the knife across the man's throat, feeling skin and tendon give. Blood spurted. Burt wasn't going to be answering anyone. He let the man drop and moved on, picking his quarry from the darker shadows moving between the trees.

Panic started among the attackers at Burt's lack of response. They started calling to each other, giving away their position. There were four, maybe five of them. All scared. Wanting contact to bolster their courage. They were in the wrong profession. A man who went hunting at night couldn't count on safety in numbers.

The man looking for Burt called out again, fear pitching his voice an octave higher. The yell ended midshout. Caden smiled and wiped the knife blade on the dead man's pants. Ace was doing his part. Ducking back into the shadows, Caden leaned against a tree and studied the situation. The claim jumpers had the campsite surrounded. Which meant they were all around Maddie. He remembered the terror in her eyes, her trust when he'd tucked her away. Fuck. She'd better keep put. She'd be fine as long as she kept put.

Like a voice from a bad dream, one of the claim jumpers called out, "Stranger."

He supposed "stranger" was him. Instead of coming out, he started working around toward that voice.

"Come on out."

Like hell.

"Do it now, stranger, or your lady friend's going to have another hole in her."

Maddie! He kept silent.

"You thinking I don't have her? Give your man a shout, sweet thing."

He heard Maddie cry out in pain. A high-pitched sound that brought him up straight. And then there was the sound of a man grunting in pain and Maddie's panicked "Run, Caden!"

She was fighting them to give him time to escape? Who the hell asked her to do that! As he pushed away from the tree, Caden heard the distinct sound of a fist connecting with flesh.

"Maddie," he whispered, knowing what that sound meant.

The next sound he heard was a groan.

Goddamn… Maddie!

"If you don't want me cutting off one of her pretty little fingers, you'll come out now, mister."

"I'm coming." But not that fast, and not without buying Ace as much time as he could.

"I'm going to start counting," the claim jumper warned.

Caden walked through the woods until he reached the clearing. It was just a few steps. He could see Maddie standing in the firelight, her shadow blending with another, her yellow skirts wrapping around his legs. She was holding her cheek. He could see the darker stain of blood on her jaw. Rage flared hot before settling into icy resolve. Just five minutes ago, she'd been asleep in his arms, her soft breath blowing over his skin, and now she was in the arms of scum, scared out of her wits. It was the way of things out here. Survival was for those who had the strength to maintain their position, and Maddie didn't have any strength at all. She depended on him and he'd failed her. He wouldn't again.

"Did you find out his name, Maddie?" he asked, keeping his voice calm.

She shook her head.

"Drop your guns, mister. Right there in the dirt."

He never dropped his guns in the dirt. Caden bent down and slowly placed his revolver on a rock. "It doesn't matter. We'll add him to the list anyway."

"And that knife, too."

What was the guy, a cat? He could see in the dark? Caden set the knife down beside his revolver.

"Now stand up and put your hands over your head."

It was a plus they hadn't shot him on sight. He did, tucking them behind his neck.

"What do you want?"

The man was holding Maddie by her chin and throat, practically lifting her off the ground without a care to her comfort. He was going to pay for that.

"Well, we came for the gold, but now we got us a bonus. He'll pay extra for her alive."

"Who?"

"None of your business."

"Someone sent you here for my wife but not my gold?"

"He wants both. But we're not fools. The gold's ours."

Who the hell was "he"? "There is no gold."

"Don't play dumb. We checked around. Rumor has it there's a lot of gold here."

"Rumor has it there's a lot of gold everywhere."

The knife sheathed between his shoulder blades grew heavier and heavier with every moment. His fingers twitched with the need to grab the hilt. It would be so easy to kill the leader, just let the blade fly. Except the way Maddie was wiggling, he couldn't risk the shot.

He brushed his fingers over the hilt. In time. "Maddie," he drawled, getting her attention. "Let me handle this."

She slowly subsided. The leader pulled her higher. Caden waited. Sooner or later the man would mess up. "If you let her go, I might let you live."

It was an outright lie. That man was going to die as painfully as Caden could arrange. Nobody came into his camp and threatened his woman and tried to take his property.

The man laughed, his rotted teeth showing behind his overgrown beard. "Hardly. I haven't had anything this sweet in ages."

More shadows came out of the dark. One, two, three, four. They were definitely outnumbered.

"No sense putting up a fight. You're a bit outnumbered."

So he was, but of those shadows that came close to the fire, none of them was Ace.

"I'll ask again. What do you want?"

"And I'll tell you again. The gold and the woman."

"There is no gold."

"Come morning, we'll be finding that out. Gordon, come hog-tie this man."

A lean man whose stench was bigger than his body came over, gun trained on him, and grabbed him by the arm, yanking him forward. Caden pretended to stumble, going with the push. It never hurt for the enemy to believe you were weaker than you were. Gordon shoved him up against the nearest tree.

"Stand there."

Caden stood.

"Check him for weapons first."

The man checked his boot tops and pulled out a knife. He checked out his other boot and pulled out a derringer. He ran his hands up his sides, checked his pockets and pulled out assorted necessities. He checked his wrists, found nothing.

"Next time you go hunting in the dark, you might want to grab your gun belt."

"I'll remember that."

They grabbed his hands, put them behind his back up against the tree. The knife between his shoulder blades bruised the bone. Carelessness, pure carelessness not to check to see if he had one at the top of his back as well as the bottom, but he wasn't going to lecture them on it. Instead of tying his hands behind his back, the man punched him in the gut. Nausea pounded through his stomach right along with the pain. He didn't have to fake doubling over and gagging. That was real enough.

"Leave him alone!" Maddie called, struggling in her attacker's arms.

His "Be quiet, Maddie" ended with a grunt as Gordon brought his fist down on his back.

Maddie did no such thing. She clawed at the man's hands, snapping at his arm with her teeth, her hair flaring about her face as she fought like a wild thing.

"Keep still, bitch, or I'll put a bullet in your lover."

She froze with that particular stillness about her that told him she was slipping away. Fuck. No telling what Maddie was going to do when she slipped away.

Caden watched as Maddie changed before his eyes from terrified woman to confident seductress. The transition was eerie in its seamlessness. "Did you gentlemen come to have a good time?" she asked in a sweet, sultry voice.

The gentleman didn't answer her. He knew why. He was having the same what-the-hell moment.

"There's no need to be rough on the other patrons. There's plenty to go around." Reaching out, she stroked her fingers down Alan's beard-roughened cheek. "I can handle all you've got."

A tall, skinny man with a hooked nose backed up. "Christ, you've got one that ain't right in the head. I ain't touching no crazy woman. They're cursed."

"You're a chickenshit, Skeeter, to give up pussy over superstition."

"Fuck, I'll touch that any way she comes, right in the head or not," the man restraining Caden called out.

"You'll wait your turn, Gordon."

"I'll take Skeeter's."

"You're not going to take anything, Gordon, until you tie that bastard up."

Gordon grabbed up the leather strings from his belt. "Shit. Don't start without me."

"I'm not waiting."

Alan grabbed Maddie's breasts through her dress and squeezed hard. Skeeter grabbed at Caden's wrist, missing the first time because he was watching what his friends were doing rather than Caden.

"You like that, huh?" Alan squeezed again. Maddie moaned and melted into his hands.

"Oh."

Just that. *Oh.* But Caden was willing to bet every man's cock jumped.

Alan let her go and laughed over his shoulder at Caden.

"You came out of the woods for a goddamn whore?"

Caden snarled under his breath, "I came for her."

"Must be a damn good lay. Open that dress, let me see those titties, pretty."

Maddie smiled a seductive smile and turned around. Every eye was upon her. Caden just needed their attention to slip a bit further.

As if she heard his thought, Maddie started to sway, just a little, as if there was music in the night that only she could hear. Her fingers toyed with the ties on her camisole. The strings slid though her fingers in a silky glide that made a man think of those fingers on his cock.

"Of course." Maddie started unbuttoning her bodice without an inch of modesty or hesitation. Caden had a glimpse of the woman he'd accused her of being. He didn't recognize her. She took a step to the side, turning so slightly all he could see was her back, but that little seductive sway as she was unbuttoning was damn potent and he could only imagine what the rest were feeling. As much as he needed their attention diverted, this price was too high. And then he noticed something else. That little move put her directly in the line of fire. She was sacrificing herself for him. Again.

"Goddamn it, Maddie."

"I'll be with you in just a minute, Caden. I just need to take care of these gentlemen first. They seem very... hungry."

The filth spilling from her mouth in that sweet singsong voice made Caden want to puke. Maddie shrugged and the dress fell off her shoulders, revealing her undone camisole beneath. She hadn't had time to button it back up.

"My, my, now, there's a pretty sight."

Where the hell is Ace?

"Throw some wood on the fire, give us some light."

"What color are her nipples, Alan?" Gordon called out. "Are they pretty pink or are they brown?"

Maddie stepped out of her gown, her white petticoat and camisole gleaming as white as her shoulders in the faint light. She looked like a goddess of the forest.

"Can't tell right yet," the leader said. "We've got another layer. Undo the rest of those strings, baby. Let me see those breasts."

Maddie giggled a purely seductive giggle. It floated in the night and stabbed like a knife into something soft inside Caden.

"Maddie, don't you dare."

The leader lifted his gun and pointed over Maddie's shoulder straight at Caden. The barrel glinted in the firelight. "Shut the hell up."

Maddie laughed again. "So impatient." Her fingers trailed up to the gun. She fondled the barrel of the revolver as if it was a cock, thumb and forefinger pinching delicately, stroking along. Alan groaned. To say Gordon's tying of Caden's hands was half-assed was an understatement. All his attention was on those fingers on that gun and those white shoulders, that waist and that plump ass. Caden was going to kill her. Flat-out kill her. That body she was flaunting was *his*.

Instead of stepping back, she took a step in and then

another and another until her shadow blended with Alan's. Alan didn't drop the gun, but he dropped his gaze.

"Hello, pretty little thing. Let me and my friends see those breasts."

"Naturally. Do you have money?"

She paid him and his orders no mind. Reaching up, she knocked the leader's hat off his head, running her fingers through even what Caden could see from here was greasy hair without a shudder. What the hell was she used to that this man didn't make her cringe with his smell and his dirt? He shook his head again. It was one thing to know Maddie had been a whore. It was a horrible thing to see her being one.

"If you don't put that gun down, there's not much we can do."

"You got him tied there, Gordon?"

Gordon quickly came from behind the tree and ran forward. "Yep."

Alan put the gun back in its holster. "Then I guess we got us a way to entertain ourselves while we wait for sunrise."

Sunrise would be another two hours. Caden didn't want to know what men like these could do to a woman in two hours.

Alan was happy to show him. He grabbed Maddie's braid, yanking at it until she arched back, her breasts lifted like offerings. Maddie didn't even flinch, though it had to hurt. She just kept rubbing her body against his, talking to him and enticing him. She turned again, distracting him, Caden realized, as Alan turned with her. She was using her body to buy them time.

Fuck.

Caden went to work on his bonds, methodically working the poorly tied knot.

"Now, take off that camisole," Alan ordered, his voice rough with lust.

Maddie playfully tugged at the strings, not quite pulling them free, her breasts jiggling as she laughed seductively. Alan cursed and grabbed the edges of the material from her shoulder and wrenched downward. The material parted with a harsh rip, Maddie's breasts spilled free, large and white, so very lush in the night. Caden couldn't see the color of her nipples, but he found he was as curious as everyone else. What the hell did that say about him?

"Get your goddamn hands off her."

"I'm not touching her," Alan mocked. "Yet."

And he wasn't. Maddie was the one doing the touching, running her fingers over her breasts from nipple to base, drawing the man's attention, pinching the peaks, tugging them away from her breasts, jiggling those fleshy mounds. Where the fuck was Ace?

"It's two dollars a tumble," she told them.

"Honey, I ain't paying you shit."

She didn't even blink.

"But you'll want to."

"Why? Because you're that good?"

She nodded and ran her tongue over her lips as she pinched her nipples again, drawing her breasts up and out, suspending them from the small red points. "Yes. But that's not why."

"Then why?"

She nodded toward Caden. "He'll kill you if you don't."

Any other woman would be screaming, but Maddie, Christ, only Maddie could think he was her pimp.

Alan spat. "He's not going to do a goddamn thing."

Caden felt the knot start to give. Like hell he wasn't.

Maddie smiled and twirled around, her braid sweeping around. "You don't know him. I've seen him kill men with his bare hands, and you know how Madam Tia is. He works for Madam Tia."

Christ, now she had Tia in the game.

"She doesn't tolerate anybody messing with what's hers."

And that was the truth. Tia was like a lioness when it came to anyone she loved.

"Well, Tia isn't here right now, pretty lady, and your guardian is tied up over there. He can't do shit, so why don't you bring that pretty mouth here and kiss me."

She shook her head. "I don't kiss men."

He blinked. "Well, honey, you're kissing me."

"Not on the mouth," she said. "I never kiss on the mouth."

Gordon chuckled and unbuttoned his belt. "I can live with that."

Caden couldn't, but he didn't have any choice. He was forced to watch as Maddie, his sweet, fragile Maddie, drooped as graceful as a dove to her knees.

"Goddamn it, Maddie, get up."

"In a minute, Caden."

"Now!"

He might as well have been talking to the wind. Where the fuck was Ace?

Alan pulled his cock from his pants, stroking his fingers along its length. "It's going to take more than a minute to satisfy me, pretty."

"Oh."

Again with the "oh." Caden didn't want to hear it. He didn't want to see Alan's hand cup Maggie's head, see his dirty fingers sink into her fiery hair and draw her in. He didn't want to remember Maddie kneeling in the dirt, servicing a man to save him. He ripped at his bonds, tearing his flesh. Blood soaked his skin, wetting the leather strings. Fuck.

"I don't want this, Maddie," he snapped at her. "You're never a trade. Not ever. For anything."

He thought he saw her flinch, but she didn't stop.

Alan sneered at him over her head. "You might as well watch, mister. It's the only pleasure you're going to get tonight."

"Fuck you."

"It's this little lady we're all going to be fucking."

And he was the first one Caden was going to kill. The knife chafed against his spine as he strained at the restraints, rubbing them up and down the tree, the muscles in his shoulders burning with the effort. Sweat stung his eyes. Agony lanced up his arms as the leather cut to the bone, but it was giving. It was giving.

"Dammit, Maddie, stop."

She didn't listen this time any better than the last. He wanted to close his eyes as Maddie leaned forward, but he didn't. He owed her more than the bliss of ignorance, so he stayed with her, watching it all, wanting to kill Alan, hug her. He watched as she parted her plump red lips in a seductive smile, wrapped her delicate fingers around the base of his cock and leaned in. When her mouth spread over the tip, Alan groaned. Caden had to look away. He couldn't watch another piece of her soul be stolen away. To save him.

"I'm not worth it, Maddie."

"Son of a bitch," Gordon whispered, his hand fumbling in his pants, going for his own cock.

With a cry of rage, Caden tore his hands free. Blood sprayed as the leather gave way. He let out a snarl of victory, lunging toward Alan just as the other man let out an unearthly scream of agony. He writhed, holding Maddie's head.

"You crazy bitch!" He looked around wildly, a scream carrying his words. Not holding, Caden realized, but pushing her away. "Get her off me! Get her off!"

Maddie was on her feet, fast as lightning, grabbing for Alan's hand. They struggled. A gunshot rang out. Alan went down. Gordon yanked his hand out of his pants and fumbled for his guns. From the woods came another man's scream. Ace. Caden grabbed the knife from his back and threw it. It buried in Gordon's throat.

Maddie spun around. He could see the dark red stain of blood on her lips, then a gun shaking in her hand.

"Easy, Maddie."

"Ace!" Caden called. "Any more?" There was a choked-off cry and then Ace called back, "No more."

Caden grabbed one of the blankets off the ground and headed to Maddie. She stood over Alan, looking like a broken angel, her camisole falling down over her petti-coats, the gun still in her hand, a slight wildness about her as she kept turning and looking as if there must be more. He didn't know if she was with him or not. It didn't matter.

Alan writhed on the ground, moaning, his hands clutching at his dick as blood pumped from his chest. It wasn't a clean shot, but it was a mortal one. He'd be dead soon enough.

Caden carefully took the gun from Maddie's hands before draping the blanket around her shoulders. With the edge he wiped the blood from her mouth. Damn. If he hadn't been there, she might have just saved herself.

"You're quite a woman, Maddie Miller." Hooking his hand behind her neck, he drew her to him. "Where the hell did you learn to do that?"

She looked at him then, all the pain and knowledge of her life in her eyes as she said quite simply, "Men always seem to forget that a whore knows how to take care of herself."

CHAPTER TEN

A WHORE KNOWS how to take care of herself.

Caden had opportunity to debate those words over the next two days and to study the possible meanings and for whom they were intended. He'd always known how Maddie had lived her life before coming to Hell's Eight, but watching her do what she'd done, taking the chance that she'd taken to protect him, he shook his head as he put a rope around another rock and started hauling it away from the mine. In the process, he'd come to realize he didn't know shit.

Maddie Miller was a very complicated woman. Part lost child, part avenging angel, part loving, passionate woman, she was a mix of contradictions wrapped up in a package of total honesty. And he hadn't been able to get near her since that night. Immediately after the attack, she'd let him hold her while she'd cried and shaken. He'd needed that. Needed to comfort her and take away her pain. He still did, but then she'd pulled back behind an invisible wall and he hadn't been able to touch her since. He didn't know if her reaction was because of how she saw herself or how she thought he saw her, but either way he was getting tired of her hiding. She was his wife. It was his right to care for her.

He looked over to where she was working on clearing her own small, self-assigned section of the mine. The skirt of her yellow dress was torn, her hands dirty, and her hair was tumbling around her sweaty face. She was working herself into the ground. Had been ever since that night. As if she had something to prove to herself. Or to him. He glanced over to where Ace was sifting through a mountain of rubble. Ace gave him that same look he'd been giving him for two days. The one that said, "Fix it."

Maddie suddenly cried out. She was holding her hand, shaking it. Smashed her fingers again, no doubt. He knew if he went over there she'd tell him to go to hell. Well, maybe not *go to hell* in so many words, but a look would say it. She hadn't slipped away since that night. She was firmly planted in the here and now. It was kind of a shame. That steady beat of her anger was wearing.

He shortened up the harness. Ace put down his sifting tray and came over.

"How long are you going to take to fix this?" Ace asked.

Caden ran his thumb under the harness. "My wife, my business."

Ace shook his head. "She's Hell's Eight. She proved that the other night doing what she did to save your sorry ass."

"I know."

Ace continued as if he hadn't spoken. "She had no way of knowing I was out there. She's never worked with us before. They were tying you up and hurting you, so she sacrificed herself for you because that's what she fucking does. It's all she knows how to do."

"What do you want me to do about it, Ace?"

"Make her stop punishing herself. You're her goddamn husband. If anybody in this world should make her feel like something, it should be you."

Ace thought he had all the answers. "One of these days, Ace, someone's going to come along and knock you six ways to Sunday and you're not going to know if you're coming or going."

"Yeah?"

"And when she does," Caden said, "I hope to hell I'm around to watch you spin."

Ace laughed. "Never gonna happen."

"Never say never, my friend." He looked over at Maddie. Because there was no way in hell he ever thought he'd end up being married to Maddie, no way in hell he thought he'd be able to hurt her, but he'd done both. She stopped and wiped the sweat from her brow. The morning sun was giving way to the intensity of the afternoon. Plain and simple, it was too hot to be doing what she was doing. "Now, if you'll excuse me, I think my wife needs rescuing."

"From what?"

Caden shook his head. "Herself."

SHE WAS STILL nursing her finger when he approached. He saw her tense, but she didn't turn around.

"Let me see," he said when he got close enough.

She shook her head and tucked her hand behind her back. "It's fine."

As if he'd let her get away with that. "I want to see, Maddie."

"It's nothing."

"It's my job to take care of you."

She opened her mouth, and he knew goddamn well what was going to come out of it. She was going to tell him again that a whore knew how to take care of herself.

He put his finger over her mouth. "Maddie."

She glared at him.

"Don't say it."

Her mouth snapped shut. He slid his finger down to her shoulder, over her elbow, to her hand. She stood rigidly with none of the melting he was used to. He didn't like it. Lifting her hand to his, he could see that she'd smashed the nail.

"You're probably going to lose that."

She didn't say a word, just stared past his shoulder. He sighed.

"Come with me."

She didn't move. "I have work to do."

"I'm calling a break."

"If we take a break, we'll never get done. More of those claim jumpers might come."

He knew she was afraid of that. He was more afraid of the unknown person who'd sent them.

"We're ready for them."

She didn't say anything. Just stiffened.

"We will protect you."

"I can protect myself."

Ignoring the provocation, Caden took her hand, running his thumb along the back of her hand. "But now you don't need to."

With a tug he pulled her behind him, leading her down the narrow path to the swimming hole. The dappled sunlight of the trees was so much cooler than the unrelenting force of the sun.

"I am thinking I probably should have come up with this idea a few months earlier or a few months later."

"Why?" she asked as he helped her over a rough part in the path.

"Because it's damn hot to be hauling rock."

That honesty earned him a chuckle. It was a small victory, but he'd take it.

The trees ended at the small pond. The water looked cool and inviting with the sun sparkling off the top. Maddie stopped short of the edge. Caden let her, taking one more step than her, turning around so he could face her.

"What are we doing?"

"I told you. We're taking a break."

She looked at the pond as if it were poison. She'd been looking at him that same way the past two nights he'd come to bed, lying rigid in his arms until she'd fallen asleep. It wasn't the Maddie he was used to. He was used to the Maddie who reached for him no matter what, who put up with his moods no matter what. He was used to the Maddie who loved him. He wanted her back.

He wiped a smudge of dirt from her cheek with his thumb. It didn't really come off, just kind of smeared along the sweat. Her nails were dirty and cracked. Dirt was caked into the creases in her hands. She smelled of sweat and woman and despair, he thought. A despair she didn't deserve.

"Maddie, I'm sorry." The words just came naturally because he was. A sorry son of a bitch.

"Why?"

"I'm sorry for everything I did. For calling you names, for calling you a whore." He shook his head. "For not knowing what that meant."

"You know what it means." She stepped back out of his reach. He had to take another step to follow.

"I can be a pigheaded ass when I get mad."

She raised both brows but didn't say a word.

"Say what you want. I'm not going to tear you up for it."

He started unbuttoning her dress, and she stood there as she always did, as she had for the past two days, just letting him do what he wanted, no response on her part. Where before she'd hidden away in make-believe, now she just stood there and dared him. He didn't understand what she was thinking, but he understood the dare.

Caden continued unbuttoning Maddie's dress, one at a time, not stopping until he was all the way down the row. Sweat beaded her ample cleavage. He couldn't believe she was working as hard as she was with so many layers of clothing. He'd really never thought of it before, but feeling the heat pound his back through his thin shirt and looking at her wool dress, the petticoats beneath, the corset, the camisole… Christ, it was a wonder she hadn't passed out.

He pushed the dress over her shoulders and then down off over her hips. It caught halfway down on her petticoats.

"I don't want you wearing all this shit anymore."

She didn't meet his eyes, just nodded.

He grabbed the string that held her petticoats up and gave it a tug. It didn't give. He saw it was double-knotted. He guessed a woman would have to be careful that her drawers didn't drop to her ankles in an embarrassing moment. He worked those knots through, too, and slid that off her shoulder.

She stood before him, skirts a puddle at her feet, in her pantaloons, corset and camisole.

"I bet that corset is hot."

She looked at him and said, "I got used to it."

Like hell anyone got used to it. It, too, was soaked through with sweat. He started to untie it. As he did, he started to talk. She was so far away from him.

"As I was saying, I'm a pigheaded ass. You've always treated me like gold, always understood me." The corset was hard to unhook. He got it done. The heat that came off her skin was incredible. He looked at her face again. She was pale, paler than normal. Oh, Christ, had she given herself sun sickness?

He tossed the corset to the side and lifted her out of the skirts. At least she grabbed for his shoulders. It was a sign she knew he was there. He hoped she was listening. He'd never needed anybody to listen to him as much as he needed her to listen to him right now.

"Sit down."

She looked at him.

"The grass is fine."

She sat down. Crouching in front of her, he untied her shoes, first the left and then the right, slipped them off her feet. When he saw the blisters along the heel and the toes, he wanted to shoot himself. Cradling her foot in his hand, he asked, "Why didn't you tell me?"

"You told me you didn't want to hear any complaints from me."

"That's not a complaint. Blisters like that can turn sour. You can lose a foot, for Christ's sake."

"They don't hurt anymore."

"F— Damn." He looked at them again. They were deep, broad, angry looking.

Picking her up, he carried her to a rock by the edge of the pond. She struggled for a second when he stepped to the pond and tried to lower her into it.

"I don't want to go there," she told him.

"Tough."

He let her feet dangle in the water, holding her as her breath hissed, feeling her pain escape across his chest, and then feeling her relaxation as the coolness of the water on her hot feet started having an effect.

"I'm fine, Caden."

He pushed the hair out of her face and untied the braid.

"No, you're not. You're hurt and you're sad and

you're mad as hell but you're far from being fine." But he wanted to make her fine. He wanted his Maddie back. The one who baked him cookies, who worried about him, who ran her fingers down the inside of his wrist and held on to him as if he was the only solid thing in her world.

"I guess you stopped worshipping me, huh?"

"I never worshipped you."

Cupping the cool water in his hand, he poured it over her calves. "It felt like it."

"You should have told me you minded."

"I didn't. I should have, but I didn't. You're a very complex woman, Maddie. You keep a man on his toes."

"What you're trying to say is I'm crazy."

He shook his head. "Nah. Even at your flightiest you're talking common sense."

"*Flighty* is a nice way of saying *crazy*."

"Yeah, well, you seem to have forgotten how to take flight."

"I don't want to do that anymore."

"Why not?"

"Children run away. Women stand their ground."

"That sounds like Bella."

"She's a smart woman."

She was so tense. He took her right calf in his hand and massaged it gently. She moaned under her breath but he heard it. "You two have gotten close, haven't you?"

She nodded. "I like her."

"I like her, too. She's a good match for Sam."

"She's very kind."

"Yes, she is."

"She knows how to fight for what she wants."

"Yes, she does. Is that why you like her, Maddie? Because you want to know how to fight for what you want?"

She shook her head. "I just want to know what I want, and I want what I want to be good for me and not like poison in my veins."

Caden kicked off his boots. He'd have shucked his pants except for the fact he didn't have anything on underneath. He stepped into the water.

"Your clothes will get wet," she observed.

"Yeah." The water felt cool and blissful against his feet, the muddy bottom cushioning the soreness. Maybe it was time they all took a break. The sun beat down on his shoulders. It was so much more tolerable with his legs in the water.

"You can take them off, you know. I've seen naked men before."

"What makes you think I'd be naked?"

"You don't like underwear."

"How the hell do you know that?" Just how much had she been spying on him?

"When we do laundry, you don't have a lot of that to add to the pile."

"Oh." So simple an explanation. Once again, so mean-spirited his suspicion.

"You may have seen naked men before, but between us there needs to be better respect."

Her gaze darted to his.

"Whores—"

"Don't say it, Maddie."

"Why not?"

"Because it's not true. Because I don't think it."

"You said it." And those words had sunk into her soul. He understood that.

"I was mad."

"That just means you speak the truth."

"The hell it does. I can spout more nonsense mad than a drunk on a Saturday night."

"Why?"

He shrugged. "Because when I'm mad I just want to hurt somebody."

"Oh."

"Yeah, I wanted to hurt you."

"I know. I deserve it. I should've—"

Dammit, he didn't want to go here. Why did they have to keep rehashing this?

"You shouldn't have done anything other than what you did, Maddie. I came here to rescue you, and you pretty much rescued yourself."

"I didn't—"

"I don't want to hear it, Maddie. I'm just telling you and I want to get this out. I don't want to go over it. I don't want to get mad over it again. I don't know what happened between you and Culbart. I don't want to know how you wrapped him around your finger. Just let it be."

He didn't. He didn't want to hear how she'd slept with Culbart, how she'd fucked him into giving her what she'd wanted. He didn't want to think of that big bear of a man sweating over her. He shook his head, shedding the image.

"How are your feet feeling?"

"Better."

"Good."

He picked her up off the rocks, carried her to a deep part of the water. She grabbed his neck, holding on tightly.

"Maddie, I won't let you drop."

She shook her head. "It's not that."

"What, then?"

"I don't want to be here. It's too hard."

"What's hard about this?" He bent his legs, dipping her in the water, letting the coolness run over her flushed body. Her legs came around his waist and his cock hardened despite the cool water and tension within. There was something about Maddie that was soft and smooth and inviting like the first kiss of summer that brought him alive inside. He sat down in the water. It came up to Maddie's shoulders, floated in her hair. He took a scoop of water and dripped it over her head. Her eyes closed and she sighed.

"Feels good, huh?"

She nodded. He pulled her hair over her shoulder, leaving her sitting in his lap.

"You're working too hard."

"No harder than you."

"Honey, I've got a hundred pounds on you, and all of that is muscle. It's not as hard work for me. On top of that, you cook supper."

"That's not much of a contribution."

He smiled. "You care for the campsite."

"You take care of the animals."

He just looked at her. "Maddie, I'm trying to tell you this isn't what I want for you."

Her lips thinned. "I don't want a divorce."

Ah, hell, she was pushing him faster than he wanted to where he wanted to go.

"We'll cross that bridge when we get to it, but right now—" He fluffed her hair around her shoulders, leaning her back. She grabbed his shoulders with desperate hands, her eyes flying wide.

"Don't."

"Why not?"

Her mouth worked. He pulled her back up, studied her face.

"What is it, Maddie?"

She shook her head. "Ponds are dangerous."

"Maybe down Louisiana way, but besides the odd snake or two, we're good here. I'll protect you."

She shook her head again. Her mouth worked. She couldn't get any words out, but he could see she was trying. Whatever had her upset was deep-seated.

"It's all right, then. I'll just scoop the water over you." And he did, cupping his hand and pouring water over her head, gently wiping at her cheeks and face.

"I should have brought soap."

She shook her head. "This feels good."

Yeah, it did. He rubbed his hands up and down her back. It felt very good to have her sitting so trustingly in his arms, to have her not looking through him.

"I was wrong, Maddie. Wrong in what I said, wrong

in how I treated you, and I've got no excuse except I had
a mad on. I thought you'd betrayed me."

"I don't understand you."

"It's okay. I don't understand myself."

"What do you want me to do?"

"Right now I just want you to sit here and let me take
care of you the way I haven't, so just close your eyes, put
your head against my chest and let's just relax a minute, all right?"

She didn't put her head against his chest, but she did
sit there without another word. He scooped handful after
handful of water over her head until her hair was plastered to her skull, revealing the purity of her features
and the bruise on her cheek from where Alan had struck
her. Many people would say that Maddie was ordinary
looking, but if they thought that, they weren't looking
deep enough. She had a beautiful soul, a big heart and
a hell of a life.

Giving in to impulse, he kissed the slight frown between her brows. She jumped.

"You want sex." She said that as if she'd found the
explanation to everything. She couldn't be more wrong.
Yes, he was hard, but sex wasn't what he wanted. What
he wanted was what he'd had a couple seconds before:
her trusting him.

"If you're talking about the fact that I'm as hard as a
rock, I'm not going to deny it, but this isn't about sex."

"Then what's it about?"

"I want you back, Maddie."

"You've got me."

"You're here physically but you took your heart away."

She winced and blushed. "That was just girlish foolishness."

He traced her eyebrows. "Maybe, but I want it back."

"Why? So you can use it against me some more? So when you get a mad on you can hurt me with whatever I've revealed to you?" She shook her head. "I don't want that."

He shook his head, sliding his fingers through her hair. "Nobody wants that. You'd be a fool if you did."

He kissed her eyes closed, not wanting to see the fear as he confessed this. "I want to be gentle with you always, Maddie."

She asked again, but differently, "Why do you want me?"

He stroked his finger across her cheekbone, the sprinkling of freckles that just invited his kiss. He gave in to the impulse and kissed the tip of her nose, holding her head there while he moved his lips down to hers. *I don't kiss,* she'd told Gordon, and from the way her lips were still under his, he guessed she really didn't.

"Because you're the one who makes me smile."

He kissed the left corner of her mouth and then the right, keeping it gentle and easy, tapping into that part of him that went tender when she was around. She didn't move, didn't breathe, and that gave him hope, because she wasn't sucking in a breath to tell him to go to hell. He fitted his mouth to hers, tilting her head sideways, kissing her with all the gentleness he felt inside, with all the softness of the day around them.

When he pulled back, her eyes were closed and that frown was back between her eyes. A good or bad sign? He had no idea, but she didn't double up a fist and hit him.

He waited until she opened her eyes.

"Maddie?"

She licked her lips and her eyes darkened to a deeper green.

"Why don't you kiss?"

She frowned and took a shuddering breath. "I don't know. Before I went in with my first customer, one of the other whores told me to never kiss a man."

"And you never have?"

She shook her head. "No, she said it's giving away your soul to kiss somebody."

He touched his thumb to her lips. Such pretty lips. "That's all you got, huh?"

She nodded.

"How old were you?"

"Eight or nine, I'm not sure. My mom wasn't real specific on my birthday. We kind of knew the year and made up the month."

"Did your mom raise you?"

She shook her head. "No. She had other interests. There was a rancher who was in love with her, and she planned on leaving with him."

"Did she?"

"I don't know."

That was sad. He remembered his mother with a smile and sadness but always love. He didn't have to ask whether the madam was good to her. Anybody that put a little girl to work… Hell.

"I hope she's miserable," he said.

"She's dead."

"Not miserable enough. Do you hate her?"

"Why would I hate her? Everybody has to earn their keep."

"Is that why you're hauling those rocks, because you're earning your keep?"

She nodded. "I don't want to be indebted."

"You're my wife. How can you be indebted? What's mine is yours."

"Only inasmuch as you want to give it to me. Men discard women all the time. Just drop them wherever and leave them to fend for themselves."

He supposed that was true.

"That's why you were learning to bake, right?"

She nodded. "Yes. I like it, it's fun and baked goods are always popular."

"Good."

It was peaceful sitting there, the water cooling their bodies and the sun warming their shoulders. Around them birds sang and bees buzzed. A perfect summer day.

Out of the blue she announced, "I think I'm going to open a bakery."

He didn't ask with what. Everyone needed their dreams. "Where?"

"I haven't decided yet."

Leaning back against the bank, he worked on containing the flare of anger that she was making plans without him.

"Any plans for me in this baking future?"

Her silence gave him his answer. He sighed.

"Tell me something, are you not including me because you don't think I'll want to be there or you don't want me there?"

He was going to have a hell of a lot of mud in his hair, but it didn't matter. He pulled her down until her cheek rested against his shoulder. The water was cool, her skin was warm, and any other time he'd lift her up, free his cock and slide it into the slit of her pantaloons up into that warm, moist pussy. But he had a feeling that Maddie's pussy wouldn't be moist, that such an act would irrevocably damage her. He needed her trust back, and after he had that, he could go looking for her passion.

She laid against him stiffly, letting him do what he wanted, but not participating, and her fingers didn't slide down his arm and circle his wrist the way he wanted. He'd thought his wife was crazy, but the truth was she was just very, very damaged. Crazy would have been easier.

Resting his cheek against the top of her head, he wrapped his arms around her back and hugged her, holding her tightly, rocking her in his arms, just holding her.

"You don't have to worry anymore, Maddie. No one's going to hurt you."

And before he could say it, she said it for him, but she said it with a question mark he would have left off.

"Not even you?"

CHAPTER ELEVEN

MADDIE WAITED FOR the answer that didn't come. On one level she had to respect a man who wouldn't make a promise he couldn't keep. On the other, she wanted to hate him for bringing alive that hope she'd tried so hard to kill. One day she was truly going to learn to stop loving Caden Miller.

"That's what I thought."

Maddie scrambled out of Caden's arms, pushed to her feet, stumbling as the soft bottom sucked at her feet. He reached out but she shook off his hand and slogged to the bank, ignoring his call of her name. Who did he think he was? Blowing hot and cold, promising not to hurt her when he'd already hurt her so much. She'd never forget the way he said *whore* that time, the same way that other men did with such contempt. And now he wanted her to forget, because he felt guilty. But that would only last until he got mad again. She might not know husbands, but she did know men. They always got mad. She heard him behind her. She walked faster.

Yes, she'd been a whore. She'd never had a chance to be anything else, but she did now and she was going to be better than what they all thought she could be. She was going to be who she wanted to be.

Caden caught up to her as soon as she got up on the bank. She stood there dripping and reached for her petticoats. He took them away from her. She grabbed them back.

"I'll wear what I want."

"It's too damn hot, Maddie."

She held out her hand. "It's not proper."

If he made one smart comment about that, she was going to slap him. She couldn't ever remember feeling this angry. Who did he think he was, trying to make her vulnerable by acting so nice? In the end, she let him have his way, not because she was giving in but because she wasn't up to struggling into layers and layers of wet cotton.

When she reached for her dress, his hand was there first. When she grabbed it, his finger went under her chin.

"What the hell are you so mad at?"

She turned away. "You."

She could feel the call of the pond, not this pond but her pond, her sanctuary, and she pushed that away, too. It used to be easy to slip away, but now it was easier to stay because goddamn it, as completely messed up as it was, she was going to have a life. Turning away, she struggled to stay calm.

He grabbed her arm and swung her back.

"Why?"

How dare he ask her that? After all he'd done. "Because this is just a game to you, but it's my life."

"I'm your husband."

The truth lay flat between them.

"Not for much longer if you're to be believed."

Just another thing to hold against him. Caden let go of her arm and ran his hand through his hair. She stepped into her dress and turned her back, yanking it on. His arms came around her from behind, sliding over her wet camisole, pulling her back against the lure of his body. Who the hell did he think he was, making her care, making her feel? She didn't have her pond, but she had that wall of hate and she didn't want that coming down.

"Maddie."

She didn't answer.

"Maddie mine."

She stomped on his toe. "Don't call me that!"

She didn't ever want him to call her that again.

He didn't even grunt. He pushed her hair back from her face with his fingertips in that way that used to make her knees weak.

"Maddie?"

"What?"

"I've been an ass."

"Yes."

"A fool."

She wasn't going to argue with him.

"But I'm still your husband."

"For what, a day? A week? A month?"

He jerked her around. "Till death do us part."

She didn't want him holding out her dream. Not anymore.

She lifted her chin. "Until the next time you decide

that I'm a whore, you mean, and that I'm in your way, and then you'll be telling me you're going to end it again or you'll get on your horse and you'll ride off and you'll leave me just like everyone else and I'll be alone because I stupidly believed you."

He jerked back as if she'd struck him. "The hell I will."

"The hell you won't. You do it all the time."

He frowned. "What are you talking about?"

"Every time you start to feel comfortable, every time you start to feel like you belong, you pack up and you leave. Well, fine, just go, but don't make me care about you. Don't make me want to be with you so much that it rips my heart out when you do. I don't want that. I see who you are now."

"And who am I?"

"A selfish man who cares only about himself."

"That's not true."

"Well, you can't prove it by me. And my infatuation with you, it's just—" she made a slash with her hand "—gone." She put her hands on her hips and stomped her foot. "And now I want you gone."

"Tough."

That one syllable contained more emotion than all her yelling. Despite her resolve, she looked at him. He wasn't looking at her face anymore. She looked down and knew why. Her camisole was plastered to her breasts, hugging the round curves. Her nipples, drawn tight with cold, pressed against the fabric in small, inviting peaks. She crossed her arms over her chest, hiding the sight.

"I'm a whore, remember?"

He didn't blink. "I remember a lot of things, Maddie mine."

He took a step forward; she took a step back. She took another back; he took another forward. When she would have taken the next, he shook his head.

"Another step and you're going to be flat on your back in that pond."

She looked over her shoulder. Sure enough, she was on the edge.

"Then you stop coming."

"No." And he kept walking. "You were right about some things, Maddie, wrong about others. I can be stubborn and pigheaded, but I can also be loving and loyal."

"Not to me."

"That's a lie and you know it."

She bit her lip. "Not anymore."

He sighed. "I want you, Maddie."

"You had me."

"Yeah, I did. And I took it for granted." His eyes were still on her breasts; the pond was still behind her. Maddie gathered up her skirts. Caden shook his head.

"Don't."

She lifted her chin. "I don't have to listen to you." It was pure bravado.

He smiled that smile that made her heart skip a beat. "Yeah, you do."

The next step he was right there in front of her, so close she swore she could feel the heat of his body over the heat of the day. The sun glinted off his eyes, those beautiful eyes. She didn't let herself stare into them. She didn't let herself care. But it was hard.

She thought of her pond, the coolness of it, the smooth surface that rippled when she tossed a rock, the peace and quiet. His hand touched her cheek and the illusion shattered and she was right there where she didn't want to be, standing in front of Caden, the focus of his attention.

"You're my wife, Maddie."

"*Now* you remember."

"I never forgot."

"Tomorrow you will, when it's convenient, when you're in town, when you see some nice, respectable lady. You'll remember who and what I am, and you'll *want* to forget."

His fingers slid across her cheek to anchor in her hair.

"You're wrong about that." He pulled her closer until she had no choice but to lean up against his chest, and then, with an ease that made her want to slap him, he pulled her up into his kiss.

"No."

His breath caressed her lips. "Yes."

"I don't kiss."

She felt his smile as his lips touched hers. "You do with me."

She had no choice but to put her hands against his chest. No choice but to wrap her fingers in the cloth of his wet shirt as he leaned her back, taking her off balance, no choice but to accept what was happening. She tried to build her wall, but with a soft bussing of lips over hers, he destroyed that effort at the first imaginary stone.

His kiss was tender, sweet, like nothing she'd imagined. His mouth moved over hers, and she waited for him to pry her lips apart as most men always did when she refused to give them what they wanted, but he didn't. He kissed her softly and gently as if she mattered.

"This is cruel," she whispered. The words flowed into his mouth, riding his breath. So intimate. She shivered.

"No, this is how I see you, Maddie."

She gasped. Outrage, hope. She didn't know what she was feeling. Everything was a jumble. But good. So good. Everything she'd dreamed of when she'd dared to dream. Closing her eyes against the glare of the sun, she moaned as it all became more intense. The power in his grip, the tenderness of his kiss, the heat of his body seeping through the dampness of his clothes. Her lips started tingling the way they had before.

She opened her palms against his chest and braced herself against the illusion. This was no more real than her pond. This was Caden getting what he wanted. He was making a fool of her the way men always made a fool of whores. Because they could. Because no matter how worthless a woman thought herself, there always was a part of her that wanted to matter to someone somewhere. That need made her vulnerable and weak. And Caden was too good at understanding people not to see that in her. And she was too weak to push him way. Real or not, she wanted this memory.

He continued to kiss her sweetly and gently, and she

continued to let him, moaning as he grazed his lips over
hers, touched the tip of his tongue to the corner of her
mouth, absorbed the burst of sensation as it shot through
her with a sense of wonder. She felt his smile against her
lips when she jumped and gasped.

"I like that little sound."

She'd bet he did. She liked it, too. And when he did
it again, she couldn't help making that sound he so enjoyed. It felt so good to have his mouth on hers. So right.
So intimate. No wonder whores didn't kiss. Kisses truly
could steal a person's soul. As if he knew what she was
feeling, he pushed the skirt back down over her hips. It
tumbled to her feet. His arms slipped behind her knees
and lifted her up. She squealed and grabbed his neck. He
laughed and gave her a little toss. She gripped tighter.
He smiled wider.

"What are you doing?"

"Smooching on my wife."

Smooching! It was simply not a word she'd ever connected with Caden. Caden was just…Caden. Hard. Hard-
headed. Determined. Protective. Virile. Her dream. But
she didn't trust him now that he was being her dream
with her.

She clung to his neck as he carried her across the
clearing, expecting to be jarred, but even carrying her
he moved with his usual grace. He sat down under the
shade of a tree, taking her with him as if she weighed
nothing. She went to stand up, feeling awkward as she
struggled out of his lap. When she was standing, she
breathed a sigh of relief. One second too soon, because

in the next, he tugged her back down. She fell forward into his chest. He laughed as he caught her and lowered her slowly, so slowly until she was straddling his lap. She could feel his cock hard beneath the heavy cotton of his trousers. Her wet pantaloons were no barrier as he pushed up, wedging the thick length against her pussy.

"You want to fuck me." She threw the words out like knives. He took them like a kiss.

"Of course."

One of his big hands held hers, keeping her put through the tension. The other slid back behind her head, cupping her skull in an oddly tender gesture even as he pulled her forward.

"But not today, Maddie mine. Today I want to kiss you."

"You already have."

He shook his head. "No." He ran his thumb across her lips, bringing up tingles of excitement. He had such big hands. She used to be excited by that. Big hands that could protect her and keep her safe. Now they were keeping her prisoner. But they were still exciting. The ache between her thighs, in her breasts, intensified as he pressed on her lower lip, separating it just a little from the top. The tingle became unbearable. When he released her lip, she couldn't help but touch the spot with her tongue.

His chuckle wafted around her like the gentlest of breezes. He leaned in until his breath was hers and hers his, but he didn't kiss her the way she expected. He just stroked his fingers down her nape and smiled, while she…she couldn't seem to catch her breath, couldn't seem to find her will. Her gaze dropped to his mouth, and she stopped breathing altogether. He had a beautiful mouth. Not so full but just perfectly shaped the way she liked it. A man's mouth. A seducer's mouth.

"Your husband's mouth," he finished for her.

Dear heavens, she'd said that out loud.

"Put your arms around my neck."

It was an order any prudent woman would have ignored. Maddie slid her fingers up his chest, riding the thick pad of muscle, everything feminine in her responding to everything male in him. When her fingers linked behind his neck, he smiled, and somewhere in her the urge to smile back grew.

"Now, come here, Maddie mine."

A tug on her head and he had what he wanted, her tumbling forward into his embrace, arms sliding farther around his neck, her head tilting to the side at the press of his fingers. The tingle in her lips met with the ache in her pussy right at the point of her nipples. Such a delicious sensation. She squirmed. He pressed. He kissed the corner of her mouth when she was expecting full contact, throwing her off balance. Threading her fingers through the wet strands of his hair, she clung.

"I've been an ass, Maddie."

"You keep saying that."

He kissed the other corner. "A full-out fool."

She wasn't going to argue the point. He smiled and cocked an eyebrow at her. This close he was even more appealing.

"Not arguing?"

"No."

"Good. I like an obedient woman."

She wanted to bite his lip. "Then you need to find one."

"I know."

He pushed her camisole down off her breasts, exposing her puckered nipples to the warm air. She didn't know whether to cover them or flaunt them.

"I know what you're thinking," he told her as he unbuttoned his shirt and pushed it aside, ignoring her struggles because, well, they were nothing compared to his strength. His chest was well muscled, darkened from the sun, enhanced by a light growth of dark hair. In short, beautiful. "But I need to know what those pretty breasts feel like against my skin as we kiss this first time. Just that, honey."

She bit back a moan. "We've already kissed."

He shook his head. "I've been coaxing you, but we haven't gotten to the kissing yet."

She lifted her chin. "Fine."

He laughed and shook his head, a stray kiss landing on the tip of her nose. "Maddie, Maddie, Maddie. This isn't me using you. This isn't you using me. This isn't you enduring. This is a husband showing his wife how he feels about her."

"You think I'm a whore."

"I think you're sweet."

"You're punishing yourself."

"I'm rewarding myself."

"Why?"

"Because I can."

That she believed. "I don't want to be your reward."

"I don't want to be your punishment," he countered.

"So where does that leave us?"

"Sitting here sparking in the sunshine."

"We're in the shade."

"So we are." He eased her forward until her breasts flattened into the hair-roughened skin of his chest. "Are you done arguing?"

Heat. Pressure. Beauty. She had to clear her throat before she could demand, "Are you going to give up on this ridiculous notion?"

"No."

"Fine. Then I'm done."

But he wasn't going to get anywhere. He could take what he wanted for a kiss, and just because he could force her to sit there didn't mean he could force her to accept it or to like it.

"Good." Pressure on her back urged her forward. It was just a scant inch for his mouth to meet hers. She had to shift or fall forward. She chose the former. His cock settled deeper between her thighs, dragging across that so-sensitive spot before throbbing against her pussy. The ache in her breasts spread downward, and that slight pressure became so much more significant. She rocked her hips. Caden moaned. A sound she never thought to draw from him. She liked it.

Her breath caught as his mouth pressed against hers with those chaste little kisses that she knew were a lie, but he wouldn't stop. He just kept kissing her as they sat groin to groin, chest to chest, lips to lips. Gentle, tender kisses until she couldn't hold on to her rancor because this moment with him was sweet. And tender, and after five minutes or so a little boring. She relaxed further, his cock pressed harder, and it was her turn to groan.

"Done fighting?" he asked again.

What was the point in lying. "Yes." There wasn't really anything to fight.

"Good."

He continued touching her, but something within that touch changed. Something that found that womanly part of her and dragged it forward with a harsh gasp as his hips pressed up and his tongue slid between her lips, teasing the moist inside, and she knew then, right then, why whores never kissed. Because kissing was a window to the soul. It allowed a man in, gave him access to things they had no business touching. It gave him access to her heart.

Too late she tried to push away, but it wasn't Caden that stopped her. It was her foolish love for him. It wanted this. It took control the way her pretend never could. Absolutely, completely, melting her against him, making her pliant and responsive where she should have been mad and hateful.

"Good girl."

Oh, God, when he spoke to her in that voice, common sense left. It made her want to give him her heart, her soul, everything just so he would say it to her again in exactly that tone. He nibbled at her lips, smiling when she rocked against him, not saying a word, just letting her feel.

His kiss, his smile. She didn't know what to identify as his emotion. The only word that came to mind was *tenderness.* But men weren't tender with her. Caden had never been tender with her. Cautious, careful, yes, but not tender. But he was tender now and it wasn't enough. She needed more. She reached down between them. He caught her hand in his and put it back around his neck.

"I want my kiss, Maddie." The words flowed into her with her next breath.

"We don't have to just kiss."

"I'm the husband and I want my kiss."

She was kissing him. "I am kissing you."

"Mmm, you're starting to."

Starting to? What the heck did he want from her?

"Then show me what you want."

"I am."

"Now."

He laughed. "You greedy woman. I'll get to it at my own pace, thank you very much."

She wanted a faster pace. She didn't know if that was because she wanted it over or if she wanted to find out what was beyond this tenderness, but in the end it didn't matter. She just wanted his hands on her body, his mouth on hers. She wanted his taste, his scent, his passion, and the more he kissed her, the higher that want went until she was the one who parted her lips, until she was the one who ran them over his mouth, until she was the one who made him gasp.

"Oh, yes," he drawled in a deep voice that was just one more stroke of pleasure. "Now you're starting to kiss me."

"You wanted me to be in charge?"

"No, honey. I wanted you to want."

And with that, the kiss changed again. It became hotter, more insistent. His hand slid down her back toward her buttocks, feeling like a brand against her hip as his fingers dug in and pulled her up into his embrace. His tongue slid inside, finding hers. She could feel the passion behind the slow, gentle gesture, feel it raging, and knew that this tenderness wasn't what he wanted, either, but he was giving it to her. A gift she couldn't comprehend.

"I don't understand."

He shook his head slightly. "And that's the shame of it. Just hold on to this. I like kissing you, Maddie mine. I like hearing you gasp. I like feeling your lips flutter against mine. I like that little sound you make in your throat when I touch my tongue to yours. I like the way you make me feel when you come alive in my arms."

Come alive. What an apt way of putting it because she did feel as if she was, for the first time in her life, alive. She rocked her hips on his and he stilled them, not letting her move.

"No. We're just kissing, Maddie. There's no need."

"It's not like I'm not—"

His lips bit at hers, cutting the rest of the statement, and his tongue thrust into her mouth, finding hers, tangling with it, teasing it, luring it until she was digging her nails into the nape of his neck and kissing him back. Then it was her tongue in his mouth and her lips on his making the demands, and he chuckled and let her. His hands skimmed up her arms, over her shoulders and down her back and then back up, skimming the side of her hips, her waist, her breasts, just a light caress that made her kiss him harder, press against him more firmly.

She couldn't rock on him. She couldn't do anything with her body. She only had her mouth to share how her body burned and ached in this new way, to beg for him to make it go away, but he had no mercy. He just drove the feeling harder. His kiss so skillful she wanted to cry. Not because of how he yearned but because he was taking care to show himself to her, his passion and desire. His caring.

"This is how a man kisses a woman he respects," he told her. "This is how a man kisses a woman he cares for."

The kiss deepened, burned out of control, destroyed time until there was only flesh on flesh, lip on lip, passion on passion. Finally, when her nails were digging into his neck and she was moaning incessantly, he pulled back, kissing her left cheek, her right cheek, her nose, and then finally pressing his mouth to her forehead as his chest soughed in and out against hers.

"That, Maddie mine, is how a man kisses a woman with whom he intends to have a future."

It took the longest time to make sense of the words, and as their meaning sank in, all that lovely heated passion chilled to ice. Maddie scrambled off Caden's lap.

How dare he offer her her dream, make a mockery of reality, treat her like a child? Maybe now, in this moment, he was thinking of a future, but tomorrow or next week, the first time somebody recognized her and sneered at him, that pride of his would rear its head.

He sighed. "Maddie." She shook her head and retied her camisole, grabbing her dress. Kissing was dangerous. It made her so weak she wanted to believe the lunacy he spouted against all common sense.

She remembered back to when she'd been twelve and had been sweet on a boy and the other girls made fun of her. She'd run home looking for sympathy, and Hilda, the girl she thought of as her best friend at the time, an older whore, had looked at her and asked her, "What did you expect? Whores are for fucking. Nothing more."

And that reality was never going to go away, would always stand between her and anything she wanted.

"Whores are for fucking," she told him. He winced as if she'd struck a blow. "So if you want to fuck me, feel free. I'm your wife and I can't stop you, but I don't want to hear fairy tales and I don't want to hear promises that won't hold water."

"Goddamn it, Maddie."

"No, goddamn you for thinking I'm stupid enough to believe a lie."

He sighed again, drawing up his knee and resting his arm across it, watching her with eyes that saw too much. "Why would I do that, Maddie?"

"I don't know. Maybe you just need to feel like you win."

"And for that to happen, you have to lose, is that it?"

She shook her head and repeated, "Whores are for fucking. There's no losing."

"You say that one more time, I'm going to wash your mouth out with soap."

"You kiss me one more time and I'm going to cut off your cock."

His eyebrows rose at the harsh language. She didn't care.

"Are you, now?"

She turned on her heel and stomped away. He had no right to take away her safety.

"Count on it."

CHAPTER TWELVE

CADEN WANTED TO follow Maddie, needed to, actually, but he held himself back. He wasn't a man known for rushing his fences, and he wasn't going to start now. He'd much rather see her vague and smiling, making up fairy tales, than see that wall of hurt rising around her. Yet another thing he hadn't recognized. How much he'd come to rely on her hiding to shield herself from hurt. He rubbed his wrist, breath hissing in as he reopened the tears from the rope. It was going to take some getting used to the fact that Maddie didn't run away anymore, that she stood her ground and hurt just like the rest of them. He'd have to be more careful.

Hell. He ran his fingers through his hair, feeling the mud and leaves clinging to it. Grimacing, he shook his head. For a man who came to the swimming hole to cool off, he'd ended up a whole lot more hot and bothered. He shucked out of his wet pants. His cock fell hard and hungry into his hand, so sensitive the warm air in itself felt like a caress. Stroking his thumb across the tip, he imagined the kiss of Maddie's sweet pussy and shivered. He just knew her pussy was going to fit him like a glove. Everything about the woman was made for him, from the softness of her breasts to the softness of her nature.

Another stroke of his thumb, another shiver of sensation. It would be so easy to seek release this way, thinking of her, but he wouldn't. Not until Maddie was ready would he come. And then they'd come together. It was a form of atonement she probably wouldn't appreciate even if she were aware of it, but it mattered to him that they share something, even if it was just frustration. With a groan and a muttered "Fuck," he jumped into the water. It felt like heaven to his overheated senses. He stayed under until his lungs felt as if they would burst, trying to will the fire in his blood to cool. He had marginal success. He broke through the surface, shaking his hair out of his eyes. A few laps across the pond took the edge off his hunger. Swimming back to where he could stand, he dunked his head and combed his fingers through his hair.

"You should have brought soap," he heard from the bank.

"What the hell do you want, Ace?"

Ace walked a coin across his fingers, looking as though he hadn't a care in the world. In some ways Ace was a master of illusion. "Well, I would say a better result than you got here, by the look on Maddie's face when she came back to the camp."

"But?" He knew that tone of Ace's. It always heralded trouble.

"But we've got trouble."

"Shit." He stood up straight. "Culbart?"

"In a way."

"Don't be beating around the bush."

"One of his men rode in to give you a warning."

"Dickens?"

"No."

"About what?" If Culbart thought he was going to dictate to him anymore, he had another think coming.

Ace pushed his hat. "Injun trouble. They're on the rise, burned out a settlement a few miles beyond Culbart's."

That had to be New Haven. Ten families had banded together to build that town. It was remote but well armed. If the Comanche had taken that out, they were serious. "Shit."

"He sent a message, said it's not safe for us to stay here," Ace added.

Caden didn't kid himself that Culbart had any fondness for him, but he clearly still saw Maddie as his concern. First chance he got, Caden would disabuse the man of the notion, but in this case, Culbart was right. It wasn't safe for Maddie here anymore. If it ever had been. Caden combed his hair back from his face, sloughing the water from it with his palms. "How long ago?"

"Three days."

It was a two-day ride back to Hell's Eight. A day's ride to Culbart's and an equal distance to the town of Simple.

"Culbart says you can leave Maddie at his place," Ace added.

Culbart had a lot of men, but if the Comanche were truly rising up, all the men Culbart had would be nothing. And point-blank, he didn't trust anybody else with Maddie's safety.

"No, she's not going there."

"It's a two-day ride back to Hell's Eight."

"I know."

"We might be able to make it."

"Maybe, but that's straight through hostile territory, and you said you saw Indian sign earlier."

Ace nodded. "A lot of riders moving fast. Likely that war party that took out New Haven riding through."

"Any indication they know we're up here?"

"I think it'd be foolish to think they didn't."

Yeah, it was. He wasn't a foolish man, and he wasn't taking chances with Maddie. "Simple's only a day's ride away."

"That's big enough the Comanche won't raid there. They might hit a few settlers on the outskirts, but they're not going to take a chance on that many white men."

"True." But that didn't mean that one of the other threats wasn't lying in wait.

Caden ran his hands through his hair. He couldn't leave the claim. Hell's Eight needed that gold to survive. He'd promised away the foal to Culbart, which meant he was going to have to stay, and Maddie was going to have to leave. "I'm going to have to send Maddie to Simple." Stash her in the hotel and hope like hell she stayed low.

"She's not going to be happy."

"I know. She's been avoiding going to town ever since she came to Hell's Eight."

"Can't really blame her for hiding out."

No, he couldn't.

"When do you want to leave?"

"First thing in the morning."

"When are you going to break it to her?" Ace asked.

Caden sloshed out of the water and grabbed his clothes, shrugging his shirt on over his wet shoulders, shoving his hands into the sleeves, yanking at them when they stuck.

"First thing in the morning."

Ace laughed. "Either you're a chicken or you're hoping to make some progress."

Caden buttoned his shirt. "What do you think?"

"I think I'm going to be on guard duty tonight."

"I want to move the campsite to that holler in the ledge. At least that way nobody will be able to sneak up on us."

"I already have Maddie packing."

"Does she know why?"

"She assumed because the claim jumpers had found us."

Caden didn't know whether to smile or sigh that Maddie was so flustered. "They're dead."

"That'll occur to her eventually, but right now she's peaceably packing up the camp, getting ready to move to a different location."

"She scared?"

"Not that she's admitting to. She didn't run and hide."

Caden tugged on his pants. It was hard work getting the cotton up over his wet thighs.

"She doesn't do that so much anymore."

"No?"

Caden shrugged. "I guess she's outgrown the need."

"I gotta admit it'd be easier right now if she'd just slip away into some compliant fantasy."

"I don't think so."

"Why not?"

"Believe it or not—" he grabbed his boots and socks, tugging one onto his left foot first and then his right "—I like her angry."

"You do?"

"Yeah. I do." There was a lot of passion in Maddie and he enjoyed all its manifestations.

Ace tossed the coin in the air and caught it with a subtle flourish. "Should I be checking you for fever?"

Caden smiled. "No."

"What are you going to do?"

"Help her get packed."

"What are you going to tell her?"

"I don't know."

Ace chuckled and tossed him his hat. "It's good to know you've got a plan."

He settled his hat on his head. "I've always got a plan," he lied.

Ace's laughter followed him up the trail.

WHEN CADEN GOT back to the campsite, Maddie had it pretty much under control, which shouldn't have surprised him. Looking around, he saw all that was required was for the packs to be wrapped and tied. And to soothe Maddie if the nervous glance she cut him from under her lashes as she motioned to the gear was anything to go by.

"I don't know how to tie it."

And that explained the nervousness. Maddie always worried about doing things right. Likely because there hadn't been a lot of tolerance in her past for mistakes. "It's all right. I'll show you."

She scooted quickly over when he hunkered down. He pretended not to notice. "You do it like this."

Taking the corners, he folded them into the middle before rolling it up over the rope and then tying it off into a finished package.

She frowned at him. "That's it?"

"We're not going that far. I'd do it a bit differently if we were putting it on the horse for the long haul."

"Ace said we had to move because the claim jumpers found us."

"I'd feel better with a wall at our back. It'll be hotter 'cause the cliff blocks the breeze, but it's safer." It wasn't strictly a lie.

Maddie licked her lips. Caden couldn't take his eyes away from the moistness of her tongue as it passed over. He actually saw her breath catch. He looked up. She was watching his mouth. He smiled. She was as aware of him as he was of her.

"You're sweet to kiss." He said that just to rattle her more, but it was the truth. "Sweet Maddie mine, never been kissed."

Until him.

He started on the second pack, letting her silence linger uncontested. She broke it with "I'm not a virgin."

He shook his head. "It doesn't matter how many men used you, Maddie. To me you're a virgin. No one's touched your heart. No one's brought out that passion in you." He finished tying up the second pack and moved over to the first. She was still standing in the same spot, staring at him, but now her hands were clenched at her sides. "The part of you that matters is untouched, waiting for the right man to bring it to life." He met her gaze. "I'm going to be that man. The one who makes you burn from the inside out. The one you can't look at without getting wet. The one who makes you scream with pleasure."

She looked away. "I know how to fake it."

She was firmly on the defensive. "Do you? Let me hear it."

"What?"

He folded his arms across his chest. "Let me hear you fake it."

"Why?"

"Because I'm curious how a woman who's never felt pleasure imitates it."

"Here?"

"What's wrong with here? It's not real, so what does it matter where you do it?"

She looked distinctly uncomfortable, and she should be. As defenses went, that was a pretty poor one.

"I don't want to."

"Why? Afraid it's not going to sound real to me?"

"I just don't want to."

"Because you can't."

"I can."

He smiled and took a step forward, expected her to

take a step back. She didn't, and for some reason that made him smile bigger. Maddie was determined to find her feet, and he wasn't going to get in her way, but he'd be there to catch her if she fell. In time she'd come to understand she wasn't alone anymore. It was easier than it should have been to slide his fingers over her cheek, to hook them behind her neck, to draw her up into his embrace, easier and beyond sweet.

"What are you doing?"

"You know what I'm doing. What's more, you want it."

"No, I don't." She whispered the denial against his lips.

He smiled his acceptance against hers and then he kissed her the way he kissed a woman that he wanted: deeply, hotly, passionately, separating her lips with a thrust of his tongue, coaxing hers into play with his, tickling the inside of her mouth until she couldn't help but smile, keeping that smile as his own, tempting her more until she moaned and leaned in, taking her passion as the gift it was. His poor sweet Maddie.

He didn't pull back until she was breathless, and then he rested his forehead against hers and smiled into her eyes. She looked stunned, like a wild creature surprised from the safety of its nest, and he guessed that was what Maddie's little pretend world was: her nest. Without it, life was just an onslaught of experiences with which she didn't know how to cope.

"I tell you what."

"What?" she asked in a husky voice that stroked along

his cock. He wanted to hear her say his name like that, preferably when his cock was sliding inside her that first time. He was going to make it so good for her.

"Tonight when we're lying down together, I want you to show me how you fake it."

"I don't lie down with you. I sleep."

"All right, tonight when you're lying beside me, trying to pretend that I'm not there, I want you to show me how you fake it."

"No."

He kissed her mouth, running his tongue on the underside of her upper lip, stroking his fingers along the nape of her neck.

"Yes. And, Maddie?"

"What?"

"Next time I kiss you—"

"There's not going to be a next time."

He had to smile at her stubbornness. He tapped his finger to her cheek, drawing her eyes to his. She was so cute. "Breathe through your nose."

MADDIE WAS AS NERVOUS as a cat all afternoon, watching the sun like a doomed man watched a scaffold. Caden shook his head again. What did she think was going to happen? That he was going to turn into some monster intent on hurting her? He shook his head. Clearly he had a long way to go to gain her trust. And now that supper was over, the dishes had been scrubbed and the fire banked down, and Ace was off on guard duty up on the ledge above, he had his first opportunity to start building it. Standing, he brushed off his pants. Maddie jumped so fast to her feet, her skirts swung about her ankles. He remembered how pretty her legs were with the slim calves leading to plump thighs that ended at delightfully full hips.

"I'm going to make a pass around and make sure everything's fine."

She looked at him.

"Maddie—" he shook his head at her wide-eyed stare "—I'm giving you time to do whatever a woman does before her lover comes to her."

"You're my husband."

"And your lover." He wanted to shake his head again. "You'd do well to remember that."

"I don't have anything."

"What do you mean you don't—" That pulled him up short, *have anything.* "It's okay, I don't need scented creams and ribbons."

She blinked as if he was speaking another language.

"What do you think you need that you don't have?"

She shook her head, and he had to think about it a bit and still he couldn't come up with anything.

"Maddie?"

"I don't have my—" And her jaw set in a way that told him she wasn't going to tell him. He supposed he could push, but what did he care?

"Then we'll just do without it."

Her eyes grew wide.

"I assure you, the lack of whatever it is is not going to stop me."

She licked her lips again and folded her arms across her chest, hardly the image of the eager bride. "I can't prevent a baby."

The answer left him stunned and then a little excited. He'd love to make a little red-haired baby with Maddie, to see her grow round with his child. "Who said I wanted you to?"

"It's just, I mean, I'm—"

He cut her off. "My wife," he finished for her before adding, "and, Maddie, I'd take you right now, as you are, and be delighted at the possibility of a child, but I'm being a gentleman."

"Why?"

"Because you deserve kindness and consideration."

She shook her head. A wave of her hand dismissed the higher feelings he was trying to give her.

"Why would you take me now?"

"Because I desire you. Why does any man?"

She shook her head. "What is it about me that makes me desirable to you?"

She wanted to know what he saw in her. A very reasonable request from a woman feeling very skittish.

"You're beautiful, Maddie."

"I'm plain. I have freckles."

"You're beautiful, Maddie. Inside and out, and if you'd come to us any other way than how you did, I'd have been on your doorstep courting your favor, but for a long time you were healing and I didn't let myself see you until it got to the point I'd learned to do some pretending of my own. And then Culbart had you, and I had to come get you. I expected to find a shattered woman, lost in fantasy, the same lost child you were when you came to Hell's Eight. Instead, I found a strong woman playing at fantasy, doing what she had to do to get us all out of the situation. And the fantasy I protected you with shattered."

She wrung her hands until the knuckles were white. "I didn't know he was going to make me marry you."

"I know, and it's occurred to me that one of the reasons you might have gone along with it is because any bullheaded thing I might have done could have gotten me killed."

She looked stunned at the revelation.

He pretended not to notice. "I do think sometimes, Maddie. Not always before I talk, but I do work on things until they make sense. Your going along with him to marry me, to betray Hell's Eight? You, who has a deeply ingrained sense of loyalty?" He shook his head. "That doesn't make sense."

"And because of that, now you want to have sex with me?"

"Don't make me come over there, because if I do you're not going to get the time you need to be comfortable."

She took a step back. He stepped forward, grabbed her hand and pulled her precisely the same distance back toward him.

"One of the lessons you need to learn is the difference between a threat of passion and a threat of danger."

"What's the difference?"

"The first one should make you smile."

She licked her lips. "You want me to like this, I know."

"I do."

"I don't like this."

He smiled, slid his finger up her neck and along her jaw, up over her lips so he could tap her nose. "Then, I'm giving you permission to show me how you fake it."

"But now you know I can fake it."

"Honey, every man knows a woman can fake it."

"They do?"

"It's part of the challenge, to see if you can get them past it to the real thing."

"And you think you can get me past it to the real thing?"

"I don't know if I can tonight, but I'm hoping. There's so much passion and beauty in you. But if I can't, I'm going to do my best to prove to you that what we have is good."

"I don't know what we have."

"We're husband and wife. We have the future that builds for us."

"You said you're going to get rid of me."

"I changed my mind."

He ignored her "Well, maybe I haven't" and turned away, a smile tugging at his lips.

She really wasn't that good at faking it.

MADDIE STOOD AT the foot of the bedroll and concentrated on breathing. Five minutes. He was giving her five minutes. Five minutes to remember—no, not even to remember, to *learn* how to be a wife. What did he want from her? He'd talked about her as if she was a virgin, but they both knew she wasn't. She'd been with men who wanted her to pretend they were her first. Was that what he wanted her to do? She could probably do that with him. He made it so easy for her to feel...new.

The more she thought about it, the better the idea seemed. Playing the virgin wasn't that hard. Men had firm ideas how virgins acted, clear preferences in what they desired.

Let me loosen your hair. First she needed to braid her hair. Not too tightly. They might want her to look virginal, but men also wanted the hint of passion. Men who liked virgins liked to loosen her hair from that braid, the same way they liked to think they loosed her passion.

Don't be shy.

And they liked to undress her, too. Liked to think they had the power to make her lose any inhibitions she harbored. *Don't be afraid.* More voices popped into her head. *Just be still. I know what to do. Just lie there.*

She took a breath and put all that together in her head until her confidence came back. Caden was a man like any other, and she knew what men wanted from virgins. She knew what Caden wanted. Taking her brush out of her pack, she ran it through her hair, pulling it back into a sloppy braid. Untouchable, yet available was what men wanted. One of her clients talked a lot about seeing her pulse pound in her throat. He liked the fear and he had been someone to be afraid of. He hadn't been a gentle man. She unbuttoned the top two buttons of her bodice.

Well, she couldn't remember back to when she'd actually been a virgin; those early years had just been so painful she'd fought to forget, until now it was as if they didn't exist anymore. Whoever she had been before her customer didn't exist, either.

She heard Caden's steps. A twig snapped as he came closer. She settled herself on the bedroll, fluffing her skirts around her, smoothing them, settling her hands on her lap, straightening her spine, looking as prim and proper as she could. She didn't have to fake the fear. She was very nervous and very afraid. She didn't want to disappoint him.

He stepped into the faint light of the fire, shadows casting a more sinister aspect, until she looked at his face. There was no anger in his eyes, just softness. She didn't know what to do with softness, didn't know how she was supposed to take it, but it was better than hatred, so she smiled at him timidly, not having to fake the shyness, either. It was strange to think of bedding Caden, stranger still to think of him as her husband. She knew this wasn't going to last, that this was just a game that he wanted to play as all men did, but it would be a memory she would have to hold on to in the years to come, and she wanted it to be a good one.

"Hi."

He looked at her and frowned. "This is you ready?"

"Yes."

He sighed. "Maybe you'd better fake it for me after all."

The panic clotted her stomach. "I don't understand."

He sat down beside her, and her breath stuck in her throat. He was displeased. He kicked off one boot, then the other, the second being a little more stubborn than the first.

"Maddie?"

"What?"

He looked over at her, his expression unreadable. "How do you think things are going to go tonight?"

"I'm going to pretend to be a virgin." The words *and you're going to pretend to be happy* stuck in her throat.

"That's what you think I want? Pretense?"

"You told me to fake it."

"You know damn well I was being sarcastic."

She shook her head. "I don't know anything." She clenched her fists in her lap, the rage coming out of nowhere. "You seem to think I should know everything when I know nothing. I don't know what you want. I don't know how you want me to be. I don't know how long this is going to last. I don't know how I'm going to survive it when it ends, and I—"

His arm slid around her shoulder and he pulled her against his chest. She wanted to smash her fists into his shoulder. Instead, she just opened her palm and laid it over his heart, feeling its steady beat, feeling the warmth of his body seep into hers.

She closed her eyes, unable to resist the hug. There'd been so few in her life. It threw her off balance every time he did it. His lips brushed her hair.

"Maddie?"

She was beginning to not like the way he said her

name. It always led to more probing, more pain, more
revelations of the person she was but didn't want to be.

"What?"

"I want to make love to you, not…fuck you."

She'd had men that liked that, too.

"Just tell me how you want me to be and I'll be it."

"I don't want you to be anything." He tipped her chin
up. She couldn't see his expression clearly in the shadows, but she was pretty sure he could see hers from the
way they were sitting. "I want whatever happens between us to be honest. If you feel nothing, then just lie
there like a blob."

"Men don't like that." Well, unless they wanted her
to pretend to be dead, but that just made her skin crawl.

"I don't like pretending to be dead," she told him.

He drew back. She could tell she'd shocked him.

"What the hell makes you think I want that?"

"You said you want me to just lie there and—"

"Fuck," he muttered. "Maddie."

"What?"

"Can we start with a hug?"

She could do hugs. She nodded.

"Good."

He lay down and she lay beside him. He waited a minute and then sighed and put his arm out. "Come here."

She went as she always did and rested her cheek on
his shoulder. She couldn't seem to breathe until his arms
came around her, and once her body was touching his,
the panic inside her melted away. He didn't do anything
except hold her and rub his hand up and down her back.

She was so nervous she didn't think she could take her next breath. She couldn't take the waiting, the pressure of the silence; as a result she just blurted out, "Do you want to hear me fake it now?"

He laughed and squeezed her tight, shaking his head, and wonder of wonders, she felt the tension leave his side.

"I think I'll save that for a little bit later."

Wonderful.

CHAPTER THIRTEEN

DO YOU WANT to hear me fake it now?

Caden shook his head. How could the woman lie in his arms as soft and as sweet as a dream and ask such a ridiculous question? He didn't want her to fake it at all, but judging by how stiffly she lay there in his arms, he had a feeling telling her that wasn't going to get him to where he wanted to go. And he very badly wanted to get there with Maddie.

He kissed the top of her head and ran his fingers down her arm, and she pressed closer. She gasped. He reached for the top button of her dress, and she stopped breathing altogether.

Rolling her over, he propped himself above her. He could still see her face in the dying light of the fire.

"What exactly do you think I'm going to do, Maddie?"

"I don't know." He felt her shrug up the length of his body. "Whatever makes you happy."

The plan was to make them both happy. And soon. His cock was so hard his pants were an erotic chafing.

"Do you think I'm so different from other men?" He winced and wanted to kick his own ass. The one thing he didn't want Maddie thinking about was her past experiences.

She shook her head. "No."

"Then why are you so scared?"

"I don't know what pleases you."

"You don't think I can tell you?"

She shrugged again. He stroked his fingers down her cheek, brushing his thumb across that spattering of freckles.

"I'm your husband, Maddie. Nothing that happens between us is going to shame you or hurt you or make you cry."

"You don't know that."

He cocked his head to the side and pulled her braid over her shoulder, sliding his hand down, his knuckles brushing the side of her breast.

"Of all that, which is the one you think I don't know?"

"Whether I'll cry."

He supposed she was right. "Well, if you cry, you can take me out to the shed and shoot me."

"You don't have a shed."

"Then behind the rock yonder."

Not even a smile.

"Is there anything I can say to calm you down?"

She shook her head.

"In that case, maybe I should just do what I do, and we'll see how it goes."

She nodded. "Oh, please."

Not the hottest invite he'd had into a bed, but it was still an invite. He leaned up over her.

"What are you doing?"

"I thought I'd have a kiss." He considered it a vic-

tory she didn't remind him that she didn't kiss. Leaning
down, he gently brushed his lips across hers, rubbing
them softly, licking at them, bussing the corners and
the middle before fitting the edges together. And she
lay there and let him. Obviously he was going to have to
bring his patience along with his best tonight.

Sliding his palm back up her side, he cupped her
breast through her dress. He took her gasp to his soul.
Maddie, the hardened prostitute who gasped when a man
touched her breast. He shook his head. Such a crime
she'd known so little pleasure. Keeping the pressure light
and easy, he teased at her lips until they parted, inviting his in. With the same gentle persistence, he coaxed
a response from her, keeping his hand on her breast, his
thumb on her nipple, not forcing anything. He let her
get used to the weight and feel, searching for that passion she'd felt before that, right now, was buried under
so much fear.

It took a few minutes of soft kisses, delicious kisses,
sweet kisses, Maddie kisses, for her muscles to relax.
Caden smiled at the subtle shift of her body into his
hand. He killed the instinct to squeeze and fondle. It was
too soon. But damn, he wanted to. Maddie had the sexi-
est body, plump, delicious, soft, curved in all the right
places. A feast for a man's senses. *His* senses.

He kissed her again, pulling back just a little, seeing
her eyes open, smiling down into her face.

"Hello, Maddie mine."

She blinked and smiled back.

"You feel up to giving me a hug now?"

Another blink. Then those little hands came up around his neck and pulled him down, holding him incredibly tight, clinging to him as if he was her sanity.

"That's it, Maddie. Hold on to me."

Her mouth worked and he shook his head, forestalling whatever it was she wanted to throw between them. "You don't need to say anything, honey."

"I'm sorry."

"What are you sorry for?"

"You want wild and exciting."

He kissed her quiet. "I want you, Maddie. However it is between us. You can lie there stiff as a board and it'll be all right."

She frowned at him. "You're lying."

He shrugged. "A little. But the truth is, this is just the first time. It's not every time. It's a beginning, not an ending. I'm going to make love with you as sweet as I can, and I'm going to give you as much pleasure as I can."

He could tell from the look in her eye she had no idea what he was talking about.

"And when it's over, I'm going to hold you and fall asleep with you in my arms a happy man. And when you wake up in the morning, I'm still going to be here, holding you, waiting."

She looked at him as if she wanted to hope, shoving the pain from her eyes. He wanted her to start thinking in give-and-take and not just him taking and her giving, but both of them together.

"What would you be waiting for?" she asked.

He could tell she already knew, but if she wanted to hear it, that was fine with him. He'd tell her every day how much he wanted her kiss if that's what it took. "For my morning kiss."

Moisture gathered in her eyes. *Shit.* If she cried, he'd lose his hard-on for sure. But she didn't cry and she didn't run away to that place she escaped to. Instead, she scooted closer and lifted her face to his. "I'd like that."

Ah, his Maddie was one in a million. "Good."

This kiss wasn't as shy, but he liked that, too. Cupping the back of her head in his hand, sliding his fingers gently over the sides of her breasts, he tilted his mouth to hers.

"Like this."

She not only followed, but she participated, too, copying his moves, sliding her tongue across his, tickling the insides of his upper lip, biting at his lower one, her nails digging into the back of his neck. And it was his turn to moan, her turn to smile. She liked pleasing him the same way he liked pleasing her.

"Shit, you are one hot woman, Maddie Miller."

She jumped at the sound of her married name. He smiled at it. He liked that she was his, wore his name. If he had his way, he'd put his brand all over that hot body. *His.*

He kissed his way across her cheek to her ear, catching the lobe between his teeth, biting gently. She shivered from head to toe and gasped and then did the most incredible thing: she turned her head a little, inviting him to do more.

"Ah, Maddie. You are so mine."

He did it again, obliging her, running his tongue behind her ear, nibbling his way down her neck, walking that delicate line between passion and calm because this was new to her. He could tell. It was there in every hesitant sigh, every pause before every action. She'd have him believe she'd done it all, but what he saw was a woman trapped in memories, trying to break free, and he wanted to be there to catch her when she did, to bring her into the sun, to teach her to fly, to watch her burn in his arms.

"I can't imagine going to bed without you in my arms," he told her, unfastening the buttons on her dress as he kissed the hollow of her throat. "To wake up in the morning and not have your hug, and not hear you laugh, to not see your smile, I don't want to know what that feels like."

But he would because tomorrow he was going to drop her off in town. It wasn't safe for her here. And that was going to kill him.

"I'll never leave you," she told him, her fingers twisting in his hair, her body twisting under his mouth, her legs parting unconsciously. He settled himself between, his cock throbbing, his pulse pounding. His balls aching. He caught her lower lip between his teeth, imagining what it would feel like to slide his cock into that pretty mouth.

"Say you're mine." He needed that at least.

She sighed into his mouth. "Yes."

The buttons on her dress gave easily. So did Maddie,

lifting her breasts into his hands, the tension in her fingers telling him what she wanted to do.

"Go ahead," he said. "You know you want to."

"What?"

"Invite my mouth to your breasts."

She shook her head, bit her lip.

"I'm not going to do it if you don't ask me, Maddie. Nothing's going to happen tonight unless you ask me."

She moaned and looked around. "Ace."

"Ace is on guard duty."

She moaned again.

"What do you want, Maddie? This is for you. Tell me what you want."

Her fingers grazed his lip. It was enough. He undid the ties on her camisole, pushed it down beneath her breasts. Such beautiful breasts. He wanted to see them in daylight, but this wasn't bad. Pink. Her nipples were the palest pink set atop high, white breasts. Plump, soft nipples he wanted to feel harden against his tongue. Her hand slid between them. He shook his head.

"No, honey." Taking her hands in his, he pinned them over her head beside her shoulders before taking her nipple into his mouth. He sucked softly, gently, the same way he kissed her, teasing and coaxing until he got the response he wanted and it hardened on his tongue. On the flick of his tongue, her breath stuck in her throat.

He let go of her hands. They didn't move and he smiled. Cupping her left breast in his hand, he rubbed his thumb over that nipple as he sucked the right one.

He started out light, very light, just the barest of sensation. He could tell it wasn't enough.

"Ask me," he told her, giving her just a little bit more pressure, letting her sense what could happen if it was just right.

"Oh."

He'd give her anything she wanted, but she had to ask. He wasn't going to force her, and he didn't want her looking back thinking she was forced.

"Caden..." The throaty purr in her voice made his cock throb and jerk against the inside of his pants.

"What?"

She shook her head.

"What?"

Her fingers yanked in his hair. "I don't know what."

He hadn't considered that.

"Would you like it harder, Maddie mine? Do you need me," he asked against her nipple, "to suck your breasts harder?"

"Yes."

"Then ask me."

There was only a slight hesitation. "Please, do it harder."

At last, the permission he wanted. He took the tip of her lush breast in his mouth, plumping the nipple against his tongue, settling his teeth slightly around it, feeling her arch immediately. Fear, not passion. He stroked his finger down her cheek, catching it on the corner of her mouth, sliding it inside.

"Easy, baby. This isn't about me taking or you hurting. This is about a husband showing his wife how much he appreciates her and making her feel good."

Her start at the word *wife* was a mystery until she whispered, "I'm supposed to be making you feel good."

"What makes you think this doesn't?"

"I'm not touching you."

"If I'm not enjoying myself, then explain to me why I'm about to come."

She didn't have an answer for that, and it was just as well. He was about out of sensible talk.

He unbuttoned her dress the rest of the way.

"Lift up." He tugged it down her hips. She lay before him in her pantaloons and camisole, lush and beautiful, everything he wanted.

"Do you mind if I undo this braid?"

She looked up at him. "I did it so you could."

It took him a minute, busy as he was at her breasts, to process that.

"Maddie, you aren't by any chance playing a role for me, are you? Slipping into your fantasy?"

"I'm not pretending."

"But you are playing a role for me."

"You said I was a virgin. You know I'm not."

Yes, he did. "Honey, I said you were a virgin in the context of you don't know what this is all about."

"I know what to do."

He took one of her hands, clenched as it was beside her head, and brought it to his lips.

"You don't know shit. You know what it's like to be taken. You know what it's like to be forced. You know what it's like to service a man, but you don't know shit about how it should be between us."

"Should it be different?"

"Between us it needs to be natural, an even give-and-take of pleasure."

She was licking her lips again, a sure sign she was nervous.

"What now?"

"I don't feel pleasure."

How the hell could she have? No one had bothered to give it to her. "No reason you should up till now. But now is different. Now is us going forward."

"Making our own life," she said, her tone lightening.

He could tell she liked that. "Yes. Making *our* life."

Her expression grew serious. "What do you want me to do?"

He'd say *nothing,* except he had a feeling that wasn't going to get him where he wanted to go.

"I want you to close your eyes and relax, and every time it feels good, I want you to let me know."

"How?"

Screaming, biting, scratching, all those came to his mind. "How about giving me one of those little sighs and smiles I like so much."

She nodded. "All right. But what if it doesn't feel good?"

"Then I'm going to have to change my technique until it does. That's all. Nothing too difficult about that."

He touched his tongue to her breast and looked up.

He had to wait a heartbeat and give it a little wiggle, but then he got that smile he was looking for.

"You like that."

She nodded. "I don't know why. It just kind of feels good."

"Real good or a little good?"

"Little good."

So he needed a bit more pressure. "Wonderful. Let's see if we can add to that little good now."

She was like a banked fire in his arms. All it would take was the right touch, the right persuasion, and she'd burn out of control. He wanted to find that for her, that spark that would crackle into flame.

Rolling onto his back until she was propped above him, her pussy cushioning his cock, he whispered, "Come here, baby."

She went, her mouth finding his with an enthusiasm that had him pushing up. "That's it."

She licked her lips, giving him a view of that little pink tongue. He had visions of it stroking across his cock. He groaned as her hips wiggled on his. Her eyes widened as the sensation streaking through him shot through her. He smiled into her face.

"You have that effect on me. You make me crazy, baby."

"Any woman could do that."

He shook his head. "I'm not saying I don't enjoy bed sport as much as the next man, but lately fucking for fucking's sake just doesn't work for me. I find—" he pushed loose tendrils of hair back from her face, taking her braid in his hand as she propped herself above his chest, working the tie free before slowly sorting the strands out "—that I've been wanting something special, someone special."

"I'm not special."

He shook his head at her. "That's for me to decide."

"But I get to find—"

This time he put his finger over her mouth more firmly. "You're my wife. Our future starts here, and I need you to pay attention, because I want to do this right so it's a good beginning, so when you look back and our daughter asks you what to expect on her wedding night, you'll smile."

"Oh, dear."

"What?"

She shook her head, her nails digging into his chest. "Hold me."

"Why?"

"Just do it."

He did. "I'll do better than that. I'm going to love you."

He worked her pantaloons over her hips, pushing them down until he could catch them with his toes, taking them the rest of the way off. She lay passively on top of him when he wanted fire. Sliding his hands down her back, he cupped them on the inside of her thighs and pulled them apart, nestling his cock between, pushing up until she was sitting in his lap, his cock still trapped in his pants, pressing hard against her pussy. He rocked his hips, catching her gasp in his mouth as the rough fabric of his trousers abraded her intimately.

"Feels good?"

She nodded and gasped, "Very good."

He groaned when she wiggled. It'd been a long time for him and she was so hot, so sexy.

"Easy, honey."

In response she wiggled again.

"Fuck."

She laughed.

"Wench."

She leaned down and whispered in his ear, "You have too many clothes on."

So he did. Setting her to the side, he stripped so fast a button popped. Before he could come back down, she reached out and caught his cock in her hand. He covered hers with his, shaking his head.

"This time's for you."

She looked at him and smiled a witchy smile that sank deep into his lust, stoking it almost as much as her throaty "I know."

She didn't let go of his cock. Instead, she moved that soft hand up and down his shaft, from base to tip, palming the head, coaxing a bead of pre-come to the tip. It'd take a better man than him to move right then. He closed his eyes and let her have her way. He expected her to touch him with a whore's practiced hand, but instead she seemed to be experimenting, even playing, and he realized for her this was another first. Enjoying a man rather than servicing him.

She looked up. It was his turn to smile. "Nothing better than your hand on my cock."

She licked her lips, those full lips, and dropped her lashes over her eyes. Though she leaned in and he'd seen her take another, he'd swear that shyness wasn't feigned. And maybe it wasn't. He was far from a virgin, but he felt shy with her. Because this mattered. He stopped her before her mouth could touch him. One touch of those lips and it would all be over for him, and there was a whole lot of pleasure he wanted to give her before that happened.

"Later." At her look he explained, "I want to taste you first."

She blinked.

"Hasn't anyone ever tasted that sweet pussy of yours?"

She shook her head.

"Ah, honey, we're going to have so much fun." A twist of his body was all it took to flip her over onto the bedroll. Her hair tumbled about her face, adding a luminosity to her eyes. Peace surrounded by fire. He leaned down and kissed her.

"Maddie mine." Trailing that kiss across her cheek to her neck and her shoulder. Her nipples pressed against his chest, little points of heat. More evidence of that fire he wanted to coax from her. He worked his way down, sliding one hand under her thigh, wrapping it around his hips, getting her to hold on to him, to cling to him.

When she moaned, he whispered, "Good girl."

"I'm not a child."

He cupped her full breast in his hand, plumping the

nipple to his mouth. "No, you're not, but you're still good."

She moaned and nodded. He drew on her nipple hard. She arched off the ground, giving him the opportunity to slide his hand under her back and press her closer still.

He worked her nipple with his tongue and his lips until her moans grew higher, rougher, and then he worked it harder, adding the edge of his teeth, making her burn for him.

"Good, baby?"

She was so lost he didn't think she'd heard him, but then there was that little smile and her hands wrapped in his hair, pulling him closer still. He kissed his way over to the other breast, pinching that nipple first, snapping it to attention, starting the fire going there before curling his tongue around it and drawing it into the heat of his mouth. Maddie dug her heels into his back, pulling him closer. His cock ground against the roughness of the blankets when he wanted the heat and silk of her pussy. He'd get there eventually. But first…

He kissed his way down her stomach, following the dip as she sucked in her breath, nibbling when he got to her navel, circling it with his tongue, pressing down with his chest, pinning her as he slipped one arm and then the other under her knees, lifting her legs over his shoulders, exposing her to him.

Her pussy lips were plump and covered with fine red hair. Between, the sweetest of pink greeted his eyes, wet and moist—not nearly wet enough, though. He

wanted her dripping for him, screaming for him before he took her.

Her scent rose to his nostrils. Musky, clean, sweet
woman. He couldn't believe nobody'd ever loved this
pussy. It was so perfect. The inner petals as delicate as
her spirit, sweet, sexy... His.

As he leaned in, she tugged at his hair. He ignored
the order and placed his tongue against the little V surrounding her clit, working inside, licking it and rubbing
it, coaxing that bundle of nerves tight, feeling the tension
radiate through her legs. Bracing his hands on the back
of her knees, he pushed her legs back farther, arching her
up to his mouth, exposing all of her, keeping her open
and vulnerable to the assault of his tongue and teeth. He
loved her tenderly and sweetly, following her moans and
her gasps, giving her more pressure, more joy, feeling
that first delicious tension enter her muscles. Waiting as
it built, hearing the desperate gasp that signaled she was
teetering on the edge before he sucked her clit into his
mouth and clamped it with his teeth, he felt the shock go
through her, heard the scream rip out of her as her first
orgasm pulsed through her body. He lapped at her clit
as she convulsed, drinking her cream, his cock swollen
to bursting as she sobbed his name. Sweet. So sweet.

He continued to suckle lightly until the last ripple
shuddered through her and she was pushing at him,
twisting away because she thought it was too much. She
had yet to learn that it could never be enough. She could
never come enough for him.

He did, however, gentle his approach, focusing more

on the outer lips as he coaxed her back into the fire, sliding his finger gently into her pussy, feeling it clench down around him, working his way back up to her clit again, just resting his tongue against it until she stopped shivering, and then he began to work her in earnest, slipping another finger into her pussy when she lifted up, fucking her slowly as he sucked her swollen clit.

"What are you doing to me?" she asked, her fingers raking over his shoulders, drawing blood. The pain just added to the passion. Fuck, he needed to be in her.

"Loving you." He kissed his way back up her body, biting at her stomach and her breasts, kissing her mouth.

She opened her legs to him immediately. The instinctive submission soothing that wild part of him that wanted to fuck her so hard she'd be feeling him for a week, giving him the strength to find tenderness. The thick head of his cock slid over her clit before settling into the well of her pussy, and for a second she stiffened.

He kissed her cheeks, her nose, her eyes.

"No, honey. Just more pleasure."

She opened her eyes; he saw the fear in them and then saw the trust push it away. His Maddie mine, who should have been broken beyond repair, reaching out to him. He cupped her head in his hands and rested his forehead against hers as he slowly, gently joined them.

"Mine." The word whispered out on a breath so soft he didn't know if she heard. Her pussy was hot and tight, liquid fire surrounding his cock. He wanted to hold back. He wanted to make it last, but it was too much. He started to withdraw, gritting his teeth against the need to plunge wildly.

"Come with me."

She shook her head. "I can't."

"Yes." He dropped his hand between them, settled his thumb on her clit. It was still swollen and hot and wet. He rubbed in time with his strokes, starting out slow, feeling the tingles rush up his spine, the tensing in his balls, as the need to come, to fill her with his seed, to brand her his overwhelmed him. He fought it back, wanting her with him all the way. Wanting to come with her this first time. Wanting it to be perfect.

Her breath caught, her back arched.

"That's it."

He fucked her harder. She pulled him closer. Him riding her, she riding him. Both of them striving for the moment when they both had what they wanted. Him, her, each other, possession.

The climax flashed over him like fire, drawing her name from his lips. Her pussy clamped around his cock as her body convulsed, tearing his seed from his balls. She whispered his name on a soundless scream and he exploded, his world narrowing to this moment, this woman. His lover. His wife.

His Maddie.

CHAPTER FOURTEEN

FOR THE FIRST time in her memory, Maddie woke up feeling content. She smiled and took a deep breath, breathing in Caden's scent and the reality of being naked in his arms and feeling good about it. He made her feel safe. She thought back to the night before, the passion, the tenderness, the kissing. Reaching up, she touched her fingers to his lips. She did love kissing. Against her fingers, his lips pulled into a smile. She stretched up, he leaned down and she got to kiss again.

"Such a marvelous thing," she murmured against his mouth.

"What?"

"Kissing."

His fingers touched her temple and slid down to her ear before moving with that familiar caress to the nape of her neck.

"And the other?"

"That's probably the most amazing thing of all," she said. "I never liked that before."

"No surprise."

"But I like it with you." She smiled. "It feels natural."

"Natural?"

"Like it's the way it should be."

"Like maybe you were made to burn for me, baby."

There was a time when that kind of talk would have made her uncomfortable, but with her pussy still feeling the imprint of his cock, and her nipples so tender from his kisses, it was hard to be uncomfortable with anything. She was like warm porridge, all mushy and gushy on the inside.

She slipped her arms around his neck. Against her will the words just slipped past her lips. "I love you."

"Aw." This time when he kissed her it was more passionate, and this time she responded without hesitation, her legs parting as he settled between them, taking his cock easily into her body, moaning as she stretched deliciously around him. Not a bit of dread in her, just a lot of expectation. She knew where this was going to lead and it was heaven.

She dug her heels into the ground and pushed up. His fingers twisted in her hair and pulled her head back, his mouth found her neck, her collarbone, the top of her breast, skimming the surface until he reached her nipple, taking it into his hot mouth even as his cock pushed farther into her hot pussy.

Heat. Everywhere there was heat. He moaned her name. She sighed his, opening her body and soul to him, giving him the emotion that was pouring through her. He was her husband. She belonged to him. She'd never be alone again. It was good, so good.

His finger found her clit and rubbed. Fire streaked through her body. His teeth found her nipple and bit ever so delicately, just enough to bring her to that edge. He thrust harder, bit harder, rubbed harder, not giving her a break, sending her catapulting into that maelstrom of emotion. She embraced it with everything she had, coming hard, screaming his name, forgetting about everything, where they were, who she was, Ace, Hell's Eight, everything. There was only Caden and the way he made her feel. Perfect. Just perfect.

When it was over, he was still there, holding her, kissing her, joined to her, giving her the one thing she'd always wanted: a sense of belonging. And she clung to it as hard as she clung to him, letting the security of that pour over her like the morning sun. Bright and strong.

Bella was right. She had needed to find out who she wanted to be, and who she wanted to be was Caden's wife. Clenching her pussy around his softening cock, feeling his seed between her thighs, she smiled. She was most definitely that.

She didn't know how long they lay there. It felt like an eternity in a good way. She didn't want it to end, but from the woods to the left there came a lot of stomping and breaking of branches and some very heavy whistling.

Ace. She grabbed the blanket up to her chest.

Caden laughed. "That, I believe, is Ace trying in his own discreet way to tell us he's coming back."

"Well, tell him to come back a little slower!" She didn't even remember where Caden had thrown her clothes. She grabbed her camisole and pulled it over her head, but she couldn't find her pantaloons anywhere. Caden, damn his hide, just sat there and chuckled, watching her. She opened her mouth to yell. He forestalled her.

"We'll be with you in a minute, Ace."

"Well, hurry up, dammit. My stomach's empty. Not everybody can live on love."

Maddie smiled to hear it put that way. Even Ace knew this was love.

"Where are my pantaloons?" she hissed.

Caden shrugged. "Might want to crawl out and look for them."

She started to before she realized his motive. "You just want to stare at my—" She blushed. She actually blushed.

"Your ass? You're damn right." He pointed to the foot of the bedroll. "Wouldn't hurt my feelings at all if you crawled on down to the bottom there to start your search."

"I'll do no such thing!" Not with Ace standing just on the other side of the bushes. She sat and untangled herself from the covers before getting to her feet. Before she was halfway upright, Caden slapped her on the butt. The tingle went right through her and she gasped. His hand lingered, stroking over the sting.

"Like that, huh?"

What was the point of lying? His fingers slipped around and tested her clit with a touch so delicate, her knees almost buckled. He smacked her butt again.

"Oh, yeah, you do." He grinned a devil's grin that just made her want to kiss him. "We'll have to experiment with that a little bit later."

Her clit or spanking? She didn't know which, but then again, she didn't care. Maybe it'd be both. She'd never been spanked before, and it wasn't something she thought she'd enjoy, but there was no denying the heat that ripped through her with that swat, and since the one who'd be doing the spanking would be Caden...

She eyed him lying there on the blanket like a pagan god, another blanket just barely covering his modesty, his wide shoulders, broad chest, well-muscled stomach and that intriguing line of hair that went from his navel down to... Licking her lips, she reached forward and twitched the blanket off him. His cock rose before her eyes, filling and expanding to its impressive size.

She curled her fingers around it, smiling at him.

"I think we'll have to."

He moaned and pulled her down across his lap, pushing her thighs aside so his cock slid between, tucking up against her pussy before he slapped her three times hard on her ass. His fingers dipped between her cheeks, finding her pussy wet with their come, taking their juices and sliding them back to her asshole. She'd been violated there before, but this wasn't a violation. This was seduction, and what hurt before made her gasp with pleasure now as he circled the tight hole, inching his finger in, holding her down until she was taking it all, drawing it out before shoving it back in, stretching her to his pleasure. Making her feel.

"God, baby, you make me burn."

She moaned in response.

"Tell me you like that." It was all she could do to nod. He pumped his finger in and out two or three times, letting her imagine how it would be if it was his cock. More stomping came from the woods. His finger withdrew. Her ass clenched on air, wanting it back. Another slap on her ass, this one more tender, followed by a soothing rub.

"Stop seducing me, woman. We've got company."

He rolled her off his lap, laughing as she pushed her hair out of her face and glared at him. He dragged her forward for a kiss. Reaching underneath him, he handed her her pantaloons. She snatched them from him, fire in her cheeks, fire in her eyes, everything about her burning.

She just had time to pull her dress over her head and turn her back and button it before Ace came out of the woods. She quickly stuffed her pantaloons down her bodice.

"You could have given us a few more minutes," Caden said.

"Hell, if I gave you a few more minutes, my stomach would be gnawing on my backbone. Besides, no matter how long I gave you two, I can see it wouldn't be enough."

Embarrassment and desire warred for dominance inside Maddie. "I'm going to go to the creek and wash up."

Ace handed her a pot. "I'll make some oatmeal if you fill that up."

She grabbed it along with some soap and disappeared down to the water. She made short work of cleaning up, braiding her hair quickly, washing her face and arms, between her legs and under her arms, freshening as best she could until the day warmed up and a swim would be comfortable. Then she'd have Caden come down with her and guard her while she took a full bath. She imagined how he'd look sitting on the bank. Those gray-blue eyes of his studying her, looking so beautiful in the sunshine. Maybe she'd invite him in and bathe him, too.

Heavens, she was turning into a wanton woman, something she'd often been called but had never had a clue as to what it really meant. But with her husband, oh, she defined the word, and it was just another supposedly bad thing that was incredibly good. With the right person. Caden was correct. The right person made all the difference

Gathering up her soap before filling the pot with water, as requested, she hurried back to the campsite. When she was almost to the edge of the woods, she heard Ace ask Caden, "Did you tell her yet?"

There was a pause before Caden said, "No."

She assumed he was shaking his head.

"When do you plan on springing it on her?"

"When it's time."

"We're packing up in an hour. You going to wait until she's on the horse?"

"She'll ask herself before then."

"So why not tell her now?"

She stepped a little closer, wanting to see Caden's face when he answered whatever Ace was asking. With a wave of his hand, he said, "She'll figure it out long before that."

"When she does, what are you going to tell her?"

"The truth."

"Which is?"

"None of your damn business."

"I'm thinking you should have told her before you made love to her."

"Why?"

"So she had a choice."

"She has a choice."

"I'm thinking maybe she wouldn't have wanted to be on the love-'em-and-leave-'em list."

"Love 'em and leave 'em?" Caden scoffed.

Inside, the ice started, freezing over her warm glow of happiness. "What do you call it? You probably spent the whole night making her depend on you, open up to you, care about you, and six hours from now you're going to drop her off in town by herself. How the hell do you think she's going to feel?"

"She's my wife. She'll be fine."

"She's a woman. She's going to be mad as hell."

"Then she'll be mad. It's the way it's gotta be."

"Why, because you say so?"

Caden slammed his hat on his head. "Mind your own business, Ace."

Maddie stood there, pot in hand, and let the horrible reality sink in. He was leaving her?

"Maddie's Hell's Eight. She is my business."

"She's my wife. My hand trumps yours."

"Just because you say so doesn't make it a fact."

"In this case, it does."

Maddie took another step into the campsite. Ace and Caden were facing each other, shoulders set, feet braced.

Water sloshed over the pot onto her foot. It was cold, just adding to the chill taking her over.

"You're leaving me?" she asked Caden.

"You can't stay here."

"Why?"

"It's not safe."

"It's been safe enough for the last two days."

Caden looked at Ace. Ace folded his arms across his chest; Caden made a sound like a growl under his breath.

"No, it hasn't. I didn't want you to worry, but the Comanche have been raiding."

"So? They won't bother us here."

Caden ran his fingers through his hair. "Honey, they'd bother you wherever you were."

"So we can go to Culbart's." Anywhere but a town full of judgmental people.

"The hell you will."

"What's wrong with Culbart's?"

"He doesn't have enough men to protect you."

"He's got practically an army and he gets along with the Comanche. He gives them beef."

A dark expression passed over Caden's face. "Honey, the anger these boys are carrying, a few head of beef isn't going to make any difference."

She looked at Ace. He had the same dark expression on his face that Caden did.

"He's right. The only place you'll be safe is in town."

Damn him for siding with Caden, but what did she expect? They were like brothers.

"I don't want to go to town." Strangers were in town.

People who might know her were in town. Shame was in town.

"You need to go."

"You're going to stay with me?"

Caden shook his head. "I can't leave the claim right now. I found a place where the collapse made a fresh tunnel. If I can get in there, I might be able to get to the gold."

"And that matters." *Unlike me.*

"Honey, that's our future."

No. Their future was him and her together.

"You never said you loved me..."

He didn't say a word, and it suddenly became vitally important that when she'd told him she loved him, he hadn't said the words back.

"Aw, hell, Caden," Ace said.

Ace's reprimand was like a nail in the coffin of her dreams. She just shook her head. He'd played her for a fool. And she'd let him.

Without a word, she put the pot on the fire and started packing up the bedroll. Everything in her waited for Caden to come to her, but he didn't. It was worse that Ace was there to see it, but not by much. Not much could make what was horrible any worse.

When she had the bedrolls rolled up tight and tied closed, leaving enough rope to tie it to the saddle, she stood.

Caden took a step forward and reached out. "Maddie..."

It was too little too late. She shook her head and

clutched the bedroll to her chest, meeting his gaze dead on, feeling that buzz in the outside of her mind, unable to touch it the way she used to be able to, unable to escape and to pretend. She just had to stand here and feel the humiliation and pain crash over her. She had to endure it, and it was all his fault.

With a shake of her head, she took another step back. "You should never have kissed me."

THE RIDE TO Simple was accomplished in silence, during which Caden shot her assessing looks and Ace concerned ones, but neither man spoke, not that she wanted them to. Her hold on her composure was so delicate she felt as if she was broken into a million pieces inside, her heart lost somewhere among the fragments. There was a reason whores didn't kiss. She thought that rule didn't apply to her because she had a husband, but it wasn't the truth. Husbands were the most dangerous of all.

She let him lead her through town. She let him bring her to the hotel. She listened as he told the hotelier that he wanted a room for a month. She watched the money change hands, took the receipt when Caden gave it to her.

"You might need that."

She nodded. A woman alone was vulnerable to a lot of things, including the dishonesty of a hotel clerk who might want to pocket the difference and kick her out. She let Caden lead her up to her room. It was clean and functional. A vase of flowers on the bed stand added a touch of color. They didn't cheer her up.

Caden sighed. "Maddie, look at me."

Instead of looking at him, she walked past him, opened the door and stood by it. If he wanted to leave, then he needed to be about it.

"There's nothing to say."

"I'm not abandoning you."

He'd paid for a month in advance, and he was leaving. She knew how this worked. At the end of that month, he wouldn't be back. At the end of that month, she'd either have a new protector or she'd be on the street. This was the way men said goodbye when they wanted to pretend they didn't have anything to be guilty for. Temporary safety followed by nothing. How could she have been so wrong about him?

"Do you like the room?" he asked.

She nodded. "It's fine."

"I'll be back for you, Maddie. I need to get that claim tied up, but I'll be back."

She shook her head, giving him the acceptance that he seemed to want, knowing in her heart he wouldn't. They never came back.

"Goddamn it." He crossed the room, his boots making hollow thumps with every step. Grabbing her by the shoulders, he pulled her up into his embrace. His mouth slammed down on hers with a passion that had so excited her last night but right now just left her cold. Fake. It was all fake. Love on her side, convenience on his.

He stepped back, giving her a shake. "I'm goddamn well coming back for you, Maddie, and your ass had better be here."

She just stared at him and nodded, giving him again

what he wanted to hear, knowing the truth behind his statements.

"I'll be here." Where else would she go? She didn't have money or family. Simple was as good a place as any to start over. Right now it was the only place she had.

"Good. You've got the receipt. The clerk gives you any guff, you show it to the sheriff, but don't you give it over. You hold on to it. It's your proof."

She nodded. He wouldn't be so worried about that if he really planned on coming back. Caden took some more coin out of his bag and put it in her hand.

"That should give you plenty to eat. Just don't let anybody scam you. A meal should be no more than two bits. And try to stay in the room as much as possible. I don't want anyone to know you're here."

She nodded again. "Thank you."

The money burned her palm. Payoff for a guilty conscience. She wanted to throw it in his face.

"I gotta go, Maddie. I gotta get back to the claim. Can't leave it for too long in case jumpers find it."

"Or the Comanche."

His response was a bit too slow, but he nodded, "Yeah, or the Comanche."

"If it's that dangerous where you're going, how will I know whether you've survived?"

"If I don't come back in six weeks, notify Hell's Eight."

"And tell them what?"

"That I didn't keep my promise."

"You never keep your promises to me."

"Like hell!"

"You told me you wouldn't leave without saying good-bye."

"Okay, once. One time, Maddie. It didn't seem that important."

No, probably it didn't to him. To her it had been a promise that mattered.

"But that's the only time."

She shook her head. No. There were more. He'd promised not to hurt her, and right now she felt as if she was dying inside.

"Maddie."

"What?"

"Honey." His fingers stroked from her temple to her cheek down to her chin. "I'm coming back. I promise."

"All right."

His gaze dropped to her breasts; she folded her arms over them. If he wanted anything sexual from her again, he was going to have to take it. He'd raped her heart—what did it matter if he raped her body?

"I didn't want you to worry."

"You didn't want me to whine at you. You didn't want my distress to get in the way of your fun. You got what you wanted. Now just leave me alone."

"I can see there's no talking to you right now."

"No." No amount of talk would change reality.

He pointed his finger at her. "You be here when I get back."

She resisted the urge to bite it. "I already said I would be."

She was done running. If this was where she had to make her stand, this was where she was making it.

"Do you need anything else?"

A man I can believe in. It hurt her to look at him, to see what could have been, what she thought was, but what hurt worse was knowing that if she were a respectable woman this never would have happened. But she was a whore. They didn't command the same kind of decency. It was okay to trick a whore. It was okay to lie to a whore. Many men even considered it sport. But play those games with a decent woman? A man could expect her kin would come calling. Men didn't play those games with a respectable woman for the simple reason the price was too high.

A knock interrupted them. Ace stood in the open doorway.

"We're all set." Ace smiled at Maddie. "We gave you an account at the mercantile, paid them in advance." He handed her a receipt. She looked at the amount. It'd be enough for a few nice dresses. More guilt money.

"We'll be back in about a month," Ace said.

What did she expect? That he wouldn't back Caden's lie? Or maybe he actually believed it. It was hard to tell. More than once a friend had fooled a friend, but she knew even if he did, in the end it wouldn't matter. Ace would always be Caden's friend, and she would always be the whore that turned up at Hell's Eight and tried to make something out of nothing.

She looked out the window. The afternoon was pass-ing. "Don't you need to go?"

Ace looked at Caden and frowned. She looked at both of them and felt nothing. She was so numb inside, so blessedly numb, and she hadn't even had to escape to her pretend world to achieve it.

"Yeah. We do." Still, Caden lingered. Finally, he put his hat on his head in that way that said he'd reached his limit. "Remember, Maddie, if you need help, send a telegram to Caine Allen care of Padre Bernard in San Antonio."

She nodded.

"Write that down."

She didn't bother. She was never going to send a tele-gram to the padre.

He ended up writing it down for her. There wasn't anything else to say, and after a long, awkward pause, Ace left. Caden paused a little bit longer, then with the brush of his fingers over her cheek he said, "You take care of yourself, and remember, I *am* coming back."

She nodded, closed the door behind him. A turn of the key and the door locked, the soft click signaling the end. After all the work of the past year, she was right back where she'd started. Alone.

FOR THREE DAYS, Maddie didn't come out of that room. For three days she drank the tea the owner's wife sent up and nibbled on some jerky from the saddlebags. She wasn't hungry. She wasn't sad. She wasn't mad. She wasn't anything. She was alone in a strange town the way whores always ended up.

On the fourth day, she started to get mad. It began with a dream, the one she'd often had as a child in which her mother wasn't her mother but someone else, someone soft and caring, someone who protected her from the world, who cooked her meals, who smiled at her achievements. That dream always angered her because when she opened her eyes, the contrast between what she wanted and what she had was so vivid it was like a smack in the face.

She sat by the window that day, watching everybody outside going about their lives, women and men moving from building to building with purpose, children gathering in the street to play hoop and stick, tag or hide-and-seek. Everybody, it seemed—except her—had a purpose. If she listened to Caden, her purpose was to sit and wait. But she knew what that would get her. If she listened to her mother, her purpose was to serve men. She knew what that wouldn't get her. If she listened to Tia, it was to be a good wife. If she listened to Desi and Bella, it was to be whoever she wanted to be. She continued to stare out the window and watch people with lives go about living them.

That day she ordered up dinner, eating alone in her room, chewing food that had no taste, wishing for bread that wasn't there, her mind going around and around.

On the fifth day, when she woke up she took her seat by the window and studied the scene again. Carriages bustled up and down the streets, families gathered at the restaurant.

The next day she did the same. Doing nothing but watch as the hours ground by.

By the seventh day, she couldn't stand it anymore. She had to leave her room, and the excuse sat on the table. They hadn't sent bread again with her lunch.

Taking her remaining coins and putting them into the pocket on the inside of her skirt, she marched down the stairs, stopping at the front desk to ask where the restaurant was. The clerk pointed two doors down on the right. She thanked him and headed that way.

When she entered, it was obvious the proprietors were gearing up for lunch. She could hear the sounds of chopping, and the smell of oil heating and onions cooking filled the restaurant. She went to the back. A harried woman in her forties looked up.

"I'm sorry. If you're looking for work, I don't have anything."

"I'm not looking for work, I'm staying at the hotel. I'm Maddie Miller." It felt strange to introduce herself as that.

"I'm Lucia Salinger, and the man at the stove is my husband, Antonio." She was attractive in a homey sort of way. She made Maddie think of hugs and kisses and the comforts of home. She had big brown eyes, an olive complexion to her skin, a red mouth and dark hair that was just showing streaks of gray. "What can I do for you? Lunch service isn't for another hour."

Maddie shook her head. "I don't want lunch. I want bread."

"Excuse me?"

"I've ordered meals from here for three days, and every single time you've forgotten to send the bread."

Lucia straightened and slid her hands down her stained apron.

"I'm sorry the meal wasn't to your liking."

Maddie shook her head again. "The meal was fine, but my bread was missing."

"I haven't had time to bake it, and there's no bakery in town, so it's not that we've forgotten. There just hasn't been any. We gave you an extra helping to make up the difference."

"Don't usually serve bread?"

"Heck," Antonio said. "We've been so busy, what with a new crop of miners coming through every day, just putting food on the table has been a challenge."

She hadn't considered that, but as she did, a possibility occurred. "Would you sell it if you could?"

"Hell, yeah. Nothing a man likes better than fresh baked bread. Could probably sell all we had and make a fortune off it, too. Nothing like baked goods to make a man start thinking of home." He turned the meat he was cooking. "Problem is, we don't have a baker."

She nodded and looked around, a wild idea taking hold. "I can bake."

The claim came out so faintly she wasn't surprised when Antonio said, "Excuse me?"

She swallowed and tried again. She'd never shot for

a respectable job, never been among respectable people, but in a month her money ran out and so would her options. If there was ever a time for bold moves, this was it. "I can bake."

"Why would you want to be baking? You're staying at the hotel."

She swallowed and cleared her throat. "That situation is temporary."

Lucia's eyebrows went up; Antonio took the skillet off the fire and put it to the side. He was a heavyset man with fleshy features, but he had kind eyes.

"Did you lose your husband?"

"Yes." It wasn't a lie. She'd never really had him and now he was gone. "And I've only got enough money to last until the end of the month."

Lucia set her hands on her hips. With doubt clearly in her voice, she said, "But you can bake."

If the subject had been anything other than her baking abilities, Maddie would have been cowed, but this she knew. "Yes, I can bake."

The woman frowned and said something to her husband in a language Maddie didn't understand. Antonio answered her in the same language. Lucia turned back to her. "You wouldn't be lying to me, would you?"

Maddie walked over to the wall where the supplies were stacked behind a well-used wooden table. The supplies in the kitchen were stored the same way they were at Tia's. It wasn't hard to find the flour.

"Do you have starter?"

A little of the tension left Lucia's stance. Pulling a

crock from the side, she slid it across the wooden table. "Yes, I kept that alive at least."

That was good. Maddie grabbed an apron off the hook.

"Rather than telling you, why don't I just show you?"

CHAPTER FIFTEEN

A WEEK LATER Maddie was exhausted. What Antonio had said was true—whatever bread she baked was gone before half the evening was over. She couldn't keep up with the demand. If she had more oven time, she might have been able to, or even if she'd had more space to work in, but in the Salingers' cramped kitchen, there was only so much she could do. If she had a place of her own, though, her baked goods would be the real gold.

She fingered the money in her pocket. Part of her deal with the Salingers was she got free meals. She hadn't spent much of the money Caden had left her for food, so on top of that she had the percentage of receipts from her baked goods. She didn't know if it was enough to open her own business, but it might be a start.

Once she had the thought about starting her own business it wouldn't let go. A home of her own. A future of her own. She remembered the phrase *I was going to* that had haunted her life for so long. Her own "going to" list sat completely neglected: start a business, buy a house, travel the world. All that took money. Money she didn't have. Money she'd never have if she stayed as she was. Money she *might* have if she took a chance.

Maddie clutched the new money in her hand and

looked out the window of her hotel room at all those
people going to all those places with all that purpose,
leading lives of which she had always been envious. She
came to a decision. She was tired of being on the outside.
It was time she did something about it. She left her room
and went downstairs, stopping at the front desk as she
always did to see if there was a telegram from Caden,
some recognition that she existed. There was none. She
thanked the clerk, straightened her skirts and stepped
out into the sunlight. The first piece of business was to
find a place in which she could work.

   She wandered down the street, going from house to
house, and learned the truth of a boomtown. Housing
was scarce. At the edge of the alley beside the mercantile was a for-rent sign with an arrow pointing down
the alley. She thought it might be a room, but when she
went down the narrow passage, she discovered a little
house at the end. No one was about, so she let herself in
and looked around. It was small, just two rooms—a living room with a couch, an end table and kerosene light,
with a kitchen beyond. Through the kitchen window she
could make out an outhouse in the back. It was a tiny
place, but the stove was big and there was enough room
for two worktables. Her heart started pounding faster
in her chest. The sign outside said to inquire at the mercantile. She headed over, walked up to the front counter
and waited, her breath catching in her throat, butterflies
tumbling about in her belly. A balding gentleman with
spectacles perched on the end of his nose came over.

   "Can I help you, ma'am?"

She still couldn't get used to being called *ma'am.*

"There's a house out back for rent."

"Ah, that was my mother-in-law's. God rest her soul."

"She died?"

"Wife said not to admit this, but yeah, she died on that couch."

Maddie didn't care about the couch.

"How much?"

He named a price for a month that made her blink. It was double the cost of her hotel room.

He shrugged at her gasp. "Property's expensive around here, ma'am. Town's booming, growing fast."

Yes, it was. "For that price, I'd need somebody to chop wood."

"Wood, ma'am?"

She looked around the store. The shelves containing sweets were almost bare. Maybe she could haggle.

"Yes, I'm a baker."

"You don't say." As casual as the statement was, there was some interest in his face.

"I could give you some baked goods to sell in exchange for the services."

"I got a boy old enough to split wood."

"He would need to be reliable."

"So would you."

"I am."

He looked at her, considering her words. "Are you any good?"

She nodded. "Yes."

"Still going to need the rent up front."

The money Caden had given her for food would cover
supplies, but the rent—

"I'll pay you three weeks' in advance and a week's
baked goods free."

He looked at her. "I could rent that place out for more."

"And likely have it filled with miners. Do you really
want those wild men that close to your wife and children?"

It was a guess that he had both. A guess that paid off.

"Nah, that's why it's still sitting empty."

"Then do we have a deal?"

He eyed her again, looked at her bare ring finger, her
dusty clothes. "We have a deal. But before we finalize
it, I want to sample your baking. If I don't like what you
produce, the deal's off."

She nodded. "You could talk to Lucia at the restaurant. She'll vouch for me. But I assure you it won't be
a problem."

His expression softened. He looked at her empty ring
finger again. "I'll settle for a week up front and weekly
rent after that."

With that she could easily afford the supplies to
get started. Relief so strong it was debilitating flowed
through her. "Thank you."

"And, ma'am? If you give me your order for what you
need to get started—sugar, flour and the like —I'll have
it delivered to the house."

Were her dire straits so obvious? Even if they were,
what did she care. She was starting her own business.

She told him what she needed, and he wrote it down. When she said *cinnamon,* his eyes lit up.

"You're gonna make rolls?"

She nodded. "If you've got enough."

"I've got a ton of the stuff. Got it off a merchant who couldn't make it all the way over to California. Too expensive for most folks around here."

He named the price.

"It's a little expensive even for me."

"You really that good?"

She borrowed a bit of Caden's confidence. "And then some."

He named a lower price. "We'll make it up in the sale of the baked goods."

She figured they would. And after the first week, they'd both be sharing the profits. Wavering between panic and excitement, her heart pounding in her throat, Maddie walked back to the hotel. If this didn't work, she'd be out on her butt in a week rather than three. It was a gamble.

I was going to... She heard Hilda's rattling whisper again.

By the end of the week she might be without a home, but at the end of the week she wouldn't be saying *I was going to* when it came to starting her own business. It would be done.

Marching up to the clerk at the front desk, she told him what she wanted. He balked at refunding her the money Caden had paid in advance. She planted her feet and brought out the Hell's Eight reputation. He caved.

She tucked the precious hoard of coins into a handkerchief and pinned it inside her bodice, then headed to the restaurant to let the Salingers know this was going to be her last night, but also to explain she was starting her own bakery and they could buy her breads separately.

They weren't happy and at first tried to keep her. She knew why. The money they were earning on bread sales would be money in Maddie's pocket after tonight, but then, with surprising good humor, Antonio wished her well and told her he'd be buying whatever she had.

It was a start.

THE FIRST THREE days, Maddie did nothing but bake. She kneaded until her arms felt as if they were going to fall off and her fingers were so stiff she couldn't even hold a hairbrush. She created loaf after loaf and then she started throwing in some sweet rolls and cinnamon rolls, drizzling them with icing and bringing them to the mercantile. It got so folks knew when she was going to be baking what, and the miners were lining up at the door to her house, sometimes drunk, sometimes sober, but always ready to buy whatever she had to offer. Though sometimes they thought she had something to offer other than breads. Those times were scary.

When Antonio got word of it, he gave her a gun. She learned to keep it strapped to her hip. It soon became easy to identify the rowdy ones and the troublemakers, and by the evening of the fifth day, she discovered something else. A hardworking woman with a product that people wanted tended to be protected by the people who wanted that product.

When one man started harassing her, it was the crowd itself that took him out, grabbing him by the arms, shoving him to the back, telling him he wasn't welcome. It was astounding to watch, and when the man was gone, two of the miners sat in front of her door, picked up sticks and started whittling. When she caught their eye, they told her to get back to work, she needn't worry at all about anything else, and she understood. She had a place here now. As long as she could crank out cinnamon buns and bread, she was valuable.

She made her rent the first week by the skin of her teeth after paying for her supplies, but the second week she had a little profit left over and the third week she had enough that she began to consider that maybe, seeing as she was a woman alone, a bank might be a better proposition for her profits than a jar on her counter. So she found time between shifts and she took a bath, put on her one clean dress and went over to the bank.

She'd never been in a bank before. She'd passed by many, but never dared to step through the imposing doors. Today was no exception. There was something intimidating about bank doors. Something so important and respectable she couldn't see herself going in. Only the amount of money in her reticule kept her from turning tail and running. It was all she had in the world. It needed to be kept in a safer place than a jar in her rented house. Besides, businesspeople had bank accounts.

"Good morning, ma'am."

She jumped and then smiled at the dapperly dressed gentleman about to enter the bank.

"Good morning."

He tipped his bowler hat slightly. He had kind eyes behind his wire-rimmed spectacles. "Are you thinking of coming or going?"

"I want to open an account."

She hadn't meant to blurt it out. She couldn't blame him for smiling.

"Well, then, I'm the man you want to see. John Laughton."

He opened the door and held it for her.

"Oh." Beyond she could see the orderly room with its heavy desks, leather chairs and railed counter. Brass gleamed on the ends of posts. Everything was clean and shiny. Prosperous. The child inside Maddie cried that she didn't belong there. The woman inside her tried to convince herself otherwise. "Maddie...Miller."

"Nice to meet you, Mrs. Miller." With a wave of his hand, he motioned her through. "After you."

She didn't have a choice then but to step inside. The place even smelled like money. And lemon oil. She clutched her reticule tightly as she followed John Laughton through the bank and into an office beyond the counter. He motioned her into the big chair in front of an equally big desk. "Have a seat."

"Thank you."

She perched on the edge of the seat. He moved around the desk and sat in the high-backed chair behind. The brown of his suit blended with the leather chair, giving him more substance.

"Have you had an account with us before?"

"No."

He opened a drawer and brought out a ledger, opening it to a marked page. Dipping a pen in the inkwell, he looked up, "Does your husband have an account with us?"

She had no ring on her finger, so he had to be fishing. She sat a little straighter. "I don't know."

His eyebrows raised. "Perhaps you should talk to him about it and come back."

"He's not available."

Another lift of those eyebrows. "We do require his signature, you understand."

"But it's my money."

"Yes, but he's your husband."

"I don't understand."

"Are you recently married, Mrs. Miller?"

She licked her lips, unsure if it mattered. "What makes you think that?"

"Your hesitation over giving your name."

"Oh. Yes."

"I have to inform you, ma'am, without his signature, you can't open an account."

"But if he signs, he has access to my money."

"He has access to your money anyway. He's your husband."

"Oh." She hadn't known that. The reticule seemed to grow heavier in her lap. Now that she'd talked herself into putting her money into the bank, she couldn't stand the thought of it being as vulnerable there as on her kitchen counter.

"He's not available," she repeated softly.

"When will he be?"

She gave him the truth. "I don't know."

"I'm sure your pin money will be safe wherever you've been keeping it."

She shook her head. "No."

"I wish I could help you, but there are rules we have to follow."

She fought back the urge to flee this place. She turned her head as the bank doors opened and Antonio came in with the deposit from the weekend. He was a foreigner yet he walked right up to the counter as if he had a right. She'd seen his money; it was no different than hers. His business was no different than hers. The only difference was in how she saw herself. And how Mr. Laughton saw her. And she asked herself a question. *How would Bella handle this?* The answer was simple. Head-on, using the leverage she had.

"I don't think you understand." Maddie placed her reticule on the desk. The bag bulged substantially. "I've started a rather successful business. *Pin money* does not quite describe my profits."

Laughton's eyes dropped to the reticule.

She opened the bag and dumped the contents on the desk. All ninety-five dollars of it. A fortune to her. And apparently not small change to him, either.

"How long have you been saving?"

"Eight days."

He reached for the money, stopping just before he touched it. "May I?"

She nodded. He deftly counted it.

He neatly stacked the bills and coins. "You earned this in eight days?"

"Business started slow, but it's picking up."

He sat back in his chair. "May I ask what sort of business you've invested in?"

His tone implied it must be unsavory. Maddie forced a smile. "I opened a bakery."

His whole demeanor changed. Leaning forward, he asked, "You're the one who made those cinnamon rolls my wife's been buying?"

"I assume so."

From across the room, Antonio spotted her and waved. When she waved back, he held up his finger indicating she should wait. Mr. Laughton watched the exchange. "You know Mr. Salinger?"

"I supply his restaurant with breads and desserts."

"I see."

Before she could say anything further, Antonio came over. Mr. Laughton discreetly covered her money with his blotter. Antonio smiled at her then Mr. Laughton. "I see you have met our own personal gold mine, yes? She makes the bread the miners cannot pay enough for." He released a kiss into the air with an expressive motion of his hand.

"We were just talking business," Laughton said.

Antonio patted her on the back. "This one has a good

sense for it. No frivolous girl, but a lioness. She will make us all rich."

"You don't say."

"I do, but I came to make a request if I may interrupt." He looked to Maddie.

Maddie smiled. "Of course."

"I would like to double our order for next weekend. The men are taking the bread home. We run out too soon."

"Of course." She'd make more money if they bought directly from her, but Antonio stayed open late on weekends and she did have to sleep. Maybe, though, if the shop made a bit more profit, she could afford help.

"You can do this? It is not too much?"

"I can do this."

"Good. Good. Lucia will be very happy."

Maddie smiled, suddenly not feeling so out of place. "Please give her my regards."

"This I will do, now back to work I must go."

As soon as he left, Maddie sighed and reached for her money. "I need to go, too."

Instead of handing her back her money, Mr. Laughton handed her a signature card. "If you'll just sign your husband's name on that line—" he tapped the middle of the card "—we'll get you squared away."

Startled, she looked up. "But…?"

He raised his brows at her. "Sometimes the rules are meant to be bent."

And right then she understood something else. Money opened doors for her that would otherwise be closed.

While she waited for Mr. Laughton to fill out her receipt, she felt the first niggles of pride. She folded the receipt carefully when he handed it to her, trying hard not to burst into laughter. She was a businesswoman. She was providing for herself. She was respectable. Standing, she held out her hand to the banker. As he took it she said, "Good day, Mr. Laughton." She smiled and squeezed his hand. "And thank you."

THE NEXT WEEK PASSED in a blur of baking and preparation. The hectic pace was only broken by a niggling sense of unease, as though someone was watching, but whenever Maddie looked, she saw nothing out of place. No matter what she did, she couldn't shake the unease that just kept growing stronger and stronger. She started going to the bank twice a day, too nervous to keep money around the house. It made her feel better, but only a little. And as every day passed, she grew more and more nervous about Caden's return until she began to connect the two.

The day he was scheduled to come back, she woke up in a sweat, her mind racing, her pulse pounding, fear vibrating through her body. Lighting the lamp, she immediately glanced toward the window, but there was only her own reflection looking back at her. Lying back on the couch, she took a breath and forced her muscles to relax. Caden had told her to stay put, but she wasn't where he'd left her. For that matter she wasn't even *who* he'd left, and she didn't kid herself that that was going to go over well. Caden wasn't a man who liked surprises, and he didn't like it when things didn't go his way.

She got off the couch, wiping the sweat from her brow. Summer was upon them full force and the heat was stifling in the little house. She poured water from the pitcher she'd set out the night before into the basin, rubbed soap onto a cloth and washed the sweat from her body. She wished it was as easy to wash the dread from her mind. She'd worked so hard for what she had. She couldn't lose it.

She glanced over at her pistol lying on the table. She hadn't carried it for a couple weeks now. It wasn't necessary. Those who'd caused trouble had gotten the message. She was under the town's protection. Today, after she got dressed, she'd wear it, though. This was her business. No one, but no one, was taking it away from her.

With a sigh she went to the back door and opened it. The kitten that had adopted her meowed and curled around her feet.

"Good morning, Precious. Today's our big day."

The cat meowed again and wandered around her feet, wanting some of the milk that she gave her every morning.

"Let's get our business taken care of and then I will." She stopped at the outhouse before heading back to the well, drawing up water, washing her hands again before filling a kitchen bucket. Precious meowed along at her side, complaining at the delay of her breakfast the way she did every day. Maddie shook her head and smiled. The kitten was a handful and demanding, but it was her kitten. Her first pet in her first house at her first job, and she'd kill anybody that hurt her.

She picked up the cat and touched her nose to hers.

"Coming right up." She set the kitten back down, picked the bucket back up and went in the house to pour a little saucer of milk. She set it outside along with some leftover stew from the night before.

The kitten licked at the stew, choosing the bits it wanted and devouring them rapidly, then lapped daintily at the milk. Precious definitely had her preferences. At first Maddie had worried that the dogs would get her kitten, but Precious was smart. She knew how to survive. Sometimes late at night Maddie thought Precious could teach her survival lessons, because it was late at night when her resolve wavered and she remembered being in Caden's arms, how close she'd felt to him, how carefully he'd made love to her, how special she'd felt, and it was hard the next morning to wake up and realize that it had all been part of a game. One she didn't understand, but a game nonetheless.

Going back out, she gathered some wood and brought it in, stoking the embers on the stove, opening the doors to both ends of the house. She couldn't wait for the day she could afford an outside stove. It was hot cooking in the little house to the level she had to.

Two hours later a knock came at the sill. Maddie smiled, seeing little Lissie Mayers with a basket on her arm.

"Are those my eggs?"

The little girl nodded. Maddie grabbed the cinnamon roll she'd wrapped and set aside the night before along with the coins.

"How much did your mama say to give you?"

She held up two fingers. Maddie gave her the coin.

"And this is for you." She handed her the bun. The little girl's face lit up and she smiled, revealing two missing front teeth.

Maddie wondered what it would be like to have a child of her own. She sighed and lifted her braid off the nape of her neck. She sighed. She needed to go back to the attorney she'd consulted with after the revelation at the bank. Before, she'd asked the lawyer all about her business, but she'd never asked him if she was truly married, and if she was, how did she get out of it because she couldn't see giving up the independence she'd forged for herself the past few weeks to a man's control. And if Caden came back, that was exactly what would happen. Everything would be his to dispose of as he willed, including her, and she couldn't have that.

She waited that whole day on pins and needles, anxiety eating at her appetite, even affecting her baking. Her bread wasn't as light as it normally was. Nobody complained, but she knew and so did some of her customers based on the looks they gave her. When darkness fell and there was still no Caden, Maddie let out a sigh of relief and started to believe that maybe he wasn't coming and all the things she worried about were not going to happen. But that night when she dreamed, it was of his hands on her face, his lips on hers, his whisper in her ear, and no matter how she tossed and turned every time she fell back asleep, she heard his promise and she cried.

She wasn't in a good mood when she got up the next

morning, so when the knock came at the door extra early, it didn't improve. Thinking it was Lissie, she grabbed the egg money and walked to the living room only to stop dead when the door opened. Frank Culbart. A different Frank than she remembered. He had shaved his beard. His hair was combed back and his clothes were clean. He still looked like a big bear and he still had that aggressive set to his shoulders, but when she looked into his eyes, she would have sworn she saw softness.

"Maddie."

She wished her face wasn't sweaty and her hair wasn't sticking to her temples. She wished her hands weren't coated in flour.

"Frank."

"I heard you were in town."

"You heard I was?"

He shrugged. "A pretty redhead named Maddie that bakes like a dream? Couldn't be that many in the state."

She smiled. "You always did have a sweet tooth for my cinnamon rolls."

"I could go for one right now and a cup of coffee if you've got time."

She didn't, but she'd make it. She considered telling him to go around back, but then she realized how that would look. She stepped back and let him in. She saw him wince at the heat in the house.

"It's the oven," she explained. "I have to have it on all day to fill orders," she explained. "But you're welcome to come sit out back. There's a nice shade tree."

He nodded. She led him through the house. He paused

in the kitchen and looked at her organized chaos. His brow went up.

"You're doing well for yourself, then."

She nodded, not sure what he wanted. She stopped and poured him a cup of coffee and handed it to him.

"I'll be right out with the cinnamon rolls. I have to take them out of the oven."

"I'll wait."

She was starting to protest. He made her uncomfortable the way he watched her, but he was a guest in her house, and even in a whorehouse that had meaning.

She pulled the cinnamon rolls out of the oven, whipped the icing, moved them to a plate and drizzled it over them. She scooped one up and handed it to him on a cloth so he wouldn't burn his fingers. He smiled and polished it off as if it wasn't piping hot, his expression melting in bliss.

"I made a mistake marrying you off."

She raised an eyebrow at him. "Is that an apology?"

"More like regret. I should have kept you for myself."

"You're not in love with me, Frank. You're in love with somebody else."

"Don't matter. It's not like she's going to bake me cinnamon rolls."

She smiled and shook her head at him. "Maybe if you let her see your sweet side."

He motioned for another roll; she motioned him out the door.

"Go sit outside. I could use a break from this heat myself."

He grunted and went out. She put four rolls on a plate

and followed him. One would be for her, the other three for him.

She joined him with a coffee on the bench under the oak tree and handed him the rolls.

"Aren't you going to have any?"

"Three is all you get."

"You usually give me four."

"You already ate one."

He sighed. "Things didn't work out with that Caden fella, huh?"

She shook her head.

"You should have told us when we took you that you weren't a working girl anymore."

"You were a scary bunch."

He looked away, and if she wasn't mistaken, that was a hint of color on his cheekbones.

"I never forced myself on a woman. It didn't sit well, you almost having me force myself on you."

"Nobody forced you to do anything."

"I was drunk."

"You were sad and lonely."

He looked at her again. "You remind me of her."

"I do?"

He nodded. "She doesn't have your spirit, though."

"How can you say that?"

"She wouldn't leave her family to be with me."

"I wouldn't leave a whorehouse to be free."

He raised his eyebrows at her. "Why not? Did you like it there?"

"Oh, heavens, no."

"Then why didn't you leave?"

"Because it was terrifying not knowing what I would face if I left. I only knew those walls, those rules, and I believed they were as set as gospel."

He nodded.

"Elsbeth lives a very comfortable life. She's used to fancy things."

"And you don't consider yourself fancy." She didn't make it a question and he didn't pretend it was.

He held up his hands, showing the calluses and the scars. Even though he'd obviously cleaned up for her, there was still a little dirt under the nails.

"These aren't the hands of a gentleman."

She took one hand in hers and gave it a squeeze. "But they're honest hands that know honest work, and the woman that holds them wouldn't be let down."

He looked down at her hand holding his. "You're holding my hand."

She shook her head. "But I'm not the one you want."

"I can learn to make do."

She let go of his hand. "Are you proposing to me?"

"Would you be interested?"

She cocked her head to the side. As soon as Frank had realized that she wasn't a willing participant, he'd kicked her out of his bed, kicked her out of his house, actually, he was so angry. Ten minutes later, he'd brought her back in and read her the riot act about not being honest with people and the dangers that can happen to a woman who played games. He'd scared her so much she'd retreated and that had scared him, too.

He hadn't known what to do with her so he'd declared her off-limits to his men and declared that she was his guest. She hadn't been comfortable being his guest; owing a man meant being in his debt, and she didn't want to work off any debts. So one day she'd made rolls, and it had grown from there. Over breakfast, coffee, lunch and dinner, she and Frank had formed a friendship, and one night when he was drunk, she'd learned about his Elsbeth, the woman he loved, the woman he saw as out of his reach. The woman for whom he was building his empire so he'd have enough money to offer her what he thought she wanted. She shook her head. And men thought women had strange notions.

"You know, Frank," she said, "you might be surprised if you go back and ask Elsbeth again."

"Nah, no reason for her to change her mind."

"Yes, there is. When you think what you want is always going to be there, you tend to take it for granted. But when it leaves—" she thought of the way Caden had left her here "—you start rethinking who you are and what you want and what you would do over."

"Sounds like experience talking."

She nodded. "I've got a lot of experience. What I don't have is a lot of practice in making it make sense."

He ran his hand through his hair. The action separated the drying strands and they began to curl. She smiled. He truly was a decent man. Not the man for her, but a good man.

"She could be married by now."

"She might not be."

"I might get my heart kicked through my teeth."

She nodded. "You might."

"You think I should go?"

"I think I would rather know than not. It's going to take you years to build up that ranch, years where you'll be alone and she'll be alone. Maybe you're supposed to be, I don't know. But if I had the chance that you do, I'd at least like to know."

He wiped his hands on his napkin and swilled down the last of his coffee. For all he was a nice man and she knew him well, he was still a gruff man. He hugged her tight. He smelled of cigarettes and musk and a slight tinge of sweat. It wasn't a bad smell.

"Are you sure you wouldn't rather just hitch your wagon to mine?"

She smiled, but it wasn't the right smell, either. "You wouldn't be happy. I'd just be a substitute for the one you wanted."

"I'd try."

She nodded. "I know. But I'd always know."

"There's also the catch she's already married," a voice added in an all-too-familiar drawl.

Caden.

Maddie spun around. He stood in the doorway to the house looking out at them, his hand on the butt of his revolver, and he didn't look happy.

Damn.

CHAPTER SIXTEEN

MADDIE JUMPED TO her feet, but Frank didn't. He calmly
finished his cinnamon roll and licked the icing from his
fingers. Maddie's breath caught in her throat and not for
any of the reasons she expected. It didn't seem possible,
but she'd forgotten how handsome he was, how rugged,
how just the sight of him made her heart skip a beat.

"Culbart." Caden nodded to him.

"Miller," Culbart replied, casually getting to his feet
and wiping his fingers on the napkin Maddie had provided. "What brings you into town?"

Caden tore his eyes from Maddie to look at Culbart.

"Seems to me that might be my question."

"Word of a redheaded woman baking cinnamon rolls
like a dream spread out to the ranch. Just thought I'd
check it out."

"Don't you have enough trouble to keep you at home?"

"I don't think—" Maddie began.

Culbart shushed her with the raise of his hand. "This
is between the menfolk, Maddie."

How could it not concern her? Before she could say
anything more, Caden jumped into the fray.

"That's my wife you're talking to."

The threat embedded in Caden's low drawl didn't

seem to have the impact on Culbart that it did on her. Whereas she wanted to retreat, Frank seemed...invigorated. She crossed her arms over her chest, shielding herself from the animosity.

"If she's your wife, why is she all alone struggling to make ends meet? Working her a—" He stopped himself. "Working her behind off trying to make ends meet? If she's your wife, why haven't you provided for her?"

Caden took a step closer to her, forcing her a step back. Away from Frank, she realized. "Nothing about my wife is your business."

Maddie immediately felt guilty. Caden had been generous. He'd made sure she had enough money to see her through.

"He takes care of me fine, Frank."

Frank looked at the dark circles under her eyes, the flour on her clothing. "I can see that."

"The business was my idea."

"Why would a woman with a good husband put her hand to work?"

"That's a good question, and as soon as you leave, Maddie and I will be discussing it."

Maddie didn't like his tone. "There's nothing to discuss."

Caden's brow went up in the way that said she was pushing him. She didn't care. Neither, apparently, did Culbart. "I don't recall the lady asking me to leave."

The last thing Maddie wanted was a showdown in her backyard. They were both big, both mean and probably both fought to the death, and for her there was no winning if either one died. She had to make a choice. Frank might be a friend, but Caden was her husband and Hell's Eight.

"It's all right, Frank. I appreciate your concern, but I do have things to discuss with my husband."

"I think," Culbart said quietly in that deep voice of his, "that you, Miller, and the rest of Hell's Eight are going to discover that there is more to little Maddie than you gave her credit for." He settled his hat on his head. "But since I care about Maddie's welfare, I'm going to give you a bit of advice."

Caden grabbed her arm and pushed her behind him with controlled violence. "Shove your advice."

Culbart's lips twitched. "Your tendency to be an arrogant bastard isn't going to get you what you want." Culbart touched his fingers to the rim of his hat. "Maddie."

"Goodbye, Frank."

He turned and headed down the alley alongside the house. Maddie watched him go, counting his steps, trying to regulate her heartbeat. It didn't help. It was pounding wildly.

"He's gone. You can stop pretending to watch him now."

Folding her arms across her chest, she faced Caden. "You're mad."

"Of course I'm mad. I left you plenty of money. What the hell happened?"

"Nothing happened. I saw an opportunity."

"To rub my name in the dirt? Everyone here knows you're my wife."

She shrugged. "Now everyone here knows I can bake."

"And this gets you what?"

"Respect."

"You had that before."

"As your wife, not as me."

"And it matters?"

Maddie scooped up the napkins and tossed them on the plate before grabbing the handles of the empty coffee cups and carried everything back into the house. When she got to the door, Caden was there ahead of her, holding it open.

"I asked you a question."

"The answer is obvious."

"I still want to hear it."

She placed the dishes on the counter and spun around. "Why? Because I didn't sit in that hotel room and wait for my money to run out?"

"I told you I was coming back."

"Men always say they're coming back."

"I'm not all men. I'm your husband."

"And you left me. You told me you wouldn't but you did, another promise broken."

"I kept my word and came back."

"Seems to me you're not too picky about what word you keep and what you break."

Caden sighed. He poured hot water from the kettle into the basin. While she watched, he lathered up a cloth and took the cups from the counter and dropped them in. She watched, stunned, as he started to wash them.

"What?" he asked, a bit of the edge leaving his drawl. "Tia made sure we all knew how to clean."

She knew that. "But why are you doing it here?"

"Because this is our home and my hands are available and it looks like you could use the help."

She didn't have anything to say to that. While he washed, she took the time to inspect him for any visible wounds. He appeared fine.

"Did all go well at the mine?"

"A couple skirmishes. Nothing we couldn't handle."

"So there was no need for you to leave me here after all."

Caden set a freshly cleaned plate on the sideboard and wiped his hands on a towel. The distance she thought so safe between them was closed in two steps. His hand snaked around the back of her neck and pulled her up against him.

"I'm madder than shit right now, Maddie. I wouldn't suggest pushing me."

"How am I pushing you?"

"You're my goddamn wife. It's my job to keep you safe, not put you in harm's way just because you don't feel like spending some time without me."

She blinked at him. She hadn't thought of it that way.

"There's going to be a lot more Indian trouble around here. All those settlers that have got their homes out there are going to find out how lonely it is to be so far from help. Blood's going to be shed before this is over. A hell of a lot of it. I'm determined not one drop of it is going to be yours."

Again she didn't know what to say. "What about Hell's Eight?"

"We may come under attack, but we have the skills to defend it. And the hands. And our location definitely helps."

"What makes you so sure there's going to be bloodshed?"

His mouth tightened. "I can read signs."

"Seeing tracks in the ground tells you this?"

He dropped his hand from her neck. "Looking at burned and scalped bodies has a way of making a point."

She reached for the chair. "You saw bodies."

"Of course. So did Culbart. I suspect that's why he's here."

"He said he came to see me."

Caden snorted. "That might have been one of his reasons, but it's not the main one. I'll lay you money he came here looking for guns. His ranch is going to be one of the first to be attacked."

"Why, if he's got so many men to defend it?"

"To put the fear of God into the enemy. Take out a ranch like the Fallen C and you strike terror into the hearts of everyone around it."

"The Indians wouldn't attack the town, would they?"

"Not Simple, but maybe the smaller ones."

"Then I was safe."

"You were safe in the hotel. Here you're off by yourself, an easy target for any no-account that gets a notion. If I'd have wanted you ripe for the plucking, I would have just left you in the middle of the plains."

"If you wanted me safe, you wouldn't have left me anywhere. You'd have kept me with you."

"There's work I had to do at the mine. Time constraints on it."

"So you chose gold over me. Same thing."

"I chose our future."

"Our future? No, it's not our future when you can, on a whim, just set me aside, take all my money, take my children and just leave me behind."

He blinked. "What in the hell are you going on about?"

"I talked to an attorney."

"You talked to an attorney? Why?"

"To see what my rights were in divorce."

"Who the hell said anything about divorce?"

"You left me. It was an option. I wanted to see what my rights were."

"And what exactly did you find out?"

"That I have none! But you know the worst part, Caden?" She folded her arms across her chest. "I had more rights as a whore than I do as a married woman."

"The hell you say."

"The hell I do. And you know what else? I don't like it. I don't like that you can tell me you love me one night and the next morning just drop me off like I'm just so much garbage you're sick of carrying around."

"I told you how it was."

"But you didn't ask me what I wanted."

"It's not my job to ask you. It's my job to keep you safe and it's your job to follow what I say."

"That's a crock of shit."

"Watch your language."

"You watch yours," she retorted.

"What the hell's gotten into you?"

She had no idea, but she was gloriously, furiously mad, and she wasn't going to take this anymore.

"Nothing that shouldn't have been there all along."

"Pack everything. We're getting out of here."

"You pack up *your* things and leave."

Caden looked around the small house. "You can't seriously want to stay here."

"You can't seriously expect me to abandon my business."

"What business?"

"I have a bakery." She waved her hand around the kitchen.

"A few loaves of bread for the locals?" The way he scoffed just grated on her nerves.

She wanted to go move that hutch, rip up the floorboards where she kept her emergency money and show him just how little her business wasn't. Instead, she gritted her teeth.

"The money that you left for me is in the bank."

"You didn't spend it?"

"Some of it, but I paid it back and it's there waiting for you."

"Can't get it without your signature."

She shook her head. "All you've got to do is walk in and tell them you're my husband and you can have anything you want."

The shock in his expression soothed a little of her anger.

"What the hell makes you think I would do that?"

"I don't know, but it grates the hell out of me that you could. That everything I've worked for my entire life could just vanish into your pocket. If you were a gambler I could lose it all with no say."

"I don't gamble."

"And if you were a drunk you could just drink it away."

"I don't drink."

"Yes, you do."

"Not more than a beer or two." He grabbed her forearms and gave her a little shake. "Maddie, are you crazy again, just in a different way?"

Yes, she was. Crazy mad at life, at the unfairness of it all, at the uncertainty of knowing that this business she'd started, that this identity she'd developed could just *disappear* on his whim. It drove her crazy. It made her crazy. She wanted to be safe, and nothing in the law provided that she would be. But she couldn't expect Caden to understand that. The advantage was all on his side, and only a fool would give up that advantage. Caden Miller was no fool.

"No. I'm not."

"You couldn't prove it by me."

"Do I need to?"

On a muttered curse, Caden turned on his heel and slammed out the back door. Maddie leaned against the counter and put her hand against her pounding chest and breathed a sigh of relief. She didn't have any doubt that he'd be back, but a day's reprieve would be nice. Running her shaking fingers through her hair, she went to the sink and quickly washed her hands. The dough she'd left earlier to rise was almost past the point of no return. She quickly punched it down, flopping it onto the board and rolling it out. Before she was on the fourth pass, Caden was back, his saddlebags slung over his shoulder, his rifles in his hands.

"What are you doing?"

"Unpacking."

"I thought you were going to the hotel."

"So did I."

He stopped in the living room and looked around for a door. "Where's the bedroom?"

"You're standing in it."

"Where do you sleep?"

She looked at the couch.

"Son of a bitch."

He dropped his gear on the floor.

"You don't have to stay if you don't like it."

"I'm staying, Maddie."

She wanted to scream. "Why? There isn't even a bed."

"Because this is where you are, and I promised to cleave unto you, forsaking all others." He looked around the tiny house again. "It'd be a hell of a lot more comfortable cleaving, though, in a hotel room with a nice big bed and a hip bath."

The bath did sound nice.

"There's a swimming hole just out of town."

He stopped and looked at her. "You saying I stink?"

He didn't. There was a slight scent of sweat about him, but mostly he smelled the way he always did, of man and good things.

She shook her head.

"I just thought you might be hot."

"I am. Maybe after dinner you and I'll go down and sample it."

She shook her head. She remembered all too clearly what happened last time they'd "cooled off." "I can't."

"Can't or won't?"

"Caden, I bake until I go to bed, and when I get up in the morning I start again."

"Why?"

What was the point of telling him? What was the point of not?

She waited too long.

He made a slashing motion with his hand. "I don't want to hear it anyway." He came into the kitchen. "Do we have anything here to eat?"

She handed him a cinnamon roll. He looked at it and sneered.

"You give all your beaus cinnamon rolls?"

She took it back. "Only the ones I like."

He looked a little stunned. Good.

"Do you want some or not?"

"How many did Culbart have?"

"Four."

"I'll take five."

She put five on a plate and handed it to him, then

poured him a cup of coffee. "After you finish that, you can either make yourself useful or leave. I have orders to fill."

The regulars were arriving at the front door with their usual commotion. "And I'm already behind."

"Hey, sweet cheeks, I'm here for my sugar!"

Caden's head snapped up at the unfamiliar voice coming from the alley. "What the hell was that?"

She groaned. Rowdy Rod. This *would* be the day he decided to show up.

"Hey, sweet thing," he yelled again. "Come bring me some sugar."

Caden's voice got very quiet. "You serving more than cinnamon buns?"

That hurt way down deep. Maddie's chin came up and she folded her arms across her chest. "Go to hell."

Caden looked at the sofa in the living room. "I think I'm already there."

"It's very comfortable." That was an outright lie.

Caden stared at her for the longest time, shook his head and swore. Rodney called out again. She heard someone in the crowd tell him to shut his ass up. It was going to be an ugly morning, maybe because of the heat, but when Caden hit the front door, it got uglier fast.

She ran after him. She couldn't afford for him to alienate her customers. Caden burst out the door and grabbed Rod by the throat, lifting him off his feet. Rodney wasn't a small man. Neither was Caden, and Caden was pissed. He kept walking with Rod dangling in his grip until he slammed him up against a tree. Rodney gasped and kicked. Caden didn't budge.

"Did you have something you want to say to my *wife,* mister?"

Rodney's eyes bulged farther as he shook his head. Caden still didn't let him go.

"You say one more disrespectful thing to her, or you even look at her disrespectful, and I'll rip off those balls that you're so proud of and shove 'em down your throat. Do we understand each other?"

The man nodded. Caden looked around at the crowd by the door. Maddie had the impression he was surprised by the numbers. There were at least twenty people waiting to buy her baking.

"That goes for the rest of you, too."

"Hell, mister, you're not going to get any complaint from us. Rowdy's had that coming for a long time."

"Sure enough that's the truth."

"We just want our cinnamon buns."

"And bread. I need two loaves of sourdough."

"Miss Maddie," Anna Lee called. "I need a dozen of the pull-apart rolls for Sunday dinner."

Orders started flowing from all around. Maddie held up her hand. "Hold on a minute. Let me get my pencil and I'll be right back. I'm a little behind today."

One of the women looked at Caden from head to toe, her eyes caressing him like a touch. "Easy enough to see why, honey."

It was Hester, one of the local soiled doves who had a penchant for cinnamon rolls.

"Heck," she continued, "if that'd be my husband, I wouldn't even be answering the door this morning."

Caden looked at the crowd, at Maddie and shook his head as if he didn't understand it all, and maybe he didn't. He'd gone away and left a terrified, cowering bride, and he came back to a businesswoman. But desperate people did desperate things, sometimes stupid, sometimes smart. She had been smart.

People walked up to Caden and started shaking his hand, welcoming him to town, telling him what a good baker Maddie was and what a lucky man he was. One older gentleman with a paunch that hung over his belt patted it and warned Caden in a few years he'd be looking like him with a wife who could bake like that. Caden laughed, but she could tell he was still mad. She could have called out and saved him, but she didn't. She wanted a few minutes of peace.

When Caden came inside fifteen minutes later, all he said was, "You were busy when I was gone."

She nodded, poured him fresh coffee and started stacking the bowls that needed to be washed for the next round of ingredients over by the basin.

He picked up a cloth and went to the sink and started filling it again.

"You don't have to do that."

"Yeah, I do. Consider it an apology."

"For what?"

"For what I said."

"You didn't say anything more than the truth."

"Shit. It's going to take me a while to live that one down, isn't it?"

"Nothing to live down. It's how you see me."

"The hell it is."

Someone knocked at the door. It was Mrs. Petittot for her cinnamon bread. Maddie quickly brought it over. Caden watched with a strange expression on his face, as if he'd never seen her before, but there was nothing in that expression to say whether he liked what he saw. Many men—most men, she had to admit—didn't like their wives working or earning money; they saw it as a shadow on their manhood

He finished the dishes. There really wasn't anything else for him to do, and quite frankly, everywhere he stood he was in her way. She had a system and he was in the middle of it. After the fourth time she bumped into him, he stepped out of the kitchen and grabbed his hat.

"I'm going to go up to the saloon."

She ignored the panicked flutter inside that said loose women were in the saloon, and nodded.

"Thank you."

"What time will you be done here?"

"I usually stop for dinner at five."

"I'll be here at five, then."

She forced a smile. "All right."

"We're going to talk, you know."

She nodded again. But not any sooner than she had to, she said to herself.

He stopped at the door and looked back.

"Did you really think I wasn't coming back for you, Maddie?"

She shrugged. "I couldn't take the chance."

He left then, slamming the door shut behind him. She had the oddest feeling she'd just hurt his feelings.

AS SOON AS CADEN entered the saloon, he noticed Ace at a table in the corner. Caden snagged the whiskey bottle off the counter as he passed. The owner complained, but Caden tossed the man a coin that would more than cover the cost. The bartender slapped another bottle in its place. Farther down the bar, Caden grabbed two glasses. When he reached the table, he set one in front of Ace and one in front of himself.

"I take it from this—" Ace motioned to the bottle and glasses "—your reunion with Maddie didn't go too well."

"She started a business."

"From what I heard, quite a successful one. She's got a nice little deposit over at the bank."

Caden growled in his throat.

"What?" Ace argued. "That's resourceful on her part."

"It was unnecessary." Caden poured the whiskey into the glasses and slammed his shot back. Ace sipped his more slowly.

"Maybe from your point of view."

"Who else's point of view matters?"

"Hers."

"My wife does not have to work."

"Maybe not, but your wife wants to."

"How the hell do you know?"

"If she really thought you weren't coming back and she really didn't want to work, she'd bat those big green eyes at that fat banker in town and have him cover her bills for her."

"Shut up and drink your whiskey."

"Why? You don't like hearing the truth?"

"No."

"What truth don't you want to hear?" Ace asked. "That you have a wife clever enough to come up with a business idea, who's more than capable of supporting herself? Or that you fucked it up so badly your own wife thought you weren't coming back for her?"

Caden tightened his fingers around the glass.

"You say it's not my business, but since you sat at my table and started chewing on my ear, I figure I'm going to make it so. Why do you think that is?"

"Because you think I'm like my father."

"For Christ's sake." Ace slammed back his shot and held the glass out for more. "You're no more your father than I'm my mother."

"You didn't know him."

"I knew him. We all knew him. He was outwardly charming and completely irresponsible. He spent more time in the bar than he did at home. He had women everywhere, and he liked to pretend that he was chasing gold when the only gold he ever found was between some loose woman's thighs."

"What the hell are you talking about?"

"Your father was a rounder, Caden. I'm not saying he didn't love you, but he was an out-and-out rounder."

"He loved me and he loved my mother."

"Yeah, he did. But he was lousy at the day-to-day part of it. He couldn't handle responsibility. The responsibility of being a dad and a husband. He'd rather play cards than put food on the table. He'd rather chase rainbows than be there with you. It didn't mean he didn't love you, but he sure as shit wasn't reliable."

"Who says?"

"Everyone says. Everyone knew. Even you if you think about it. Why the hell do you think you're so worried about being like him?"

Caden shook his head.

"He was your father and you loved him and you should've and that's the way it is. But you grew up differently and you are different and if you'd stop fucking around trying to fulfill a promise to him that he probably didn't even mean, your wife wouldn't be over there building her business."

"She's proud of it."

"Of course she's proud of it. Who wouldn't be proud of it? Hell, I'd be proud of it if I'd made it happen. Why the hell does that make you so mad?"

"I don't know, but it does."

"Then maybe you'd better chew on the why of that before you head on over there to chat with your wife again. She did what she thought she needed to do. She didn't lie on her back and spread her legs. She didn't rely on a man. She used her brain and her skills and she created a legitimate business to support herself when she thought you weren't coming back. Now, if it bothers you that your wife doesn't have any faith in you, then I suggest you look at just what the hell you've done to make her lose it. But ranting and raving about how you're like your dad? That's just bullshit and it's not going to serve either of you."

"Anybody ever tell you, you talk too much?"

"Anybody ever tell you, you don't talk enough? You hold everything inside and think your actions speak for you. Well, they don't. For as long as I can remember, for more than half the time I've known you, I haven't known why you do whatever the hell it is you're doing. I just take it on faith it's for a good reason. Your wife hasn't even known you a year and she depends on you a hell of a lot more than I do, and you seem to think she ought to be able to figure it out. Well, it's not going to happen, Caden. Sitting here drinking whiskey isn't going to solve your problems any more than standing at that house and screaming like a madman—"

"What the hell do you know about that?"

"Everybody knows. It's all over town that Maddie Miller's husband came home and he's pissed as hell at her and that is a damn shame, Caden, because somebody's going to tell her that, too. And it hurts when you love someone and they're not proud of what you accomplish."

Ace took another shot of whiskey and put his glass down before saying quietly, "It hurts like fucking hell and Maddie doesn't deserve that, Caden. You spend all those hours at the mine hunting for riches when you've already found your gold."

Ace stood.

"Where the hell are you going?"

"I find I'm bored with the present company so I thought I'd go over and say hello to Maddie."

"Stay the hell away from her."

"Why? Because you're a jealous son of a bitch?"

"That, too."

Ace picked up Caden's glass and downed its contents, too. "Then you best lay off that whiskey and start putting some shine on your image, because I'm going over and I'm going to talk to her. Maybe even do more than say hi. And when we're done conversing, I'm going to head over to the hotel, lie down on my bed and I'm going to get some much-needed sleep. And in the morning, I hope to hell I'm going to find you sober and in a better mood." Slamming the glass down on the table, he turned and walked out.

Caden watched him go, feeling all eyes in the saloon upon him. Just one more thing to blame Maddie for. He poured himself more whiskey, but this shot didn't taste as good as the last. Everything Ace had said was running around his brain. *Fuck.* All he'd wanted to do was come home and hold his wife, tell her he loved her the way he should have done, but all he'd ended up doing was yelling and cussing. He really was a sorry son of a bitch.

CHAPTER SEVENTEEN

WHEN THE KNOCK came at the door, Maddie's heart foolishly leaped. Of course it wasn't Caden. He'd gone to the saloon. He wasn't going to be back any too soon. No man did once they had a bottle in their hand. They just drank and drank until there was no more sitting up, and then they either lay on the table or on the floor until one of their friends came and scraped them up and carried them home.

She licked her lips and wondered, not for the first time, if she should go to the saloon. Caden was her husband. It was her job to scrape him up. He was also the man that had pissed her off. Wiping her hands on her skirt, she went to the front door and found Ace standing there.

"Maddie." He smiled. "I heard this is the place to come for cinnamon buns."

Disappointment and happiness warred within her. She let the latter win and smiled. "Ace, it's good to see you."

"Good to see you, too."

"Do you really want a cinnamon bun?"

"I would kill for one."

"You'd kill for biscuits."

He smiled. "No, I'd bust heads for a biscuit, but it

takes cinnamon and icing to work me up to killing." He reached behind her ear and with a flip of his fingers produced a coin. "But I'm willing to pay for this one."

She laughed. The magic trick, as always, made her smile. She took the coin from his hand and examined it, and as always, there was no indication of how he made it appear and disappear like that. When she'd questioned him about it before, he'd asked her wasn't it enough that she enjoyed it? And she decided that yes, it was.

"I'd invite you in, but—"

"But what?"

"It's deathly hot in here. With the oven going all day, I think I can start baking rolls on the counter."

He smiled. "Got a shady spot out back?"

She nodded. "Yup. And I've even got some cold coffee."

"That sounds right nice."

She motioned him through the house.

He shook his head. "I'll go around the side. No sense starting talk."

She shook her head. "As if my reputation couldn't stand any more."

He laughed. "Maddie, honey, I don't think it can. The whole town's abuzz about how you entertained two men in your house today and how they nearly came to blows over you."

"One of them *was* my husband."

"Yep, that's the juiciest part."

"Wonderful."

She went in the house and, for the third time that day,

loaded up some cinnamon rolls on a plate and poured two cups of coffee, adding cream and sugar to Ace's, leaving hers black. The man did have a sweet tooth.

He was sitting in the same seat under the big oak where Frank had sat. As she set the tray before him, she asked, "How likely is it Caden's going to pop in here and start trouble again?"

"From the way he was nursing that whiskey bottle, I'd say not likely at all."

She sighed and sat across from him. "He drinking?"

He nodded. "Yep. Seems to feel justified."

"I don't understand what he's upset about."

"Well, no man likes to come home and find another man settled in with his wife."

"He wasn't settled in. He'd just gotten into town and stopped over to say hi."

"Your *uncle* Frank."

She shook her head. "He's not my uncle."

"Yeah, I know. That's probably the part that's chewing at Caden's craw on top of the fact that you seemed happy to see Frank and unhappy to see him."

She sighed. "I can't help it."

"He didn't leave you, Maddie. Surely you understand that now. He was a day late getting back, but he's back."

She shook her head. "No, it's not that."

"Then what?"

She took a sip of coffee. She couldn't even call it cold it was so warm.

Ace took a sip of his. "You remembered how I like it."

She nodded. "I remember all things Hell's Eight."

"I know."

"Have you heard about Worth?" she asked. "How he's doing?"

He shook his head. "I haven't heard, but Hell's Eight wouldn't risk a rider for a dog."

She knew that, too. He'd only been valuable to her.

"That's not true."

She looked up. "What?"

"You said Worthless was only valuable to you."

She hadn't realized she'd said that out loud.

"Worth means the world to Tucker, too, and the fact that he took that bullet defending you just makes him a hero. Tucker will use him to beef up Boone's legend. Everybody wants one of his puppies because of how he'd tracked Desi with a bullet in him, bleeding the whole way. Takes a lot of heart to do that."

She nodded.

"Takes a lot of heart to do a lot of things," Ace said.

"You're not going to lecture me, are you?"

"On what?"

"On not staying put."

He laughed. "Hell, no. I can't blame you for breaking out of the hotel room. I'd have gone stir-crazy by the second day."

"Caden seems to think I should have stayed."

"Caden's got a lot of weird notions. Mostly all involving you."

She nodded.

"But none of them have to do with thinking less of you."

She looked up.

"Maddie. He married you."

"He didn't have a choice."

"Caden always has a choice. You know Caden can be a son of a bitch."

"He doesn't mean to be."

Ace shook his head. "Maddie."

"What?"

"You're supposed to be mad at him."

"I am."

"Then why when I say something bad about him do you turn it around and make it sound good?"

"I didn't."

"Yeah, you did."

"I don't know how to talk to him," she told him, wrapping her fingers around her cup.

"Caden's a pretty straightforward guy. You said it yourself."

She shook her head. "Not with me."

"Maybe you ought to ask yourself why."

"I irritate him."

"Don't be so foolish. The man married you, Maddie."

"He had to."

"He consummated the marriage."

She dropped her face in her hands. "There are some things I never need to know. One of them being how you know the intimate details of my marriage."

He laughed. "How about we just not look at each other for a while."

She nodded. "That would be good."

He took a bite of his cinnamon roll. She heard him chew, then heard him moan.

"Damn, they weren't exaggerating. These are good."

"Thank you."

"How many you make of these a day?"

She shook her head. "A hundred, a hundred and fifty maybe."

"And that's not keeping up with demand."

She shook her head. "No."

"It's quite a little business you've built here. How much you charge for 'em?"

She told him and his eyebrows rose.

"Damn, Maddie. You're a hell of a businesswoman."

"There are some things you pick up—" she was going to say *as a whore,* but she bit her tongue "—over the years."

"Caden's a lucky man."

She sighed. "He doesn't think so."

"Yeah, he does. He's just a little put out right now."

"Why?"

"Well, I could venture a guess, but I'm thinking that's probably something you should ask him."

"I will when he comes back."

"Yeah, that would be the time to do it. And maybe after he sobers up."

"He's drinking that much?"

"Yeah. And Caden rarely drinks. Wonder why that is, too."

She remembered the sense that she'd maybe hurt his feelings as he'd closed the door.

"Oh, damn."

"I've never heard you cuss before."

"I'm trying new things."

"Normally I'd say it doesn't look good on a woman, but on you, it's becoming." He finished his coffee and stood.

"Where'd you leave him?" she asked.

"Up at the saloon."

The saloon where no decent woman would go. She took off her apron and handed it to Ace.

"In five minutes, take the rolls out of the oven and drizzle them with the glaze that's beside it."

"You want me to bake?" He looked stricken.

"I want you to drizzle. There's a difference. Remember, five minutes."

"Five minutes. Just take them out."

"Yes, and drizzle the glaze over them."

"Okay, but you're not holding me responsible for how they come out, I hope."

She nodded her head. "Yes, I am. Those things are expensive to make."

"And where are you going?"

She sighed. "To fix a mistake."

MADDIE WAS HALFWAY to the saloon when she saw Caden coming toward her. If she didn't know him so well, she never would have recognized the signs that he'd been drinking, but his walk was a little too slow and his motions a little too controlled. Caden stopped in front of her.

"Maddie mine."

People stopped right alongside them. Ace wasn't kidding when he said she'd been the talk of the town this morning. She'd never had so much attention.

"Were you coming to see me?" he asked.

"I was coming to fetch you home."

"Why? Nothing there for me."

"Everything's there for you."

He weaved ever so slightly.

"You've been drinking."

"And you've been baking."

She touched a bruise on his knuckle and noted a slight swelling by his eye.

"You've also been fighting."

"A slight disagreement."

"With who?"

"Your uncle Frank. We had to renegotiate a deal."

"What deal?"

"He seemed to think you're for sale."

She had been. "The foal?"

"Yes."

"You decided not to honor the bargain?" She couldn't conceive of that. Hell's Eight never went back on their word.

"Hell, no. Hell's Eight doesn't renege."

She ran her thumb over his knuckle. "I don't understand."

"I gave it to him as a gift."

"How is that different?"

Sliding his finger under her chin, Caden lifted her gaze to his. The consumption of alcohol did nothing to dim the force of his personality. "A man couldn't buy a treasure like you with all the gold in the world. I don't want that bastard thinking he could."

She bit her tongue on the immediate contradiction that sprang to mind for the simple reason she didn't want to correct him. She loved the way Caden ignored her past as if only now mattered.

"But I'd sell my soul if that's what it took to get you back, Maddie mine," he finished.

"You didn't sell your soul to Frank, did you?" Frank had been kind to her but he was a ruthless man in many ways.

Caden brought her hand to his mouth. Her heart caught and her stomach dropped as his lips burned into her palm. He smiled at her gasp, the hard edge in his drawl now in his expression. "Culbart is now an ally of Hell's Eight."

She gasped again for an entirely different reason, pulling her hand away. He didn't let go. "It's too much."

An alliance was serious business. Frank could call on Hell's Eight for any reason. At any time and they would come, putting everyone she loved—Caden, Tucker, Sam—in danger. Wives could be without husbands, children without fathers because of her. She yanked at her hand again. "You have to undo it."

Instead of letting her go, Caden pulled her up against him. His body was hard and warm. He smelled of alcohol, and she tried to tell herself she should be repulsed, but she wasn't. She was too horrified by what he'd done. She wanted to smack him and cling to him at the same time.

"I'm not undoing a goddamn thing. There's no telling what could have happened to you out there. Like it or not, I owe your *uncle* more than I can ever repay."

He meant it. He really meant it. Maddie curled her nails into Caden's chest. A treasure, he'd called her. *His* treasure. Her knees nearly gave out. She was Caden Miller's treasure.

"He's not my uncle." Somehow she got the words out.

"You used to think he was."

"It was—" she shrugged, still wrestling with the reality of understanding what had been make-believe "—necessary at the time."

"And now it's not."

She shook her head. "No. A lot of things aren't necessary anymore."

"Including me, now that you've got the bakery."

The note in his voice yanked her eyes back to his.

"Why do you hate my business so much?"

"Why do you hate that I hate it?"

"Do you always do this when you're drinking?"

"What?"

"Answer a question with a question."

"I don't know."

"How can you not know?"

"I haven't been drunk in a very long time."

"Are you drunk now?"

"When those last two shots I pounded down hit me, I'm gonna say I'll be pretty far gone."

Not a good time to talk, then. About anything, especially the knot of fear and joy tightening in her stomach. She hooked her hand through his arm and held on. "Then maybe we need to go home."

"Got that couch with my name on it?"

She smiled, feeling lighter inside than she could ever remember feeling.

"I don't want to sleep there."

"Why not?" she asked, strolling beside him.

"It won't fit two."

That was sweet to hear.

"It will fit you, for now."

"Yeah, I suppose it will."

He followed meekly. Well, as meekly as Caden could do anything.

He broke the silence with "Why didn't you believe me, Maddie?"

"Because you broke your word."

"That's not it."

"Of course that's it."

She didn't reply, and instead focused on getting them home. He kept trying to help her over bumps in the sidewalk, but his balance wasn't that good, so she pretended to let him help her while she steadied him. By the time they got back to the house, Caden was noticeably stumbling. There was no sign of Ace, but the cinnamon buns were on the kitchen counter, properly drizzled. At least one man listened. With a push, she urged Caden into the living room.

"Sit on the couch."

He sat in the chair.

"That's not the couch," she pointed out.

"So?" His big body dwarfed the little wingback she'd purchased. She worried the legs would snap. It was made for a woman's delicate body, not a rawboned wrangler like him.

"That chair won't hold you."

"It'll hold." He pushed his hat back. It fell to the floor. He didn't even look, but Maddie did. Caden never tossed his hat on the floor.

"Why did you leave the hotel, Maddie mine?"

"Because you left me."

"I left you money for a month."

She nodded. "Yes."

"And at the end of the month I was going to be back."

"I didn't believe that."

"I don't believe you didn't believe that."

She knelt at his feet and tugged off his boots, first one and then the other. He moaned in relief.

"Those things are hot."

His feet looked hot. They were red and sweaty, and quite frankly they smelled.

She went into the kitchen and got the footbath out from under the cabinet. She poured a bucket of well water into it and brought it along with soap and a cloth back to the room. One by one she lifted his feet and put them in.

He moaned again. "I like you on your knees."

"Most men do."

He shook his head. "Not for that reason. I don't want you to beg. Well—" he reconsidered "—not that way."

"Then why?"

She washed his feet gently.

"Maddie. I never meant to hurt you."

"I know."

"And I did come back."

"I know."

She could tell the alcohol was taking a stronger hold on him.

"We need to get you to bed." She took his feet out of the bin and dried them gently. She might be mad at him and she might not want to be married to him, but she did love him.

He held out his hand; she took it and stood. Before she could get all the way on her feet, he tugged again and she went off balance, tumbling into his lap. The chair rocked. If the wall hadn't been behind it, they would have both gone down.

He stroked his fingers over her cheek, tucking her face into his shoulder.

"Maddie mine. Did I tell you how proud I am of you, of the way you're building this business up from nothing, finding a way to support yourself without spreading your legs?"

She winced. Did he have to be so graphic? "No, you didn't."

"I am. Proud as shit."

"Then why are you so mad?"

He didn't answer right away. She thought he'd nod-ded off. She needed to get him to the couch.

"Stand up, Caden."

He did no such thing. "I'm comfortable."

"Caden." He cracked one eye. *"Stand up."*

"Why?"

"Because I want you to."

"I'll stand up if you show me your breast."

"Oh, my God." She paused and, not seeing any other way out, asked, "Which one?"

"The right one."

Now she had to know. "Why the right one?"

"It's got a cute little dimple."

"My breast does not have a dimple."

"I say it does."

"Well, it doesn't."

"Well, that's the one I want to see."

She opened her shirt, showing him the nipple. He moaned in his throat.

"I've dreamed about those for the last month, how they melted on my tongue before they grew hard, how you sighed when I nibbled, moaned when I sucked and arched that sweet pussy onto my cock when I bit down."

Her knees almost gave out, but one of them had to be strong.

"I did my part, now you stand up."

He did, albeit while weaving. It was just four steps to the couch, but she didn't think she was going to be able to get him there. Finally he went, sitting down with a thump and sort of just falling over. The couch that fit her pretty well was way too short for him. Drunk as he was, he didn't seem to mind; he just draped his knees over the back. It didn't look comfortable.

She took a pillow and slid it between his leg and the wooden frame. At least he wouldn't be bruised.

"Thank you."

"You're welcome."

"Why did you leave me, Maddie?"

She didn't know what to say. He caught her hand when she would have moved away.

"I have to clean the kitchen."

"Stay."

"Why?"

He rubbed his thumb across the back of her hand.

"Because I missed you."

What was she supposed to say to that? There was no place to sit on the couch, so she sat on the floor beside it, resting her head against his chest, letting him stroke her hair.

"That's never happened before," he said.

"What?"

"Me missing anyone."

"I'm your wife. You're supposed to miss me."

He shook his head. "I didn't think I *could* miss anybody."

"You don't like it?"

"I do now."

"Why did you get so drunk?"

"It seemed like the thing to do," he said sleepily.

"Well, it seemed like the thing to do for me to open my own business."

"You're lying."

"So are you."

He cracked his eye at her. "I'm too damn drunk for this discussion."

On that she agreed. "You are."

She stroked the back of his fingers as his other hand smoothed over her hair. They were always touching each other.

That's why he smiles whenever you're near and you smile whenever he's near. Bella was right. There'd always been an attraction between them. It was just when they started talking that things got messed up.

"Why did you leave me, Caden?"

"Because that's what I thought I was supposed to do." He sighed. "It's what my father did."

"I didn't understand."

"Neither did I before today."

"But you understand now?"

"I've got an inkling." He cracked his eyelid again. "Ace can be damn blunt when he's pissed."

Yeah, he could.

"What do you want, Maddie?"

"The same thing I've always wanted."

"Love and respect."

She nodded. She took his hand and draped it over her shoulder, scooting up so she could lean against his chest.

"You really are too drunk for this conversation."

"So stay with me until I fall asleep."

"And then what?"

"When I wake up we'll try again." He smoothed his fingers over her temple and down over her cheekbone.

"I don't like fighting with you."

"You couldn't have proved it by me."

"I know. I tend to lash out first before I can get hurt." So did he.

"Would you divorce me if I asked?"

"Hell, no!"

"Why?"

"You're mine, Maddie. You've been mine since the day I saw you."

She remembered that day. Hell's Eight had been under attack. Caden had ridden up with Caine and Ace. Mostly she was in a fog, but she remembered him, the look of him, the feel of him. His smile. She remembered that very well.

"Go to sleep, Caden."

He opened his eye. "Will you be here when I wake up?"

"Where else would I be? I have rolls to bake."

"Yeah." He sounded sad. "That's what I figured."

And again, she had that sense that she'd hurt him.

She sighed. She didn't seem to be able to do or say anything right today. The only thing she felt sure about was baking cinnamon buns.

She got to her feet and brushed off her skirt, stroking her fingers down his cheek. He looked so relaxed lying there. His fingers caught hers. He brought her palm to his lips and, eyes still closed, a smile on his lips, pressed a kiss in the center.

WHEN CADEN WOKE UP it was dark and his head hurt. He had the vague impression it was morning. The one thing that stood out was he remembered asking Maddie if she'd been selling more than sweets.

Fuck.

He shoved himself up, groaning. His neck ached and his back ached and his head ached. He deserved a lot worse. What the hell was the matter with him? What was it about Maddie that made him so crazy that he said shit he didn't even mean?

He could see her in the kitchen, just twenty feet away, icing rolls. Dark circles rimmed her eyes. She was thinner than he remembered. Her hair was tied back in a loose knot. She was killing herself making a go of this business.

He got to his feet.

"Maddie mine."

"What?"

He could see the fear under the belligerence. She was ready for him to lash out again.

"I'm an ass when I'm pissed."

"No argument."

"I shouldn't have said what I said."

"You can't help what you believe."

"I don't believe that. I've never believed that."

"Then why did you say it?"

"Because I was mad."

"Well, now I'm mad, too. Are you happy?"

"Not a bit."

He walked over and took the knife with which she was slathering glaze over cinnamon rolls out of her hand.

"I have to finish these."

"Fuck it. And not because I don't want you to succeed, but because no wife should believe her husband thinks that about her."

"Once a whore, always a whore."

"You're my wife. Once my wife, always my wife."

"You don't respect me. You're going to divorce me."

"Like hell. Where'd you hear that?"

"It's actually a simple process for a man," she said. "You just have to make a few accusations on a piece of paper. Nobody will even check to make sure they're true."

"Maddie..."

She looked up.

"I should have told you this a long time ago."

"What?"

"I love you."

"I don't believe you."

Of all the answers she might give, that hadn't been the one he'd been expecting.

"Why the hell not?"

"You left me."

"I could point out that *you're* the one who left *me*. I left you safe in a hotel. You're the one who traded that in for drudgery."

"It's *not* drudgery."

She grabbed some flour and threw it at him. It hit him square in the face. He jerked back.

"This is *mine*. You've got your claim. You've got your reputation. You've got your confidence. You've got your respect. Well, this is *mine*. I made this. I didn't have to spread my legs to get it. *I. Made. This.* Through my hard work. Through my ambition." She threw another handful of flour at him. "I can buy a house with this. I can travel to San Francisco with this."

"I would have taken you there."

"Yes, you would've and you'd have saved me and for my whole entire life I would have been indebted to you."

"What the hell's so bad about that?"

"Nothing. If you don't mind crawling."

"When the hell have I ever asked you to crawl?"

"Never. You don't have to."

"Maddie?"

"What?"

"Come here."

"Why?" She stood there, belligerent, head down, arms folded.

"Because I want to hold you. Because I'm sorry. Because I love you."

"Stop saying that! I don't need you to lie."

"That's good, because I don't." *Usually.*

She looked up at him. He waited, but she didn't close those two steps between them, so he took them for her, getting close enough that he could reach out and touch her cheek. She had a dusting of flour on her nose, covering her freckles. He wiped it with his thumb.

"I like your freckles."

"Thank you."

"Maddie?" he asked her again. "Come here."

She went and he accepted, scooping her up in his arms and sitting in the kitchen chair. It groaned under their combined weight.

"We're going to end up on the floor."

"Don't worry, I'll cushion your fall."

She poked his chest. "There's not much softness in you."

"When it comes to you, there's a whole wagonload."

"Not that I've noticed lately. Why is that?"

He shook his head. "I don't know."

"Maybe you ought to come back when you do know."

"And maybe you ought to sit here and let me hold you while I figure it out. You're always arguing with me, Maddie mine. Do you ever wonder why?"

She shook her head.

"To everybody else you give endless patience. To me you give lectures."

"That's because you do the most foolish things."

"Nobody else thinks they're foolish."

"Yes, they do."

"Well, if they do they don't have the guts to tell me."

She nodded.

"But you do. Because you care."

"I already told you I love you," she said plainly.

"And instead of responding, I brought you to town and dropped you off at the hotel."

She nodded.

"I had some foolish idea, Maddie, that if I didn't tell you I love you, then it wouldn't hurt if I didn't come back."

"I was hurting before you left."

"I see that now."

Her breasts pressed into his chest and her breath slipped between the lapels of his shirt. He'd missed her so.

"You're a sneaky woman, Maddie mine, getting under my guard, staking your claim on my heart, slowly and surely hog-tying me until I can't see anything but being with you."

"You make it sound like an assault."

"It felt like one."

"And now?"

"Now I don't like the fact that you're planning to leave me."

CHAPTER EIGHTEEN

"I HAVEN'T MADE my mind up about anything, Caden."

"You realize that's not much comfort to me?"

"I'm sorry, but it's the truth."

That pretty much summed it up. Caden ran his fingers up and down Maddie's spine, struck once again by the differences between them. He was all hard muscle and she was all sweet softness. Everything he'd always craved. And she thought he'd let her go? Was it because she wanted someone else?

"Tell me what happened at Culbart's, Maddie."

She stiffened.

"Don't worry, I won't kill the son of a bitch." Unless he had to.

She sighed deeply. "They found me on the trail." He could hear the quiver in her voice as she remembered the fear she felt.

"Where you shouldn't have been."

She brushed his comment aside. He found it convenient the way she ignored what she didn't want to hear.

"I didn't know what else to do. I went back to my pretend world, but this time I was pretending what I already was." She shook her head as if she couldn't figure how that was.

"Maddie, you were never a whore. Not really."

"Pretending it's not true doesn't change it, Caden."
She gave him a wry smile. "I'm an expert on that."

He touched her cheek. "A whore is someone who makes a choice. You never had one."

She shook her head again, denying it. He didn't like it. He never had, probably never would, but he held on to his temper.

"I had a choice many times, Caden. There were many times I could have walked away and tried to make a life for myself like I did here."

"Make a life with what?"

"With *me*. Why don't you understand? *Me*. The same me that did this." With a wave of her hand, she indicated the messy kitchen full of pots and pans and dough that was almost ready to go into the oven.

"All right. I get your point. You had a choice. There was always a choice. You just waited for the right time to make it."

"You always try to make me look so good."

"You always try to make you look so bad. Gotta have balance in there."

She shook her head. "I didn't like being a prostitute."

"I don't imagine many do."

"I never really adjusted to it, either. But there's just no way out of it once you're in. You are what you are forever and that taint is so strong."

"Maddie." Caden grabbed her chin, jerked her face up, seeing the tears in her eyes, the belief.

"What you are forever is *you*. Maddie Miller. What

you had to do to survive along the way? That's just what you had to do."

Her fingers curled around his wrists and her nails bit into his skin. "The rest of the world doesn't see things that way, Caden. You know that."

"Fuck the rest of the world."

"There are going to be times in the future—"

"Yeah," he prompted, "finish the sentence."

She shook her head. The anguish in her face ripped out his heart. Her breath caught, and she cast her eyes down in shame, the same way he'd hated when she first arrived at Hell's Eight.

"You look at me, Maddie mine." He didn't give her a choice, tipping her face up. "You're worried that somewhere down the road some yahoo is going to recognize you?"

She nodded.

"And you think I'm not going to be able to handle it."

"What if we're with our kids or somebody else from Hell's Eight?"

"Then we'll tear the asshole from limb to limb if he dares say a word."

"Caden, you can't beat up every man who remembers me as a whore."

"I can beat up everyone who tries to cause you pain."

God help her, she actually believed him.

"Do you know what it does to me when you say things like that with such conviction?"

"It makes you happy, I hope."

She shook her head. "It makes me hope so much I want to run away."

"Why?"

"Good gosh, Caden. You're every woman's dream, and for a woman like me who wasn't expecting to have anything, ever, who thought it was all just make-believe? You're like touching the sun. I don't want to love you."

"But you said you did. You can't take it back. I'm not letting you take it back."

He wasn't hearing her. "I don't want to love you."

"Because I'm too good for you?"

"No. Because of how I want to be with you."

"You realize you're talking nonsense, right?"

"I understand it sounds that way to you."

"Maddie, it would sound that way to anybody."

She wished he could understand. "When you grow up with nothing, like me, and then you're handed everything, you just know it's going to disappear. So I need to protect myself from loving you. Protect myself from believing in you. Guard against putting my faith in you."

"Why the hell would you do that?"

"Because of who I am."

Caden's frown deepened to a scowl, but his fingers against the side of her face remained gentle. He rested his chin on top of her head, pulling her close, holding her tightly. She could feel his confidence wrap around her as strongly as his arms. He truly believed that her past couldn't hurt them, and he truly didn't understand how it would wear down on him when it did. Time after time.

"So you're telling me we're married. I love you. You love me. But none of that matters?"

"I want to be me. A woman in her own right who stands on her own two feet, who pays her own bills, who depends on no one."

"And you can't do that with me?"

She stroked her fingers down his face. "No."

"Why not?"

"Because you're so much you and there's so little me. I'd just get squashed."

"So that's why you fight me."

She nodded. "Yes. I want to know who I am before I decide who I'm going to belong to."

"Too late for that, Maddie. We're already married."

"As you said, that can be changed. I know it can be messy and it's ugly and it ruins a woman's reputation forever, but it's not like I have much to hold on to anyway."

"I won't give you a goddamn divorce."

"See? No me. All you."

"Dammit, Maddie, this is unfair."

"I know," she admitted sadly.

"What do you want from me?"

"I want you to go home, to Hell's Eight, to your gold mine, to wherever."

"And? Just leave you here?"

She nodded. "Just leave me here. I've made a place for myself here. It's not big, it's not rich, it involves a lot of work, but it's mine."

"Is it Culbart?"

"No! I need to know *me* before I go with you or go

back to Hell's Eight. When I go there I'm the old Mad-die again. Crazy Maddie. Sweet Maddie. Needy Mad-die. Helpful Maddie. Did you ever wonder, Caden, why I was so busy helping everybody all the time?"

"No."

"It was me trying to prove to you that I was worth something. All of you, not just you." She made a cutting motion with her hand. "You know, I just figured if I made myself indispensible, you wouldn't throw me away."

"I didn't throw you away, Maddie."

She made another cutting motion with her hand. "I'm not talking about you leaving me here."

"Just tell me what happened with Frank."

"This morning?"

"No, at the Fallen C."

"Nothing really. When they met me on the trail, I told them I was a working girl. It seemed the safest thing. Frank offered me a job."

"Doing what?"

"Doing what working girls do."

"Why did he shoot Worthless?"

"Because I didn't want to go with them, and Worth-less tried to save me."

"Thought it was something like that. So Culbart took you by force."

"It's hard to explain, but yes and no."

"And when you got there, Maddie?"

His fingers were incredibly tender on her cheek. His expression serious but not mean. He was braced, she re-alized, for the worst.

"He tried to take me to his bed."

"And?"

"I'm not a working girl anymore, Caden."

"You fought him?"

"Yes."

"Did he force you?"

"No. He was appalled."

"Excuse me?"

"I told you. He felt it was unfair of me to put him in a position of raping me."

"Son of a bitch. He felt he got a raw deal, huh?"

"I think for a day or two, yes."

"And then what?"

"We walked around on eggshells. He wouldn't throw me out because I had nowhere to go. He'd brought me there so he was responsible for my safety. He didn't have the men to spare to send with me on my way."

"So what happened?"

"For a while, it was just really uncomfortable and tense in the house. I kept drifting in and out of this world, out of here."

"And what did he do?"

"Stayed away a lot. He was embarrassed, I think."

"You think?"

"I don't know the man that well, Caden, and he has a very gruff exterior without a lot of revelation afterward."

She slipped her fingers between his shirt collar and his skin.

"Then one day I was so bored, I thought maybe if I

baked him something to eat, he'd soften up. So I made cinnamon rolls."

"Your cure for everything."

She nodded. "Yeah. It works."

There was something Caden really needed to know. "Did it work on Culbart?"

"Turns out men are willing to do without sex if they can have good baking." She laughed.

He laughed, too, and turned her so she straddled his lap, his fingers going to her shirt. She was so naive. "I have news for you, Maddie. I want you first, then your baked goods."

It was sweet.

"So what put marriage into Culbart's head?"

"The guilt, I think, worrying that I thought he'd force himself on me."

"What do you mean?"

"You could have knocked me over with a feather when Frank said we had to get married or he'd kill you."

"He threatened me?"

She nodded.

"Hell, I thought he threatened *you*. Why the hell did you go along with it if he threatened me?"

"Because I believed him. He said he wasn't sending any woman into a situation where she'd be raped."

"He didn't think I could rape you if I was married to you?"

"Apparently not. It would be legal then."

"Strange way of looking at it."

She rolled her eyes. "It's the way everybody looks at it, Caden. Except you."

"Maybe because I never planned on getting married."

"Maybe."

He got the fourth, fifth, sixth buttons of her shirt undone. He tugged the string of her camisole and then he pushed both aside, revealing her full breasts, with those pink nipples that made his mouth water.

"So you pretended to be in your pretend place to go through with it?"

"No. I was in and out. But deep inside I just wanted to be married to you, Caden. And that's why I went through with the ceremony and that's why I didn't warn you and that's why you were right. I did betray you."

He shoved her dress down her arms, trapping her hands at her sides. She looked pretty like that.

"Thank God."

"What?"

"I was pissed as hell at the time because of the way our marriage came about, but you notice I never did anything about it. I didn't keep my distance. I yelled. I raged and I pointed a finger at you a little bit, but I stayed close. Touching you. Sparking you."

"A *little?*"

"Okay, a lot."

He cupped her breasts in his hands, lifting them, stroking his thumb over the nipples, smiling when they rose. She had such pretty breasts. So sensitive. He knew he could make her moan just by pinching the nipple. He did, letting the soft sound stroke along his desire, settle into his cock.

"But the truth is, Maddie…"

"What?"

"I wanted to be married to you, too. So for whatever reason Culbart did what he did, it ended up being a favor."

"What are you doing?" She sighed with pleasure.

"If you don't remember, I didn't do a good enough job last time."

She shook her head. "Of course I know what you're doing."

"Good, then unbutton my pants."

"This isn't going to solve anything," she said, her hands soft on his, making short work of the buttons on his pants before reaching inside and closing like hot velvet around his cock.

He lifted her up and she freed him. He held her feet off the ground.

"Now, pull those skirts up."

She did. He knew she knew what he wanted when he lowered her, his cock naturally slipping between the slit in her pantaloons. She was wet and hot and it was easy to lower her onto his cock, to feel the silkiness of her pussy close around him as he let her weight settle onto his thighs. To feel that hot shudder slip through her.

He moaned. "Fuck, that's good, Maddie."

"Yes."

He liked that she didn't argue with him here.

"Now you can continue."

For about five minutes he might be able to keep it still. He started pinching her nipples. She started rocking on his cock. Her voice was breathless. His wasn't much better.

"So we married each other because we wanted to."

"Looks that way to me."

"But we don't know each other. I know you, you know you, but neither of us knows who I am."

"I know who you are, Maddie mine. I've known you since the first time our eyes met. Your strength, your spirit, that deep heart you have for loving."

"Well, I don't know me and I need to."

He rocked her up and down slowly. Her head fell back and her nails dug into his chest. He rolled her nipples through his fingers.

"Harder."

"What do you want harder, my cock or my hands?"

"Both."

"I think I'll just work with my hands." He liked that she was on edge and needy. He pinched her nipples harder, holding the tension until she gasped, drawing them out, letting the weight dangle from the hard tip.

"Such pretty breasts you have. I always noticed them."

"You noticed?"

"Who wouldn't?"

That seemed to be the right thing to say. She smiled.

"Offer them to me."

She slipped her hands beneath and lifted them, stroking her fingers up the sides until her fingers touched his on the nipples. He took his away. She twisted and pinched her nipples.

"That's it, baby, make them hard for my mouth."

She did without hesitation. He liked that instant response in her. That willingness to experiment.

"Good girl." He waited until she had them stretched away from her body before ordering, "Hold it."

She did, her body tense and quivering, anticipation in her eyes. Holding her gaze, he lowered his head, raking his tongue across one nipple. She moaned and her head fell back. He braced her with his hand between her shoulder blades. She brought her feet up, driving his cock deeper. As his lips closed around her nipple, she rose up on his cock, fucking him in short little jabs in time with his sucking as he nibbled at her breasts.

"Christ, I'm not going to last long, Maddie." He'd been so long without her. "I need you, honey."

"I need you, too. Harder."

"You first."

She laughed the laugh he'd always wanted to hear from her. Free and wild and happy. "No, you."

She rose up and down, maintaining the rhythm, making love to him with her eyes, her body, her smile, taking the pleasure he gave and returning it tenfold, with the grind of her hips, the squeezing of her pussy. Fuck, her pussy. So tight and hot, so wet. He thrust up, twisting her nipples between his fingers as his cock slid deep, parting her, stretching her. Son of a bitch.

"Maddie!"

She answered in a high-pitched cry, her body quivering against his. He was close. So close. "Come with me, honey. Come all over my cock, show me how you feel."

"Yes."

He drove up again, grabbing her hips and fucking her harder, deeper. Her nails raked down his chest. The pain blended with the pleasure. With a growl he gave her more. Of his cock. Of his passion. His love.

The explosion caught him by surprise, tearing his control from him. Her body convulsed around his, her pussy milking his cock, taking every spurt with greedy acceptance. God, he loved that she always did that, took whatever he gave her as a gift. And there in the midst of his orgasm, he realized what she'd been trying to tell him all along.

"Fuck!"

"Good fuck or bad fuck?" she asked a few minutes later, her arms around his neck, her face buried in his throat, her body still quivering and spasming around his.

"Good for you, bad for me."

"I don't understand."

"I finally understood what you've been trying to tell me, Maddie."

"In the middle of making love, you understand?"

"I'm funny that way."

Digging his fingers into her hair, he tilted her head back, studying her face, memorizing it for the time to come. Leaning down, he kissed her lips, not with passion but with love, because God help him, he did love her, and while it went against everything he believed in, he was going to give her what she needed.

"You pick a hell of a way to tell me to go, honey."

Resting her cheek on his chest, she sighed. "I didn't start it."

"But you sure finished it."

He ground his hips up into hers. She moaned, he moaned.

She smiled and stroked her fingertips down his cheek. "We both did."

"As a reward, I'm going to give you what you want."

The terror in her gaze hurt him, but not nearly as much as the relief.

"What does that mean?"

"Exactly what I said. You want me gone, I'm going to go. But—" he stood "—wrap your legs around my waist."

She did.

"Not until tomorrow."

He turned and realized there wasn't anyplace to go.

"And on one condition."

"What?"

"You get a bed for those times I come back."

"I don't understand."

He laid her down on the couch, coming down above her, sliding his hardening cock deep into her pussy, watching her eyes close and her expression melt at the pleasure.

"We're going to do it your way, Maddie. You're going to stay here and find out who you are, and I'm going to work the mine, but I'm going to come back. Don't you ever think I won't. I'm not leaving you. I'm going to come back, not because you're my wife, but because I need you, plain and simple. And we'll make love and we'll talk and we'll go to socials and we'll get to know each other, and when you're ready, you'll tell me what I want to hear."

"And what is that?"

"You'll know it when you say it."

"I do love you."

He shook his head. "That's not what I want to hear."

"Caden." He could see her panicking. He caught her hands in his and brought them to his mouth.

"You're right, Maddie. You need this time to discover who you are, to find out what you want, because truth be told, I don't want you unless you're sure, too. But I'm not divorcing you and I'm not abandoning you. We'll do this like adults."

"You're going to live here?"

"I can live anywhere, Maddie. What I can't do, what I don't want to do, is live without you."

She opened her mouth, but he put his finger over her lips. "I don't want to hear lies, honey. So when you know it, just give me the truth."

CADEN WAS AS GOOD AS his word. The next morning, exhausted, her body pleasantly sore from lovemaking, her heart lodged in her throat, Maddie watched Caden leave. He rode out of her life the way he rode in. A confident, powerful man as rugged and wild as the land. A man who loved her. And she'd sent him away. Dear God, maybe she really was crazy. She wanted to run after him and tell him to come back, but there was no going back. No closing the door she'd opened. Not without the knowing. Neither could be satisfied with less. Caden rode out of sight, leaving the street as empty as her heart. At her feet, Precious meowed. Maddie picked her up.

A chill went up her spine. She looked around. There was nothing.

"I truly must be crazy." So crazy she thought someone was watching her. So crazy she was letting Caden ride away. But as terrified as she was, as desolate as she felt watching Caden ride away, she hadn't chased after him, and maybe that was more significant than the fear she was feeling now. She clung to the doorjamb.

I won't abandon you, Maddie.

She hoped he wouldn't. There was so much she needed to figure out. She wanted it done yesterday, but it seemed determined to come at its own time.

Time.

"Oh, my God."

She darted back inside to take the first batch of cinnamon rolls out of the oven. Across the street she could see her first line of customers wandering over, some with coffee cups in their hands, getting ready for the first stop in their day. The satisfaction she felt replaced some of her panic. And she knew without a doubt she'd made the right decision. *They'd* made the right decision.

She took the rolls out of the oven and set the tray on the table. Whipping the glaze to a thick, creamy consistency, she drizzled it over them. She needed this. And she needed Caden. Somehow she needed to be good with both. It shouldn't be this hard, but it was. Fear churned in her stomach. She fought it back with slow, even breaths. She had to figure out what she was afraid of.

A WEEK LATER A KNOCK at the door caught her by surprise. She wasn't expecting anyone, especially this late in the evening. She looked up to see a familiar woman standing in the doorway.

"Lucia! What brings you out this late?"

"Bread, what else?" She was dressed in a crisp white shirt and a blue walking dress. In her hand she held a pair of pale blue gloves. With a smile, she motioned to the kitchen. "May I come in?"

"Of course."

The older woman came in and looked around the kitchen.

"You're very efficient at what you do," she said, the appreciation clear in her tone.

"Thank you."

"We'll need three more loaves of bread for tomorrow. There's a fresh crop of miners that came in last night, and without the extra, we're going to come up short. Can you do that?"

Maddie did a quick calculation. She didn't owe the cinnamon rolls to the mercantile anymore, so if she didn't bake those, she could add the bread. There'd be a little less profit, but Lucia was a good customer and she'd given her her first break, her first opportunity.

"Yes, I can do that."

Lucia turned to leave and then stopped. The way she

fiddled with the gloves clearly indicated she had something on her mind. "I saw your man leave."

Maddie nodded, but didn't offer anything further. How to explain her situation?

"He goes away often?"

"He will be gone for a while this time."

"You've been fighting."

It was a statement. Maddie shook her head. "No, it's just…it's just something I need."

The older woman smoothed her hair. She picked up one of the cinnamon buns.

"May I?"

Maddie nodded.

She delicately pinched off a piece and put it to her mouth.

"It's easy when you're married to forget things."

"Like what?"

"Do you have a mother, Maddie?"

She shook her head. "She…died."

"She never spoke to you of marriage and what to expect?"

Maddie shook her head and blushed. Oh, dear God, this woman wasn't going to talk to her about sex, was she?

"I'm not…afraid of my husband."

It was Lucia's turn to blush. She pulled off another piece of bun and quickly put it in her mouth, chewing it thoroughly before she responded. She was clearly choosing her words carefully.

"I don't mean between the sheets. But what happens

between a man and a wife out of bed. I've watched you, Maddie, and you have something to prove. I remember when I first married Antonio, there was so much that was suddenly 'us' I felt like I was losing who I was."

"I can't lose what I don't have."

"What do you mean?"

"I grew up differently, without a family. I was never allowed to make any decisions."

"But this is normal for young girls."

"It was extreme in my case, and if I don't know who I am outside my marriage, how can I know who I am inside it?"

"Ah, I suspected this was the case. It's easy to forget, when you worry about losing yourself, in a marriage that which you gain." Lucia took another step forward and patted Maddie's cheek and smiled gently.

"You don't lose yourself in a marriage, Maddie. You gain your other half."

CHAPTER NINETEEN

SHE GAINED HER *better half.*

Maddie was so absorbed in the concept that it took a good ten minutes after Lucia said good-night for her to recognize that uncomfortable, clammy feeling was creeping over her skin again. As if eyes were upon her. Secret eyes. Evil eyes. She hadn't felt them at all when Caden was here, but as soon as he was gone, it was back. She needed to get control.

Feeling stupid, she yanked the kitchen curtains closed. Standing in the middle of the kitchen, she waited. The feeling didn't go away. Darn it, she didn't have time for this. The last of the dishes needed doing. And her bed needed making. Both the front and back doors were open to let in the air. She could close the front, but the back had to stay open until the oven cooled down; otherwise she'd roast.

Licking her lips, she wiped her hands on her apron and quickly closed the front door and turned the lock. She stepped back and she wondered at the futility of her actions. The lock wasn't even as strong as the ones that had been on the whorehouse's door. Of course, those were meant to keep girls *in,* but studying her front door, the lock didn't look strong enough to keep a mouse out.

Maddie shook her head at her foolishness and un-locked the door, forcing herself to take a step outside and look around. She was her own woman, dependent on no one. There was nothing unusual, just the peaceful goings-on in the street past the alley, her cat chasing a bug in the patch of grass just off the front step. It was a calm summer night and she was being foolish. Besides, Lucia had just left and she would have said something if she'd seen anyone lurking about.

Shaking her head again, Maddie stepped back into the house, closed the door, debated a second and then threw the lock. If she was her own woman, she shouldn't be ashamed to lock the damn door if she wanted to.

She took a step back toward the kitchen, her eyes locked on the door. The hairs on the back of her neck lifted. On the next step she bumped into something that shouldn't have been there, some*one* who shouldn't have been there. Her scream was cut off by a hand over her mouth, her struggles ended by a knife against her throat.

She closed her eyes. Not so foolish after all. It was little comfort.

"Hello, Maddie."

It took her a minute to place the voice. Dickens. As he dragged her back into the kitchen, the heat from the oven hit her hard, wrapping around her body, bringing the acrid scent of her own fear to her nostrils. On the next breath, she drowned in the stench of his, only he wasn't afraid. He smelled of hate and sweat.

"I came to collect what's owed me."

Insanity. Dickens. He was Frank's man.

"Did Frank send you?"

"Culbart and I parted company."

"He fired you." It was a shot in the dark that hit home. He yanked her back, shifting his grip to her mouth. "Over you, you fucking bitch. We'll add that to your tab."

There was only one thing he could think she owed him. He turned, and out of the corner of her eye, she saw he closed the back door and locked it. Wild laughter rose as she realized instead of keeping the danger out, she'd locked the danger in with her.

Sweat popped out over her body, at her temples, dripping down her cheeks. Fear constricted her lungs. She opened her mouth, trying to suck in a breath, but his hand smothered the effort. His thumb pressed up under her nostrils, restricting how much air she could even inhale. Despite the knife, she had no choice; she had to struggle and she felt the sting of the cut and blood drip to join the sweat.

He changed the angle of the knife and pointed the tip up under her chin.

She held still, terror building on terror.

"Good girl."

She wanted to kick him in the balls.

"I'm going to let go of you," he told her, "but if you think I can't throw this knife faster than you can scream, you just give it a shot."

She believed him. When he took his hand from her mouth in a quick, efficient movement, she didn't move, just stood there staring at him as he stepped around in front of her. Light from the lamp caught on the blade.

She brought her hand up to her throat. The cut was a small gap in her skin, but it was too easy to think of it being so much bigger. She stared at his knife. That was her blood on the blade. She'd been close to death before, but it had never felt this real.

You gain your other half.

Lucia's words came back to her. She was just beginning to figure things out and now she might be losing everything.

"Why are you here?" Her voice was a dry rasp of sound choking off in the middle.

Dickens smiled and took his hat off and set it on the back of the chair.

"You owe me. Back at the house, you tricked the boss man into taking you off the table, but I've had a hard-on for you ever since. Dancing around, acting like you're better than the rest of us. Just a split tail that belongs on her back, and I want what you stole from me." He motioned with the knife. "My time between your thighs to start."

"You want to make love."

"I don't make love with whores."

She knew that. And it should be easy to give him what he wanted, to unbutton her dress, shrug out of it, to lie on the bed, spread her legs and go to that place where everything was good and he didn't exist.

"I think I'd rather die first."

"That's a bit dramatic even for a whore."

"I think this is a bit dramatic for a cowhand." She

motioned with her hand, indicating his knife, the room, the situation.

"Well—" he took a step forward, unbuckling his gun belt "—if I were just a cowhand, maybe it would be, but I have plans, big plans, and you weren't supposed to leave before I got them going."

"All this because you want to have sex with me?"

She thought of the weeks where she'd felt someone's eyes upon her. He had to have been stalking her from the beginning, following her, watching her, studying her. It made her skin crawl.

"Have you been watching me?"

"Yes."

The buckle came undone. He placed the gun belt over the chair. A little leap of excitement inside as she realized how close the weapons were. She licked her lips. Just an arm's length away.

"Are you crazy?"

"Nope."

He said that so calmly she was convinced he was. Only crazy people denied it in a flat tone like that, as if they'd long accepted what was inside them so much so that it was normal.

Only crazy people that lived with themselves long enough to feel that it was normal said no in a voice like that.

She took a step back.

"That's a step in the right direction."

And she realized he was looking at the big bed Caden

had bought. She shook her head. No. She wouldn't lie with him there.

His hand in the middle of her chest sent her spinning back. She caught the bedpost to stop herself from falling.

"Get out of those clothes and on that bed."

"You don't want to do this," she told him.

"The hell I don't. I told you I've had a hard-on for you since the first time I saw you."

"Caden will kill you."

"Caden ain't gonna do shit." He waved the knife. "Get out of those clothes."

He was fumbling with the buttons of his pants. She tried, she really tried. She'd been in situations like this before and a man's tensions eased once he reached his release—sometimes they had to beat you a bit before they left, but they always let their guard down once they came. It was almost like a game.

The light caught on the drop of blood bright on the blade. *Her* blood. She looked into his eyes. And her stomach sank. Dickens wasn't playing.

She dug her fingers into the bed coverings. Her eyes stuck on that knife, her mind whirling. There had to be something she could do. Some way to distract him. She had to keep him talking. "You said there was something else."

"I want the gold, Maddie."

Oh, dear God. She didn't have any gold.

"I don't have any gold."

"Your husband does and I want to know where it is."

"What makes you think he told me? I'm a whore."

"The man rode into the Fallen C for you. That means you meant something to him. A man tells things to a woman that matters."

"Maybe some men…"

He grunted a deep sound that could have meant anything.

She looked around the room for a weapon. There was nothing. The tiny oil lamp on the stand wouldn't even make a dent in Dickens's skull. She had no way to defend herself.

"Take off that dress."

She touched her throat, slid her fingers down the V to the next button. He licked his lips the way she'd seen a man do, full of greed and lust. His eyes narrowed. It should be so easy to unbutton those buttons, expose her breasts, lift them up in an offering bound to distract him. She'd done it so many times, for so many men. This was just one more time. But she couldn't work the button, and the rage that swelled inside all but choked out the fear. Clutching the material in her fist, she spat, "Go to hell."

He didn't even bat an eye. "I'm sure we'll both get there eventually."

He took a step forward, the knife in his hand pointed up. She pressed back against the bed. He smiled and pressed the blade flat against her stomach.

She gritted her teeth. "Fuck you."

"That is the plan."

She closed her eyes, biting back a sob. Words were the only weapon she had, and the ones she was throwing sounded more like jokes than threats. But since she couldn't come up with anything else to say, she clung to her defiance. She wasn't a whore. She was Caden Miller's wife. If she died, she would die an honorable woman.

Whatever you had to do to survive, that's just what you had to do.

Maybe back then that was true. But not now. She wasn't doing this. She took a step to the side. Dickens blocked her by taking a step of his own. The knife tip slid up the front of her dress.

"Get on with it."

She shook her head. "If you want me naked, you're going to have to make it happen yourself."

"Putting on airs now that you're married?"

"No." She was being who she was. Finally.

He reached out. She slapped his hand away, getting a small glimmer of satisfaction when he looked shocked. Her satisfaction was short-lived. He backhanded her across the face. Stars exploded behind her eyelids. She went tumbling backward onto the bed, right where he wanted her.

She waited for him to come down over her. They always came down over her, thinking they'd won once they had her on her back.

He laughed and climbed up over her.

"Nothing worse than an uppity whore."

And there was nothing worse than a man who thought being male entitled him to everything. Lashing out, she sank her nails into his face, going for his eyes, ripping down his cheeks. She wanted him to holler and scream, like she was, to maybe alert somebody, anybody, that she was here and that she was in trouble, but all he did was grunt and grab her wrist in one of his hands, blocking the other with his elbow as he pressed his forearm across her throat.

Instinct told her to grab his hand, but she'd been choked before. Her strength was nothing against his. Her only defense was to keep striking at his soft spots. His eyes, his balls, his throat. Opening her eyes, fighting the urge to gasp for air, she lashed out again at his face with her free arm, this time striking with her thumbs for his eyes. She grazed one, not the direct hit she wanted, but it was enough.

He jerked back and released his hold on her. She rolled to the middle of the bed. He lunged after her. She jumped for the floor but he caught her skirts just as she launched. He yanked her back. Anchored by her skirts, she fell face-first over the foot of the bed, smashing her hands into the floor and upending the bed stand. The oil lamp shattered into shards around her fingers. Maddie watched the oil spread over her clean floor as she dangled there, wheezing for breath and managing, finally, to drag past her terror, in one, two, three breaths. The fourth she let out in a scream she hoped was loud enough to wake the dead.

Somebody had to hear her. And if they heard her, someone had to care. She was Maddie Miller. Baker, wife. She was *someone*.

"Shut the fuck up."

Dickens grabbed her hair and hauled her back up,

clamping his hand over her mouth. Her back arched. It was an impossible position, a defenseless position. In the next instant she was flipped over, and once again she was on her back on the bed. The bed Caden had sent. The bed they were going to make love in. Her marriage bed. Dickens wasn't going to take her on her marriage bed. She'd die first.

Opening her mouth, she sucked in a breath to launch another scream.

"Oh, no, you don't."

His hand closed around her throat like a vise, clamping the sound within. Her face heated and her eyes bulged, but he didn't loosen his grip. "You keep doing that and I'll fuck you as you suffocate."

He meant it. *Caden.* She screamed his name in her mind. She'd sent him away to find herself and he'd gone, giving her what she'd needed. Oh, God, she'd been so selfish, thinking she couldn't be herself with him. Sending him away. Hurting him.

Caden.

Another prayer couched in a silent scream. She didn't want to think of him finding her like this. From a distance she heard hollow gasps. Pain in her shoulder and the back of her neck savaged her control. There was the sound of cloth tearing. So much distraction, but she reached for the image of her pond in her mind. The image wouldn't form, so she reached for something stronger and found...Caden. Feature by feature she built his face in her mind, from his beautiful eyes to that lower lip she loved to nibble on.

"Goddamn fucking bitch."

It was getting harder to move, harder to focus. Darkness was bleeding over Caden's face. *No!* It was a cry from her heart. As futile as all the others. She shook her head, trying to dislodge the blackness from the beauty. Caden was her one good thing and she wanted to hold on to him, whisper his name with her last breath.

"Wake up!"

Dickens shook her. She knew he shook her because she could feel her body's disjointed motion, almost as if she was bobbing on waves. Her hand flopped out. Pain lanced up her arm. She'd been cut. How odd—the world was black yet she could still feel pain. She moved her hand. The pain intensified. Sharp. The stray thought entered the void. There was something sharp by her hand. Glass…a weapon. *Yes!*

With the last of her strength, she slashed upward, using his voice as a guide, striking for his eyes, those horrible, ugly eyes full of lust. She hated the way men looked at her, hated the way *he* looked at her. It was only beautiful when Caden looked at her because he never saw her as a piece of meat he was going to buy. Caden looked at her as though she mattered.

Her hand connected with something soft, giving before slamming up against something hard. There was a scream. Agony in her palm. Agony in the scream. Agony in her heart. It was everywhere.

Dickens fell off her.

Run! Get up! Run!

The voice inside her screamed at her, but she couldn't

move, the life choked from her. All she could do was lie there and wheeze, hoping to get enough oxygen back inside so that her mind could function before Dickens recovered. *Oh, dear God, let me recover first.*

From the front door came an explosion of glass and splintered wood. Maddie opened her eyes. For a second everything was too bright, too much, but then she saw the silhouette of a man—broad-shouldered, lean-hipped, with an arrogant tilt to the chin she'd recognize anywhere.

Caden.

She wanted to warn him about Dickens, out of sight on the other side of the bed. Though her throat worked, she couldn't make a sound. She heard the soft glide of metal over leather.

"Maddie!"

She heard Dickens shift position. *No. No. No.*

She did the only thing she could think of. She just rolled right off the bed. Dickens was on the floor. If God was in his heavens, she'd land on him.

She did mostly, but she hit the floor, too, the wood slamming into her ribs. She heard Caden swear, heard a shot ring past her ear, then a thud.

Oh, God. Was that what a bullet sounded like when it hit flesh?

She was wedged between Dickens and the bed, his shoulder pressed against her back. She pushed for all she was worth, trying to get on top of him, to block him. He elbowed her off. She grabbed his arm, her wrist screaming a protest when he jerked.

"Fucking bitch! Get off me!"

She wasn't getting off him. She was going to be all over him. Screaming, clawing, doing whatever she had to. He was not going to kill Caden.

She grabbed feebly for his gun and missed. She saw his hand rise, the kitchen light gleaming off the butt as it came down toward her face. She braced herself for the pain, but the blow never came. Dickens twisted away from her, pulled her around in front of him, the full length of his body pressing on hers. She wanted to heave.

"Don't move," Caden growled. She didn't know if he was talking to her or Dickens, but if it was to her, he needn't have worried. Rolling off the bed had taken the last bit of strength she had. She hurt all over and it was hard to breathe through the constriction in her throat.

"Get back up on the bed, Maddie."

Caden's voice cut through the chaos like an anchor of calm. She shook her head. A hand grabbed her hair, yanking painfully at the roots. Her scream came out as a hoarse rasp.

"She moves, I'll shoot her."

"No, you won't."

"What makes you so damn sure?" Dickens asked.

"Because she knows where the deed to the claim is."

"I don't need her. I have you."

She could hear that taunting smile in Caden's voice, imagined it on his face as he said, "But you'd never get me to tell you."

She wanted to scream at him to shut up, this wasn't the time to be provoking. The man had a gun!

She slammed back with her elbow, hitting Dickens in the groin. He gasped and bucked against her, his grip slipping just enough. She tore out of his arms, getting up on her knees, jamming her foot back in his groin again just for good measure, hoping he'd let go of the gun, but he didn't. He kept it trained on Caden. Caden, who sounded incredibly calm as he repeated, "Maddie. Get up on the bed."

Now she could see him, his image split in sections by the strands of hair falling over her eyes. He was standing there, hands down, palms back. He didn't even have a gun.

She stood. Dickens's hand wrapped around her ankle, clamping like a vise. The gun in his hand was pointed directly at Caden.

"He wanted—"

"I know what he wanted."

"He's got—"

"I know what he's got. Get up on the bed."

"He's got my foot."

"Do what you gotta do."

Maddie looked at Caden standing there so strong, so invincible, but he was nothing against a bullet.

"There's nothing she can do that's faster than a bullet."

"Who are you going to listen to, Maddie? Me or him?"

There was no question. "You."

Dickens yanked on her leg, upsetting her balance. "Fat lot of good that will do you. I'm the man with the gun."

Yes, he was. A very big gun. If she went down, she

could cover him, lie on that gun, ruin the shot. She imagined the bullet tearing through her abdomen. Her stomach rose. She imagined it slamming into Caden, and she lost her supper, vomit splattering all over Dickens. Revulsion pulled him back, relaxed his grip on her ankle. Maddie dived for the bed. She saw Caden twitch. Saw Dickens bring up the gun. Just as she was about to throw herself back onto him, she doubled over. Her stomach heaved again.

There was a wet *thwack* and then a gunshot. By the time Maddie turned around, it was over. Dickens was lying on the floor, a knife in his throat, making horrible gurgling noises, and Caden was coming toward her. She could only stare at him.

"That was clever," he said as he knelt beside Dickens. Did he think she could vomit on command?

"I was imagining a bullet going through my stomach."

He looked up. "I know what you were planning. It was there in your eyes, and just for the record, if you'd done that, I'd have put you over my knee every day for a week. When I tell you to do something in order to keep you safe, Maddie, I expect it done."

She looked at the knife sticking out of Dickens's throat, at the blood staining her pristine floor, the vomit on the man, herself, the bed. She scrambled back when Caden reached for her.

"I'm a mess."

"Maddie. Get the hell over here."

She shook her head, grabbing the coverlet, bundling it up, wiping at her face, wiping at her dress. She stared at the blood on her hands, tiny little splatters. She'd come so close to losing everything. Her life. Caden.

The shaking started without warning. With his hands on her shoulders, Caden pushed her down on the bed. His fingers were gentle as he unbuttoned her dress and pulled it off her shoulders. Leaning over to the remaining bed stand, he took a pitcher and poured water into the basin, dipped a cloth in it and wiped at her face.

He cupped some water in his hand and held it to her lips. "Drink."

He didn't give her much choice. Holding the basin under her chin, he ordered, "Spit."

She swished the water around her mouth and did. She felt so dirty. So used. So less than what she'd thought she was. There would always be men like Dickens. Always be men that thought she was theirs for the picking.

The shaking wouldn't stop. With ruthless efficiency, Caden ripped the sheets from the bed and then he laid her down.

All she could get out of her throat was a hoarse "I'm sorry."

"No need to be sorry." He straightened. "You got fresh sheets somewhere?"

She shook her head. She only had the one set.

"Then we'll make do." He grabbed one of the sheets back up, the bottom one the vomit hadn't soaked through, and put it over her.

"You stay on that bed."

She looked at him and grabbed his hand when he would have turned away.

"Why are you here?"

"I heard you crying for me."

She jumped and opened her mouth. He couldn't mean right then. He put his fingers across her lips.

"No pride. No arguing, Maddie. I missed the hell out of you, and you don't have to say it back, but I know you missed the hell out of me, too. The plain truth is I couldn't stay away."

You gain your other half.

She caught his hand in hers and pressed a kiss to the palm, tears pouring down her cheeks, seeping between his skin and hers, sealing them together in a salty kiss.

"You all right?"

She nodded.

"I'm going to get this body out of here and then I'm going to get some cool cloths for your throat. And then—" he brushed her hair out of her face "—we're going to talk."

CHAPTER TWENTY

THE TALK HAD had to wait. By the time Caden got back with the doctor, her throat had been too swollen for speech. The doctor prescribed bed rest and cold compresses. If truth be told, Maddie thought Caden needed bed rest more than her. The man couldn't stop touching her, doing for her, worrying at her. Between him and Lucia, she'd had ice for her throat, sheets for the bed, the floor scrubbed and nonstop fussing for two days. Today she was ready to get out of bed.

Sliding off the bed, she stood for a second, checking her steadiness. The room didn't spin and her knees didn't give out. She felt...ready. Today was going to be a good day. With a smile, she donned her work dress. She walked to the kitchen window, pulled the curtain back and watched Precious chase a grasshopper, breathing deep of the faint scent of cinnamon blending with the warmth of summer. The breeze brought the sounds of town—wagons creaking as they meandered down the street, the distant laughter of children and the fussing of parents.

Putting water in the basin, she donned her apron and started on the few dishes left, her heart feeling lighter than it ever had. She looked around her little house and kitchen and smiled. This was her home, carved out of nothing by her own hand and her own effort. This was where she'd made her stand against her past, against Dickens. This was where she'd found herself. This was where she'd found her courage. And when Caden returned, this was where she wanted to talk when he got back from Lucia's with their supper. They'd let things go too long, and the tension between them was thick enough to cut with a knife.

She heard footsteps in the alley beside the house. Her heart fluttered in her chest. Caden. She took a breath and straightened her hair, smoothed her skirts. Pinched her cheeks.

Her heart skipped its usual beat as she watched Caden from the back door, looking no less tall and no less impressive on his own two feet than he did on horseback. Bending down, he pulled up a piece of grass and dragged it in the dirt. Precious scampered over to explore the potential toy. He dropped it in the dirt and straightened, switching the wicker basket with their supper to his other hand, pausing when he saw her standing in the door.

Her heart stopped beating entirely as he walked toward her, his hat shading his eyes. He stopped two feet in front of her. He didn't smile, but he took off his hat. She didn't take it as a bad sign. If the emotions in him were as strong as they were in her, a smile wasn't possible.

"You sure you up to being out of bed, Maddie mine?"

His hair was wet. He'd obviously stopped to bathe at the pond before getting supper. She liked that, too. She liked, she decided, everything about this man. His temper, his gruff ways, his sense of fair play, his tenderness, his passion and his patience. She found her smile. Taking a step toward him, she took off her apron and let it fall to the ground.

"I've been waiting two days. Don't you have a question to ask me, Caden?"

He eyed her smile and then the apron.

"I thought I'd ease into it over the next month or so."

"Why?"

His gaze fell to the bruises on her throat. "Because it's been two weeks since we've been together, two days since you were attacked and two seconds since the last time I imagined making love to you."

"You want me."

He nodded. "Always. And right now, you're looking mighty fine."

She put her hand on her hip and looked at him from under her lashes. "I could look finer naked."

He took a step toward her. She took one, too. One for her and one for him. Equal. His head tilted to the side, studying her.

"No doubt about that."

Her smile broadened. "I've got fresh sheets on the bed."

"You don't say."

"So why don't you ask me the question?"

"I'm afraid to."

She arched her brows at him. "Caden Miller, afraid?"

"It's been a long wait."

"It was the best gift that anybody could ever give me."

"Is that my answer?"

No, it wasn't. She took the next two steps, and then another, not stopping until her breasts pressed into his chest and her thighs grazed his. "You can't have an answer to a question you haven't asked."

"I can't?"

"No. That would be an assumption."

He didn't say a word. She realized he truly was nervous. There were lines of strain settled around his eyes and tension in his lips. She'd thought he'd brushed off the incident with Dickens since violence was so much a part of his life, but that wasn't the case. She took the basket from his hand and put it on the ground. "I'm sorry."

His fingers grazed her cheek as he brushed her hair off her face. "I don't ever want to go through that again."

"Then I guess you'll have to keep me by your side."

"Or something."

She leaned into his hand. They'd been together every minute for the past two days, but they hadn't talked, too busy walking on eggshells in the wake of the trauma to address what needed addressing. She couldn't wait anymore. "I'm sorry," she said again.

"For what?

"For sending you away."

"You needed it."

But it wasn't something *he* had needed, or wanted. Leaving for him hadn't been about finding something. It'd been about waiting to find out when her discovering was over whether he was going to be part of her choice.

She took his hat from his hand and dropped it on the ground beside the basket. "You missed me."

"Like I'd miss breathing."

"But you stayed away."

"You asked me to." Because he understood her better than she understood herself. What had she ever done to deserve him?

"Caden."

"What?"

She took a step back and crooked her finger at him. "Come here."

"Don't be calling me there, Maddie, if you're not serious."

She backed up another step. "Don't be stalling if you are."

He climbed the porch steps. Out of the corner of her eye, she could see the townsfolk pausing at the end of the alley behind the mercantile. They were curious, but she didn't care. Caden didn't stop until her breasts once again touched his chest and her hips cuddled his and her skirts wrapped around his legs.

She walked her fingers up his chest, stroked them over his cheek, slipped them behind his neck. With steady pressure she pulled him down, holding his gaze, letting him see her joy, her passion, letting him see everything she'd so foolishly tried to hide from him before. But mostly she let him see the love. When his lips were a hairbreadth from hers, when they were so close her breath was his, she whispered, "Ask me your question, Caden."

With a growl, he put his arms around her, lifting her off her feet, into his arms where she belonged. "Maddie, do you want to be mine?"

The answer was so obvious. So easy. It flowed from her soul. "With everything I am, with everything I have, with who I know I am, with who I intend to be, I want to be yours, Caden Miller."

His mouth crushed down on hers. No gentle kiss this. This was a claiming, passionate, perfect kiss. Digging her nails into his nape, she pulled herself deeper into the embrace, wrapping her legs around his hips as she kissed him back just as wildly, just as passionately.

"Damn well took you long enough," he muttered against her neck as he walked them into the house.

"I had to know."

"I know, but it fucking took you long enough." Caden kicked the door closed.

"How could you ever think you didn't have value, Maddie? Everybody else sees it."

"It doesn't matter what everybody else sees. I need to see it, too."

He tossed her on the bed and started stripping off his shirt. With her foot she kicked the front door closed. They really needed a bigger house.

"Get undressed or I'm going to take you right in your skirts."

She didn't want that. She wanted to feel his skin against hers. She wanted to taste him, to mark him, to love him. She was as wild as he. She stripped in record time.

"Those, too," he said as she stood in her pantaloons and camisole. "I want to see all of you. Feel all of you."

They were, as always, in perfect accord.

He stood there watching her shimmy out of her pantaloons, the muscles of his chest clearly defined. His powerful shoulders blending to his narrow waist and strong thighs. Her gaze dipped between, settling on his cock, thick and straight. He cupped it in his hands and stroked it once or twice. Tempting her.

"Come here."

She did. Gliding across the room on happiness, dropping to her knees before him, running her tongue over the head of his cock, taking that sweetness for herself.

He groaned and braced his hand on the wall. "Damn, Maddie, I missed you."

"I know."

His fingers threaded through her hair, tipping her gaze to his. "You sure, Maddie?"

She looked up, rubbing her cheek against his cock, and smiled. "A very wise woman told me that in a marriage you don't lose yourself. You gain your other half. I can't go around anymore missing the most vital part of me."

"Is that why you're doing this, because you're lonely?"

"I'm doing this because I love you. You're my partner, my friend and my lover. And I need you." Turning her head, she bit his thigh. "All of you."

"I like the last."

"You like it all."

And as she watched, Caden found his smile. His

thumb stroked over her lips, pulling them apart. "Yeah, I do."

It only took a turn of her head to press her lips against his cock. He moaned and cupped her skull in his palm, guiding her. Opening her mouth, she accepted the gift, reveling in the feel of his hard shaft sliding over her soft tongue. He pressed farther and she moaned, taking all he could give, worshipping him, loving him, telling him with each caress everything she felt inside.

"Goddamn, Maddie, I missed you."

She knew that from the way he held her to him as if he couldn't get close enough. He didn't back off and she didn't make him. Whether he wanted to admit it or not, her husband had a bit of anger in him. Waiting didn't come easily for a man like Caden. Waiting passively... She mentally shook her head. That must have just about killed him.

"Goddamn, Maddie, I want to be gentle with you," he moaned, even as he pumped his cock harder and faster than was comfortable. She stroked her hands down his hips, slipping her fingers between his thighs, cupping his balls in her hands. He might want to be gentle, but he needed this right now. She took all he gave as best she could with the pace he set, feeling his cock get harder and harder, his balls drawing up tighter. She encouraged him, sliding her fingers behind his balls, pushing up hard. She wanted him to come.

"Fuck."

He came hot and sweet on her tongue, feeding her his aggression, his pain, his love. And when it was over, he grabbed her by the shoulders and dragged her up before kissing her passionately. "Goddamn, woman, why did you let me do that?"

She wrapped her arms around his neck and hugged him, whispering in his ear, "Because I know you, too, and it about killed you to give me what I needed, and you're just the teensiest bit mad that I needed it."

"Not anymore."

She nipped playfully at his chest. "Good."

His fingers drifted down the side of her breast to her waist before finding her pussy. She spread her legs, knowing what he'd find.

His eyes were dark with passion as he said, "You're wet."

She nodded and squirmed. "That was exciting."

His brows rose. "You liked that?"

"Yes."

"What part did you like?"

"The part where you were honest with me and trusted me to handle what you needed to show."

"I liked that, too."

"I'm going to like this next part, too," she stated, smiling up at him, wiggling against his hand.

His smile broadened. "And what's that?"

"You and me, coming together, as husband and wife."

He slid two fingers inside her slowly and steadily, stretching her deliciously. "It's going to be sweet."

He added a third, pressing it against her opening, letting her contemplate the potential. "It's going to be passionate." He eased it in beside the others. It was a tight fit. A perfect fit. "I'm going to make you burn, and when you think you can't stand it anymore, I'm going to make you explode."

She moaned "Yes," spreading her legs wider, inviting him deeper. "Make me love it," she gasped as he set a steady rhythm.

"Yes," he hissed back, giving her what she wanted. What she needed. And squeezing her pussy around his fingers, she gave him what he needed back. Her acceptance. Her love.

"And when it's over—" she stroked his cheek, seeing that tiny bit of uncertainty he tried to hide inside him "—I'm going to be right here with you. I won't abandon you, either, Caden."

His hand stilled. "Fuck."

For a moment he didn't move, just stared at her with those beautiful eyes, and she worried she'd gone too far, bringing his fears into the open. She could feel the tension welling inside him, emotional, sexual, and then he crushed her to him, his mouth biting at hers.

"Goddamn, I love you."

"I love you, too." And this time when she said it, it was right. There was no hesitation. No uncertainty, no little quiver of fear. This time when she said it, it was an opening, a beginning.

He pulled back, his gaze searching hers as he settled between her thighs. Cupping his face in her hands, she stroked her thumbs over his lips the way he did to her, wrapping her legs around his hips, opening her body, her heart and soul to his possession. Sighing as she joined him, savoring the bliss before giving him that one other thing he needed. Her promise.

"Always, Caden."

* * * * *